An Amelia

A modern twist of Pride and Prejudice

A novel by L D Raylene

Copyright@2022 by L D Raylene

First Edition. September 19, 2022

Second Edition. September 30, 2022

ISBN: 13 -978 – 0645286618

Amelia is an extremely rare congenital disability marked by the absence of one or more limbs. Amniotic band syndrome is one example.

For Petra Riley Tirtawidjaja, a family friend who was born with Amniotic band syndrome. You are the source of inspiration for this story. May you continuously grow with solid determination and resilience surrounded by the warmth love of your family and friends.

Epigraph

"Pride is a very common failing, I believe. By all that I have ever read, I am convinced that it is very common indeed; that human nature is particularly prone to it, and that there are very few of us who do not cherish a feeling of self-complacency on the score of some quality or other, real or imaginary. Vanity and pride are different things, though the words are often used synonymously. A person may be proud without being vain. Pride relates more to our opinion of ourselves, vanity to what we would have others think of us". - **Mary Bennett**

"Yes, vanity is a weakness indeed. But pride — where there is a real superiority of mind, pride will be always under good regulation." - **Mr. Darcy**

Pride and Prejudice by Jane Austen

Table of Contents

CHAPTER ONE
The First Meeting

Amelia slowly opened her eyes when she felt the warmth of the sun coming from her room window touching her face. Lazily she tried to open her eyes wider and figured out on which day of the week she was living at the moment when she heard a subtle commotion from outside her room. Her mind slowly cleared, and she turned over her head to the small alarm clock on her bedside. Her eyes squinted to see the time was showing 3 o'clock in the afternoon, and she had just woken up from her unplanned afternoon nap.

Slowly she pushed her body up with her right hand and hopped down from her bed when her room door suddenly widely opened.

"Wakey, wakey! It's almost party time!"

Lana, her beautiful older sister, walked into the room and went straight to their shared wardrobe.

Amelia furrowed her brow hearing the word 'party'. Her mind clearly was not fully awake yet. She finished her casual job as a kitchen server at midnight last night and turned to bed when it was already 2 am. She woke up early this morning to fill her tummy for breakfast before turning again for another nap after lunch.

"It's Sharon's birthday party," Lana smiled, knowing that her sister's brain was still not absorbing her words fully.

"Oh yeah." Amelia nodded, still with her sleepy eyes.

"So, what are you wearing?"

Amelia did not answer the question, and her sister seemed not to mind that her question was hanging in the air. Instead, she left the room and went out to the bathroom. Soon after, she returned and, without comment, took the dark blue tank top dress lying on her bed, which her sister chose, and wore it. She took a moment to observe herself in the mirror before glancing at Lana. Her sister was also changing into a crème gold strapless sack dress, with her over-the-shoulder length dark hair sweeping across her back. Lana's elegant appearance made her ponder how any guy could resist such beauty displayed by her sister.

On the other hand, she felt her appearance was the total opposite.

Looking back in the mirror, the first thing that caught her eyes was her little left limb. She was born with a short limb on her left arm, up to slightly over her elbow. In her current arms revealing dress, that little limb became even more prominent. As she did not plan to scare away all Sharon's guests, she took her prosthetic hand and wore on her crème cardigan. When she looked at the mirror again, no one would know about her little left limb.

With a warm smile, Lana pulled her out of the room afterwards. It was the usual smile that Amelia would see from her sister every time they were going to a social event. This had happened since she was born and started school. People would look at her differently because of her birth defect.

Lana, who was 18 months older, had been a protective older sister to her. Her sister always tried to shield her from anyone who mocked her, encouraged her to show herself more, and accepted who she was. She owed a great deal of gratitude to her sister on this, as she admitted she would not have the courage to face the world if not because of Lana and her father, who had been very supportive. Sometimes she was too scared to think if any of them were gone from her life, then her world would collapse.

However, now they were not kids anymore. They completed their vocational studies and had their jobs. Lana was a visual art specialist teacher in primary school, a profession that matched well with her motherly nurturing personality. She was a caring, gentle person and beautifully attractive, which made her the centre of attention for the opposite sex. In the beginning, she seemed not to care about receiving such attention, as if she just wanted to be on Amelia's side forever. However, Amelia knew that she had to let go of her sister. One day, Lana wished to find her Mr Right, settle down and build her own family. Amelia wanted to show her sister that she was now an independent girl. She did not need to be protected all the time.

"Thank God you're wearing your hand, Liz."

Leah, her younger sister, looked at her with relief when she and Lana came down. Lana gave Leah a reprimanded look, but Leah only smiled cheekily. Amelia was used to such nasty teasing from her sister and only released a light scoff.

"You never know, Leah. I might drop it later."

Now it was her turn getting a glaring from Lana. She just giggled away while taking her car keys.

"I'm not going to be in the car that you're driving, Liz," said Leah.

Amelia smirked. "Do you think who else is going to drive?"

"Lana!" Lana shook her head.

"That's Lizzy's car."

Leah gasped in disbelief.

"Come on, Leah. It's not for the first time Lizzy drive for us."

A victorious smile was drawn on Amelia's face as she walked out towards her car. She turned her head to check whether her sisters were obediently following her. A burst of satisfactory laughter was then heard when Leah grumpily walked towards the car with Lana behind her.

"I will never sit in this car anymore once I have a boyfriend!" growled Leah once they were seated inside the car.

"If your boyfriend has a car," replied Amelia while grinning at her sister from the centre mirror.

"Of course, he will! I will meet a handsome, rich guy at the party."

Amelia only shook her head, and she was not the only one as Lana did likewise.

Their car travelled smoothly to their destination, about 20km away from their home. Sharon's house was located in an elite area in Melbourne's eastern suburb, close to the city, ironically where they lived ten years ago. However, an unfortunate event happened on their father's business, which forced him to sell their house and move to another more affordable suburb. Sharon was their close neighbour at that time. Despite their move, they stayed in touch and rarely missed each other's life occasions, either birthday, Christmas, Easter or graduation. Most of the time, it was Sharon's family would host the party. After the financial issue that Amelia's family was facing, they had a tight budget for day-to-day living, let alone for a party.

Amelia had to foot the house bill by doing multiple jobs on most weekday nights and weekends apart from her full-time job as a community worker. Lana wanted to help too. However, her body was not strong enough to afford more works apart from her day full-time job.

"I heard that Sharon is inviting a new neighbour to the party too," said Leah enthusiastically. "I heard he is a young handsome, rich guy who demolished and built a new grand double-storey house in the corner of her street."

Amelia was not interested in getting to know new people. Lana seemed excited too, but she did not display it openly like Leah. Half an hour later, they entered Sharon's grand double storey house along with other guests who had just arrived too. Amelia quietly noticed that most guests looked like Sharon's parents' business acquaintances.

Sharon sighted their presence and approached them warmly. " I'm glad to see you all here," she said while giving Amelia a warm hug. "And I'm glad to see you, Liz. It's been a while."

"You know I always work on weekends," replied Amelia while returning the hug. "Happy Birthday, Sharon."

"Thanks, Liz. I know you've been busy. I appreciate you are here today."

"It's my best friend's birthday."

Sharon had been not only their neighbour but also her best friend. Since they were born, they had been together. They went to the same kindergarten and school until Amelia and her family moved out from the suburb.

"Let me introduce you to our new neighbour." Sharon cued them into the living room. Leah's eyes were glowing with excitement. They walked together to the living room and approached two men and a woman near the fireplace.

"Hi Charlie, these are my childhood friends."

The person with the name Charlie offered his hand. Charlie was a handsome blond man with blue eyes and a friendly, sympathetic face. His warm smile was infectious, especially when his eyes landed on Lana. Amelia could sense how he was attracted to her sister. It was a typical first reaction she would expect from any guy who saw her angelic sister.

Lana welcomed the hand shyly. Meanwhile, Leah aggressively moved forward and introduced herself before Sharon opened her mouth. Then, when it was her turn to introduce herself since Charlie's eyes diverted to her, she interrupted when Sharon introduced her as Lizzy.

"I'm Amelia."

Charlie looked at them, confused.

"My full name is Elise Amelia Bettney, but I prefer to be called by my middle name. It's just my family and some of my close friends who already used to call me Lizzy."

Charlie laughed. "That's fair enough." He turned his head briefly and gestured to a man behind him to come closer. "Let me introduce my best friend. This is Fitz."

The person called Fitz only looked at them briefly, gave away a brisk smile before he turned his face away. Charlie chuckled nervously before gesturing to a woman who stood beside him.

"And this is my sister, Clare."

Clare nodded in friendly manners towards them, which Amelia and her sisters returned politely.

Amelia preferred to find her own solitude for the next hour, sat in the bar while enjoying the cocktail she ordered from the bartender hired that night. Sharon was busy entertaining her other guests. Lana was happily engaged in conversation with Charlie and Clare. Leah was already busy spreading her charm and making new 'boyfriends'.

Amelia smiled, observing her younger sister. Between the three of them, Leah looked more like her sibling rather than Lana. Lana had dark wavy hair, almond brown eyes, a sharp nose and a tall, slender body. That was why she became a source of pride for her mother. However, Amelia had to admit that her sister did look like an angel, especially with her gentle personality.

Meanwhile, she and Leah were an inch shorter than Lana. They shared about the same height, same brown eyes, and dark brown curly hair. However, her hair was much frizzier than Leah's, which sometimes gave her trouble in the morning rush. Unlike Leah, she usually just let them down on her shoulder. Leah still had time to use a straightener to make it less curly.

And Leah did not have a birth defect, unlike her.

Sometimes she wondered why only her in the family was struck with this 'luck'. Sometimes she felt grateful that Lana and Leah were born physically normal without problems. However, she did feel she was just an embarrassment to the family, though Lana and her father had constantly reprimanded her for not having such thoughts.

On the other hand, her mother seemed to resent her. Leah never hesitated to show her embarrassment of having her as a 'disabled' sister. She could not blame her sister for having such a thought. With seven years apart between them, she would forgive her anyway.

She threw her glance at the dance floor and noticed that probably Lana and Charlie had been dancing a couple of times for the last one hour. It seemed this was the first time her sister was smitten with a guy. She had to admit that Charlie was cute and looked like a nice decent guy, unlike the previous bogan who tried to pursue Lana. She could see the way they looked at each other, and she felt happy for her sister if finally, Lana could find her Mr Right. She hoped Charlie would not mind if he knew about her physical condition.

Her train of thought was severed when she saw Sharon walking towards her.

"There's so much I want to talk with you," said Sharon with her beaming smile. "But you know this is not the place." She took a deep sigh while looking at her surroundings. "I did not plan to have such a big attendance for my birthday party."

"Well, at least you know these people."

"They are my parent's friends. Not mine." Sharon rolled her eyes which made Amelia release a soft laugh.

"Your parents want you to have a decent party," she said, consoling her friend.

"It's my 25th birthday party, Liz."

"Being 25 doesn't stop anyone from having a big party."

Sharon nodded with a laugh. "Yeah, right!"

"What do you think of Lana and Charlie?" asked Sharon when their eyes landed on the mentioned couple.

"They look cute together." Amelia sipped her drink while glancing at her friend. "What do you think of Charlie? Is he a nice guy?"

"I think so. I have no idea. He just moved in with his sister two weeks ago. His parents are still in the UK."

"Right." Amelia nodded her head. "Now I understand where his accent comes from."

Their conversation was cut off as one of Sharon's parent's acquaintances approached her to wish her happy birthday and pulled her into a more formal discussion. Sharon's mouth was shaped into an inaudible sorry word, which Amelia returned with another muffled reply, 'it's alright'. She planned to go to the restroom anyway.

She was familiar with the house and knew there was a powder room under the stairs. Unfortunately, someone was occupying the room. She waited on the door side and let herself hidden under the stairs. While scrolling her mobile phone screen, reading a couple of messages from her friends, she heard a conversation from the stairs.

"What do you think of Lana, Fitz?"

A familiar voice. Amelia wondered whether that was Charlie and they were talking about her sister, Lana.

"I guess you're into her. You're lucky. She is probably the prettiest girl in this party."

Amelia smiled. She was sure they were talking about her Lana as she thought that no one could beat her sister's beauty at this party. However, the deep baritone voice came with a thick British accent, which made her wonder whether the voice belonged to Fitz, a friend that Charlie had introduced earlier.

Charlie's soft laugh was heard. "You're right. She's lovely, isn't she? I think you should have some fun here too, Fitz. What do you think of her sister?"

"Which one?"

"Amelia. The other one is Leah. Leah is still a teenager. She is too young for you. She is probably the same age as Georgie. She could be your little sister."

"Oh, that girl. She's alright."

"Aren't you going to ask her for a dance, perhaps? Getting to know her?"

"No, Charlie. I'm not interested in her. She's not good enough for me."

Amelia's heart skipped a beat. She held her breath involuntarily as if afraid of being heard or seen. She pressed her body to the wall as if it would make her disappear.

"Come on, Fitz. What a high standard you have. You should give her a chance."

Fitz replied with a slightly annoyed tone. "Don't waste your time with me. Go and enjoy yourself."

Charlie chuckled, and both gentlemen moved away from the stairs, which made her slowly take an exhale. The powder room door suddenly opened, and the previous occupant stepped out. Amelia hurried in and locked the door behind her.

She looked at the mirror for a moment, having forgotten the purpose of why she was there in the beginning. The conversation that she had heard earlier somehow made her shaken. She felt upset, and her eyes were pricked with tears. She did not understand why.

She tried to rewind the conversation and understand what made her so upset. Was it what Fitz said about her that she was not good enough for him? She did not know why she had to feel upset about it. She was not his league, not in any men's league, in fact, especially with her birth defect. She was fully aware that she was not an attractive girl and would never be, especially with her small left limb. It was not for the first time she was mocked for her physical appearance. But even without knowing about her birth defect, Fitz said those hurting comments.

She smiled bitterly, felt small and silly at the same time. She wiped her tears while laughing at herself for letting such a feeling overcome her. Like Lana and her dad always said that she was a worthy person, and that was what she wanted to be. That was the reason she worked hard to support their family's financial issues. That was also the reason she hated this kind of social gathering and always buried herself with work. She had enough of hearing such demeaning words about her.

She took a deep breath to relax her tight chest, tidying up her hair, which was unchanged from the first time she stepped into the room. After she did what she was meant to do in that restroom, she had another look at the mirror to ensure no traces of tears on her face. She took another deep breath before reaching the door handle and stepping out.

She walked towards the bar, ready to order another drink before realising that someone was approaching her.

"May I have a dance with you?" Charlie offered her his hand and the friendliest smile that Amelia would perhaps ever receive from any man in her life. She looked around to find Lana was talking with Clare.

She was hesitant for a moment, but when she listened to the upbeat songs played, she knew she had nothing to worry about.

"Sure."

Because of the song, there was no need for physical contact. She did not wish Charlie to find out about her prosthetic hand. Not now, especially. They just moved along with the music, and Amelia threw her head back laughing when Charlie made some funny moves. The laughter made her heart much lighter after her brief meltdown earlier. When the music almost ended, Charlie whispered to her ear.

"Is your sister Lana seeing anyone?"

Amelia smiled and began to like this guy. He seemed genuine and possessed a personality that would match well with her sister. His eyes were glowing like a little boy who had just received his favourite toy for his Christmas gift when she shook her head as the answer.

Charlie's hand was at the small of her back and took her back to the bar where Lana, Clare and Fitz were standing. She silently exchanged a meaningful smile with her sister and tried her best to ignore Fitz's presence. She stole a glance at him from the corner of her eyes. At this time, she paid better attention to Fitz's appearance. When they were introduced earlier, Fitz almost did not utter any words and swiftly walked away from their sight.

Fitz was a tall guy, even perhaps taller than Charlie, with an athletic figure, broad shoulders, brown hair, handsome face featured with a strong jaw, straight nose and dark eyes. She had to admit that he was probably more attractive than Charlie. Looking at his appearance, she understood why he had a high standard of the opposite sex. There was no reason for her to feel upset about his comment earlier.

Her left hand was suddenly grabbed, which made her prosthetic hand shift down, dangling inside the arm sleeves of her cardigan. A choir of gasp heard, not only from Lana and their new friends but also from the culprit who created the scene.

Leah covered her mouth, realising what she had done. Without feeling guilty, she was instead giggling in amusement. Amelia could smell the alcohol from her breath and cursed inwardly, forgetting to watch over her youngest sister. *Unbelievable*, she thought. Her sister was drunk. She could not imagine if her sister went to the party unsupervised.

She felt furious with her drunk sister than with the fact Leah had accidentally announced to the public about her birth defect. Clare looked horrified, with her mouth opened in shock. Charlie and Fitz seemed shocked but still maintained their composure.

"Are...are... you...alright?" Charlie stammered. Amelia felt terrible looking at his pale face, combined with a concerned look from Lana. Internally she wanted to laugh, but she realised that in reality, this incident could spoil the chance that Lana could have with her potential Mr Right.

"I'm alright," she smiled as sweet as possible, hoping to give enough assurance that this was just a silly incident. However, when her eyes met with Fitz's stern face still in his shock, she repressed her laugh. Somehow, she enjoyed seeing his bewildered look as if he had just seen a ghost.

"Lizzy is wearing a prosthetic hand," said Lana calmly. Charlie turned his head to her as if trying to digest her words. "She was born with a small limb on her left arm."

Amelia understood why Lana spoke up for her. Her sister wanted to show her repeatedly that there was nothing to be embarrassed about her physical condition.

Amelia did not plan to escape from the uncomfortable situation. However, she was worried about the tipsy Leah, who swingingly walked away as she had forgotten the mess she had just made. She caught her sister's hand to stop her.

"Let's go home," she hissed in annoyance. But Leah ignored it, tried to pull away from her hand and pushed her. Instead, she avoided the push and tightened her grab, which made her sister start screaming and drew more attention from the guests in the room.

What an embarrassment, Amelia thought. Poor Lana that she had to suffer from what her sisters brought to her.

"I'm sorry, but I think we need to leave now," said Lana. She came forward and grabbed Leah's other hand, ready to drag her to leave. "It was nice to see you all." She smiled at Charlie meaningfully, who only nodded still in his shock and confusion on what had just happened. On the other hand, Fitz looked like he had come to understand the situation and put his hand on Charlie's shoulder as if stopping his friend from saying or doing anything wrong. Clare was the only one who had not recovered yet from her shock, and instead, her face slowly turned into disgust.

Amelia did not want to overthink what impressions they had left. Finally, Lana seemed to agree with what she had in mind and retreated while dragging Leah, who was still protesting. Once they were in the car, Amelia could not hold her anger anymore.

"Get a hold on yourself, Leah! If you still want your pocket money, you'd better think twice the next time you start drinking."

"That's not fair!" Leah screamed with tears start streaming down her face. "Mum will not let you abuse me."

"Abusing you?!" Amelia did not realise that she had raised her voice and hadn't started her car engine. They were still in the front yard of Sharon's house. Her eyes suddenly caught a tall figure emerging from the entrance door.

Fitz! She wondered why he came out of the house as if he wanted to ensure they had gone. For a moment, their eyes met, and she did not understand why he did not break the trance. Lana's voice was the one that forced her to look away.

"Let's go home, Liz. Let's talk at home."

She agreed, turned on her car engine and fled the place with a disquietude heart.

CHAPTER TWO
The Rescue

Amelia scrolled her mobile phone screen to find a message coming from Lana. Her sister was so excited that Charlie had asked her out tonight. She only smirked reading it, while at the same time, she felt happy for her sister.

As far as she remembered, Lana did not easily fall for a guy. She wondered whether her sister had done it to protect her feeling, afraid that she might feel left out if she found a guy and got married one day. She fully understood though Lana's desire to build her own family, which matched her motherly personality. Now they were already at the age that they were ready for that. Lana had a stable job, a steady income, and she even managed to have some savings even though it was not heaps.

Now Charlie came into their life. Amelia wondered whether this guy could probably be the one for Lana. He was handsome, nice and friendly, and on top of all, he was probably wealthy, at least in a better financial position than them. He looked like a responsible guy too, and Amelia hoped he was not only toying around with her sister's feelings.

Charlie contacted Lana within a week after Sharon's birthday party and the embarrassing farewell they had. Charlie asked Sharon for Lana's contact, which Sharon politely denied and suggested passing Charlie's contact to Lana. Lana's face was glowing when Sharon passed Charlie's business card.

Charlie Bentley, Bentley Pty Ltd, CEO. That was how the business card was read, complete with his office and mobile phone number. Amelia concluded from the card that this guy was perhaps in a better financial position than them. However, she had not researched what company he had. What she heard from Sharon, Charlie was involved in multiple businesses together with Fitz, and even they had quite an established business back in England.

Lana held onto that business card for a week, unsure what she had to do with it. Finally, Amelia understood what was on her sister's mind, and the only word that she could say to her was, "Follow your heart, Lana." They had a big tight hug for quite some time afterwards, as if they were going to be separated soon.

It had been over a month since Lana saw Charlie, and she could see that her sister was in love. She only hoped things went smoothly for them.

Another message came in a few hours later, and it was from Lana again, asking her what time she would finish her shift tonight and whether she could join them. Charlie was going to take her to one of the pubs in the city, together with Clare and Fitz. She frowned, thinking about why she had to join in and be the third wheel. However, the following message that came in made her understand.

Leah was joining too. She insisted on being taken along, and their mother pleaded with her to allow her sister to join in. Lana needed help.

Amelia took a deep sigh and looked at the clock. She just came in to begin her shift, and her work would only finish in three hours. It was Friday night, and that was why people started to hang out. Luckily, she had an earlier shift today and would finish around 11 pm. She replied to the message saying she would call to check their whereabouts after work.

After seeing Leah's behaviour at Sharon's party, Amelia knew her little sister would create another problem. She knew she had to be there.

She felt pretty tired when she finished her work, though somehow her body was trained for it. Apart from her full-time job, Amelia took a casual job as a kitchen helper in an Italian restaurant in the city. She did not do that every weeknight because sometimes she also helped as a taekwondo instructor for young kids. Sometimes she also worked on Saturday and Sunday mornings as a kitchen helper for weddings and conferences. She had been taking these odd jobs since the financial crisis that hit their family nine years ago, and she was only 16 years old at the time. None of her parents demanded that she be responsible for their tight budget family. But she knew she had to do something.

Her father's health started deteriorating since his car dealership business crashed. He was no longer himself as if his life spirit had been taken away. He spent most of his time reading in the room, which had been converted into his own 'library'.

Meanwhile, her mother's behaviour did not make the situation better. Her mother was devastated when they moved out from their beautiful grand house into a small and old three-bedroom rental unit. Instead of accepting reality, on the other hand, she was living in denial. She still lived as if she had plenty of money to spend, and did not wish to compromise her lifestyle. She had multiple catch-ups with friends in expensive restaurants or cafes almost every day, plus lavish shopping spending. Though sometimes she had to bite the reality because Lana or herself reprimanded her, she still did not want to wake up from her dream. The dream that she passed on to her favourite little girl Leah, made her become a spoiled girl.

Amelia hoped she could take a break one day, but she decided not to. One of the reasons was her little left limb. Unlike Lana or Leah, she did not need to have a social life anyway. She would better spend her time earning more money for the family, hoping to repay all her father's business debts. Her father could have a decent retirement life, and perhaps Lana could have some for her first house deposit once she got married. She would fight for the people who had fought for her too.

She reached the pub that Lana had texted her. When she entered the place, the first thing that caught her eyes was Leah. Her sister was sitting in one of the bar corners, talking with a couple of blokes around her, spreading her charm again. She was concerned to see those sights but tried to remind herself that Leah had the right to choose her friends. Her sister only needed to be supervised.

Her eyes wandered around again to find Lana and Charlie sitting on one of the tables. Fitz and Clare were occupying the next table. She was thinking of joining Leah instead, rather than being the third wheel. Anyway, her purpose here was to help Lana watch over Leah. However, Lana saw her and waved to her, asking her to come over. Reluctantly she walked over.

"Hi, Amelia," greeted Clare when she was approaching. Fitz turned his head to see her coming too.

Amelia forced a smile. She did not expect Clare would greet her, especially after her disgusted looks at her after finding out her little left arm. Tonight, she was not wearing her prosthetic hand. With her jacket tied around her waist, and the short-sleeved t-shirt she was wearing for work, her little left limb was on display. A contemptuous smirk was on Clare's face.

"You're not wearing your magic hand today," said Clare with a little mocking laugh. Amelia noticed that Charlie gave a little kick to his sister.

"This is my magic hand," replied Amelia while lifting her little left limb.

Clare threw a disgusted look. "I hope you could hide it under your sleeve."

"Clare..." Charlie sighed exasperatedly.

"It's summer here, Clare. This is not the UK," retorted Amelia. It was almost 30 degrees in the afternoon, and the warm air still staying.

"Thank you for coming, Amelia," Charlie interjected. This time it worked because Clare stopped talking, who turned her head to Fitz and whispered something to his ear. Amelia could read from her lips movement that she must be cursing on her.

"I heard from Lana you just finished your shift. Would you like something to eat?" asked Charlie politely.

Amelia shook her head. "No, I'm fine. Thanks." She looked meaningfully to Lana, who felt uneasy with the little exchange she had with Clare. It was a concerned look that she would get from her sister every time someone started to mock her. In the past, Lana would step in and escort her to avoid a commotion. However, she reminded her sister not to do that anymore as they grew up, especially after taking her taekwondo lessons. She had to learn how she could react comfortably in a such confronting situation.

"I would probably join Leah," she said, and she was about to turn away when suddenly the mentioned person approached them. Her little sister turned up with a man's arm wrapped around her.

"Hi guys, just want to introduce my new friend," said Leah with a playful grin. "This is Gerald."

The person called Gerald smiled warmly at them while extending his hand to Lana, who welcomed it. Charlie stood up and gave him a cold look instead. Amelia was astonished to see such manner coming from Charlie. Was he jealous? Fitz rose from his seat, turned around to face Gerald and gave him a stern, cold look as well, which made Gerald's smile slowly fade. Amelia could feel the tense atmosphere as both men looked at each other.

"We knew him already," said Charlie in an unfriendly tone.

"Oh, are you from the UK too?" Amelia threw the question with a furrowed brow.

Gerald looked at her as if just noticing her presence. "Yeah. We're old pals."

Fitz scoffed. Amelia raised her eyebrow and exchanged a look with Lana, who seemed to understand what was happening as well. Gerald's presence was clearly unwanted.

"This is Elise. She's my sister too." Finally, Leah's excited voice broke the ice. "You see, she has a magic hand. Show it to him, Liz!"

Hearing that scorn, people must have wondered how many glasses Leah had drunk. However, Amelia was used to her sister's talking manner on her little left limb. She lifted her left limb and showed it to Gerald without hesitation.

"That's what my sister is proud of about me," she sneered while getting a glare from Lana.

Gerald chuckled nervously with this weird introduction.

"Nice seeing you all," he said while nodding slightly. His eyes stopped at Fitz and Charlie briefly. "Again."

Lana returned the gesture. "Nice to meet you. We'll have a chat later."

And he went away still with his arm wrapped around Leah's waist as if she had become his. Amelia rolled her eyes, felt annoyed again with her sister.

"You should stay away from that guy," said Charlie immediately after the mentioned person disappeared from their sight. "You should tell your sister as well to stay away from him. He's not a good person."

"Why?" asked Amelia curiously.

"Well..." Charlie threw an uneasy look at Fitz.

"He's a playboy," Fitz replied. "He's sleeping around with many girls."

Amelia exchanged a look again with Lana meaningfully. She knew what Lana expected her to do. She wondered, though, whether she had to trust Fitz's words entirely. She felt there was more than that.

"Do you have any personal experience?" She directed the question to Fitz, who was stunned, did not expect to be thrown the question.

"Amelia!" exclaimed Claire with a high pitch tone. "How could you ask such a question to Fitz? Don't you see who appears to be more credible here?"

"I do not judge people from appearance," replied Amelia flatly.

"It is entirely up to you whether you want to believe him or me," Fitz responded in a clipped tone.

Somehow, Amelia expected such a reply from him. From the first time they were introduced, Fitz had been cold and impassive towards them. She would assume Lana thought likewise. She just didn't understand why such a pleasant person like Charlie could have Fitz as his best friend.

"Every story always has two sides," murmured Amelia. Fitz pursed his lips still with his stern eyes at her. For a moment, she returned his stare, and they were in that position as if sizing up each other. Then, it was Lana who broke their eyes trance. Her sister leapt from her seat and touched her shoulder gently.

"How about if you go and check on Leah?"

Amelia understood what her sister meant. She turned around and approached Leah, who was back to the bar still with Gerald's arm wrapped around her waist.

Gerald seemed like a decent bloke. Light curly brown hair, blue oval eyes with an aquiline nose and a playful grin on his lips. His dark blue denim shirt, which unbuttoned a few on the top, showed his broad chest. He looked handsome and charming, though he did way too much touching. While walking towards them, she felt a knot in her tummy, seeing how Leah brushed her butt on his lap while giggling at him intimately. She ordered a drink from the bar and joined in their conversation uninvited.

"I'm sorry about the weird introduction we had earlier," Amelia said.

Gerald's eyes turned to her with a smile. He seemed did not mind that she was interrupting his fun time.

"No worries. It's something that you would expect from rich people, I suppose."

Amelia raised her eyebrow, wondering what he meant.

"Yes, we knew each other in the UK. We went to the same college. Fitz and Charlie are from the wealthy circle, while I am just a poor guy. They do not want to mingle with people like me."

"They are such boring people, aren't they?" Leah chimed in, followed by a burst of big laughter from Gerald too.

Amelia watched them with another annoyed sigh. They looked like mad lovers together, and she felt sick watching it. She tried to hide it by quietly sipping her beer, but her eyes never left Gerald as if waiting. Gerald turned to her again when Leah was ordering another drink.

"Don't get me wrong. I like your sister." Gerald took a sigh. "I was in love with Fitz's sister, but he disapproved and separated us. And all because I don't have as much money as him."

He gave Amelia his sad downturn mouth, which she only returned with a weak smile. She was thinking about whether she could trust this guy and his story. She knew it was too early to judge.

"How do you know them, by the way?" asked Gerald.

"At a friend's party," replied Amelia.

"Ah..." He sipped his drink while his eyes travelled from the top of Amelia's head to the bottom. Amelia could feel he was checking on her appearance. Unlike Leah or Lana, who had dressed up for tonight, she believed Gerald must have found her appearance was not up to the standard of someone who could be in Charlie's circle.

"I know what kind of people they are. No offence, but I do not think Charlie is genuine with your sister. They always prefer to be with people of similar status. But, unfortunately, you and your sister do not seem to belong to their circle."

Amelia smiled bitterly hearing that. She did have the same thought before, and she was concerned if Charlie was only toying with Lana's heart. Gerald's words made more sense to her, especially feeling the haughtiness from Clare and Fitz. However, she did not want to make Lana worried, and in the end, Lana would find out herself what kind of person Charlie was.

"Thanks for your advice," she said.

"What happened with your hand?" Gerald looked at her little left limb.

"I was born this way."

He nodded and smiled empathically. "Actually, you're pretty. You have beautiful eyes."

A puzzlement spread across her face as she did not expect such a compliment. She could feel the intensity of Gerald's blue eyes searing through her skin. She had never been looked at that way before, not by any man. She shifted uncomfortably and quietly felt relieved when Leah came back and joined them.

"What are you guys talking about while I'm away?" teased Leah while she threw her arm around Gerald's neck. "About me?"

Gerald put his arm around her waist again and pulled her closer. "Of course, it's about you."

Leah giggled, which made Amelia look away, feeling sick at the scenes in front of her.

"We are leaving soon, Leah," she ordered after she took a breath and looked back at the couple, much with a chagrin. "It's getting late."

"I can take her home later," offered Gerald.

"Thanks for the offer. But I have promised our parents to make sure she's home with me."

Gerald seemed disappointed with the reply, but he kept quiet. At the same time, Amelia gave him a firm look, indicating that she did not want to argue on this.

"Alright. Can I have a couple more minutes with Gerald to say goodbye?" muttered Leah with downturn disappointed lips.

Amelia nodded, then walked away to Lana's seat, who seemed to have anticipated her return.

"I think we need to leave now."

Lana agreed. In response, Charlie, Fitz and Clare also rose from their seat and strode towards the door. Amelia turned around to see Leah was still in Gerald's arms, having a couple of kisses before she pulled herself away, giggling happily and joining them. She waved to him for the last time before stepping out of the door Amelia held for her.

Amelia turned to Gerald, and for a moment, their eyes locked. Her heart skipped a beat, perhaps because his deep blue eyes hypnotised her. Finally, she broke the trance before turning to him again and waving her hand goodbye. Gerald waved at her too and sent her away with his charming smile.

Amelia did not understand what had just happened. Did she hear correctly when Gerald said that she was pretty? Surprisingly, despite it being the first time a man called her pretty, she was not flattered. On the other hand, it made her think that Fitz's words probably were valid that Gerald was a playboy. Because that was exactly what playboys did, flirting with any girl, even with a girl with no complete left hand like her! She had a feeling that she should keep Leah away from this guy. However, she knew it would not be an easy job as Leah would not even believe that her new boyfriend was flirting with her 'disabled' sister.

They were standing outside the pub while discussing how they should go to fetch their car. Her car was parked in the opposite direction from Charlie's car. Charlie offered to accompany them to walk to the car, but Lana politely refused it as it was not necessary. Fitz seemed impatient with the conversation and dragged Charlie away.

After walking for a couple of steps, Amelia noticed three big tall guys in black jackets walking past them and going in the same directions as Fitz and Charlie. Amelia briefly turned her head. Her eyes followed the three big guys, who started walking briskly and getting closer to Fitz. Her gut instinct was telling her something was not right. So she stopped, which made Lana and Leah look at her, confused.

Her guess was correct. A second later, they could hear a commotion. From where they stood, Amelia could see the three big guys towering Fitz. And Clare's loud squeal was filling the air.

Amelia raced toward them, and she knew her sisters were behind her. As they were getting closer, she could hear both of her sisters' gasps, Clare's hysterical screaming, and the sounds of punches and thuds. Two big guys attacked Fitz while Charles watched helplessly as the third guy restrained him. Amelia saw Fitz manage to avoid a couple of punches before she started to scream.

"Stop! The police are coming!"

She meant to scare them away. Her scream did attract the attention of the attackers; however, it was useless. They were in a quiet street, and almost there was almost no other passer-by. One of the guys who fought with Fitz laughed at her.

"Do you want to join in the party, ladies?" he mocked her.

"Clare! Lana! Run!" yelled Charlie in panic. However, he was still overpowered.

"You guys would better leave!" shouted Amelia with her heavy breathing. "The police may come anytime soon." She did not know why she kept saying things that could probably be useless, but she was still pushing her luck.

"Leave the rest alone." Fitz sluggishly tried to stand up while wiping away the blood from the corner of his lips. It seemed he got it from the first surprise punch.

The same attacker who mocked Amelia earlier laughed again. "Do you want to be a hero, proud guy?"

"How much do you want? Tell us and leave us alone!" yelled Charlie. The tall guy who restrained him laughed at him.

"We just want to have fun. So come on, ladies, join us."

The attackers laughed together, and one of them started approaching where Amelia and her sisters were standing. Lana and Leah gasped again at the same time, and Amelia screamed at them, "Go back to the pub!"

Lana knew what she meant and grasped Leah away to run towards the pub, which was a couple of meters away. One of the attackers was running after them, but Amelia blocked him by grabbing his hand and using all her strength to push him to the nearby pole. Her trick worked as the guy hit the pole hard, enough to make him faint.

Fitz took the opportunity to strike the one in front of him. Meanwhile, Charlie managed to break free briefly to take Clare away before the same guy who restrained him earlier punched him hard at the back. Amelia launched towards him before he flew his next punch and threw her kick at him, separating Charlie. The attacker did not expect her next move. She took it as another opportunity to throw another kick, this time right at his face, making him wobbly and losing his balance. Amelia delivered another kick right on his chest, making him fall to the ground.

She took a breath and surveyed her surroundings. Charlie was on the ground with Clare, who was hugging him while crying. Fitz managed to strike down his opponent and quickly reached his friend to check on him. Lana and Leah ran back towards them with some people, which Amelia guessed were from the bar, and one of them wore a security guard safety vest. She took a relieved breath that the situation seemed under control.

Lana scampered to Charlie, who was still on the ground, groaning in pain. He slowly managed to sit up while breathing heavily. Amelia felt relieved to find that at least he looked fine, though probably with some nasty bruises on his body.

"You got all of them, mate? By yourself?" queried the security guard to Fitz while looking around to see all the attackers were still lying on the ground motionless.

"No," Fitz replied. "I only had a chance to get one of them." He turned to Amelia and pointed at her. "This young lady who got the rest."

Amelia looked up and blinked a couple of times, not believing what she saw. There was a ghost of a smile on Fitz's face when he looked at her. She was astonished as perhaps it was the first time she saw him in a different expression.

The security guard looked at Fitz while frowning, then looked at Amelia. He noticed Amelia's little left limb and looked again at Fitz in disbelief. Then, slowly his lips broke into a big laughter.

"You must be joking!" He patted Fitz's shoulder hard, which made him wince. "I like your joke, mate!"

Amelia turned her face away to hide her laugh seeing that scene.

After the police came, handcuffed their attackers and interviewed them with some questions, they took Charlie to the hospital to treat his wound.

It was a long night. Leah came back home grumbling but dozed afterwards. Lana looked tired but relieved simultaneously, knowing that Charlie only suffered a light injury and would return from the hospital tomorrow.

Meanwhile, Amelia was exhausted. After a nice warm shower, she threw herself into bed and was ready to shut her eyes. It had been a busy night. She was relieved that at least all of them were fine. There was a splash of memory of Gerald's blue eyes looking at her and telling her that she was pretty while smiling at her charmingly, which made her uneasy. Then Fitz's image with a glimpse of a smile on his face came to her mind replacing Gerald. She had to admit that she liked his smile. It would be better if he could do that more often. Finally, she drifted to sleep with a smile on her face.

CHAPTER THREE

Visiting Lana

It had been three weeks since the attack. Charlie only stayed in the hospital for a night, then spent a week at home before fully recovering. During that time, Lana never failed to pay a visit, making them see each other more often. Amelia was concerned observing how her sister was getting more attached to Charlie.

Amelia was not expecting any gratitude after the heroic act that she did. A brief thank you message would be the minimum that she would expect. However, she received none despite paying a visit to Charlie's house a day after he returned from the hospital. Lana was the one who conveyed a brief thank you message from Charlie instead. Somehow Gerald's words clouded her mind and shifted her judgement on Charlie's character. She tried to shake her negative thinking and wondered whether she expected too much from these people. Or like what Gerald said, Charlie perhaps was trying to take advantage of Lana and never actually looked upon them seriously, knowing their poor financial background and her physical disability.

She did not want to mention this concern to Lana. She knew her sister was in seventh heaven at this moment. Though she was worried, at the same time, she hoped what Gerald said was untrue. If she could believe Gerald, she could also think about Fitz's side of the story about Gerald. Remembering how Gerald looked at her and seemed to flirt with her, she may have to agree or partially agree with it. She tried to find out from Leah whether she was still seeing Gerald.

What surprised her, Leah seemed scared when she popped the question to her about Gerald.

Leah was startled and replied, "I haven't seen him for a while."

Amelia wondered whether Leah was too drunk even to remember how she was so smitten with Gerald that night. Her answer somehow made her slightly relieved.

"So you're not staying in touch with him?" she kept interrogating her sister.

Leah shook her head vigorously. Too hard in Amelia's eyes which made her frown.

"Nope."

"Alright."

She dropped the subject, but she could see the fear in Leah's eyes and a sigh of relief afterwards when she asked no more questions.

She felt something was not right. She wanted to discuss that with Lana. However, Lana came to them with excitement afterwards, informing them that Charlie had asked her to join him for a business trip to Sydney for a couple of days, coinciding with the school holiday next week. That also meant that Lana did not need to work, and Leah, who had just completed her year 12, was also free. They were going with the first business class available, and Charlie offered Leah to join in as well. Amelia felt the offer was too generous and wondered whether this was a trick of a rich guy to entrap an innocent girl like Lana.

Before she expressed her scepticism about the offer, Leah's behaviour once again astonished her. Leah refused to join in! She could hardly believe her hearing.

"That would be boring stuff. I'm not interested," grumbled Leah while leaving them. She and Lana exchanged glances in disbelief.

"It's better for you if she's not joining," she commented while chewing her toast. They were having breakfast when they started the conversation. "Otherwise, you will not be able to enjoy your moment with Charlie."

"I wonder whether Leah thinks she would only be the third wheel. Fitz and Clare will be on the trip too."

"You know our little sister, Lana. She never cares about being the third wheel or not, as long as she gets what she wants."

Lana laughed. "Yeah, you're right. But what happens to her? I thought she would take this opportunity. She has never been to Sydney before ."

Amelia shrugged. "Leave her be."

"Do you want to join in?" Lana looked at her expectantly. "You have not been on holiday for ages, Liz. I think it's time for you to have a little break. "

Amelia shook her head. "Thanks for the offer, but I'm good. I don't like someone else paying for my holiday trip." She looked at her sister carefully. "No offence. I suppose he's officially your boyfriend by now."

Lana smiled timidly. "I'm not sure if there's anything official between us. But he's so sweet. And well, we have been holding hands in public. He even has taken me to some of his business events and introduced me as his girlfriend."

Amelia was quiet for a moment listening to that. She was in dilemma of expressing her thoughts or not. She was surprised that Lana did not pick it up from her facial expression this time. Love had blinded her sister, and she could not blame her.

When the school holiday arrived, Amelia managed to get a casual job for Leah as a waiter in one of the restaurants that she worked for. Her dad was proud that she influenced her little sister to do some hard work rather than happily spending money shopping like their mother. However, her mother instead felt pity for Leah, telling her that she might damage her beautiful soft hands if she went to work.

Amelia remembered how Lana was excitedly preparing her suitcase for the Sydney trip. She did not have a chance to send her off when Charlie came to pick her up. Then, one night, when it was already 10 pm, and she had just finished her night shift, she received a call from an unknown number. Hesitantly, she answered it.

"Hi, Amelia. This is Charlie."

Amelia recognised Charlie's voice. However, she was surprised, wondering why he called her.

"Yes, Charlie. How are you going?"

"I'm well. Well...I'm calling you because of Lana...."

Her heart skipped a beat. She knew something was not right. "What happened to Lana?"

"She's alright. Don't panic." But Charlie's voice did not sound convincing." I don't want to call your mother and make her worry. But

Lana is sick. We went to a seafood restaurant for dinner, and she came back looking ashen. She vomited a couple of times."

"Have you called a doctor for her?"

"I want to take her to the emergency, but she is reluctant. So she is in her bed now, sleeping."

Amelia was thinking about what sickness her sister may suffer. She knew that her sister must felt terrible that she had become a burden instead. Tomorrow was Monday, and that meant Charlie needed to go to work. The purpose of this trip was actually for Charlie's work meeting. Lana must felt helpless but, at the same time, did not want Charlie to worry about her. Knowing how her sister must be thinking, Amelia knew she needed to be on her side to help her.

"I think she should be fine. Does she have a fever?"

"I don't think so. But I have paracetamol if needed." Charlie took a deep sigh. "Look, I don't mean to make you worry. I think you're right. She should be fine."

"Yeah, I would think so. I think it could probably be just a stomach bug. I know she doesn't have any allergies to seafood. She only needs plenty of liquid. She should be fine. Let her sleep, and perhaps she will be better tomorrow."

"Yeah, you're probably right, Amelia. I'll keep watching her. Have a good night."

"Have a good night."

Once the phone hung up, Amelia's first act was to get into her car as soon as possible. It would take her about 30 minutes to get back to the house and pack her luggage. She was thinking of driving straight to Sydney instead. She could borrow some of Lana's clothes, though they would be slightly bigger for her, which she could worry about later.

She texted her dad, informing him about her plan to drive 12 hours tonight to Sydney to see Lana. Unfortunately, her dad would not see the message until the next morning.

She remembered Lana did mention to her where they were staying. It was somewhere in Sydney CBD, in one of the high-class service apartments. She would find the information from google later when she took a break from driving. Based on her estimate, she would reach around noon tomorrow.

Her drive was dull, but she managed to get herself to stay awake with a can of instant coffee she bought from one of the servo, plus loud, upbeat music from the radio. When the morning sun started peeking up, she felt fresher. She stopped at one of the cafés for another coffee and breakfast before starting her journey again. She managed to reach her destination slightly before noon.

Once she arrived at the apartment lobby, her mind focused only on seeing Lana as soon as possible. She did not pay much attention to her surroundings. As a result, she bumped into someone. Her body froze to recognise the familiar face in front of her, who was equally shocked to see her.

"Amelia? What are you doing here?" Fitz looked at her with astonishment. He blinked a couple of times as if just seeing a ghost.

Amelia forced a vague smile but could not help her sudden nervousness. Looking at Fitz's sleek appearance in his business suit and tie, she felt small in her track pants and t-shirt. She had not even showered and felt her body sticky and dusty after the long drive. Only then she noticed the glamorous interior of the lobby, with a grand chandelier in the middle, which made her feel out of place.

"I'm visiting Lana. I heard she's sick," she replied. "Could you take me to her room?"

"Of course. But..." Fitz still looked at her in disbelief with squinted eyes. "How did you get here?"

"I drove."

Fitz was even more astonished. His eyes grew wide. "Drove? For 12 hours?"

She nodded, forcing another faint smile. "Would you be so kind as to take me to Lana now?" She pushed the question again impatiently. She felt people around them start staring at her. Her little left limb was prominent as she was wearing a short sleeve.

Fitz was instead giving her an impassive look and scrutinising her appearance. Her apprehension intensified when a man, she would guess as the office manager, approached them with a knitted brow.

"Is there any problem, Mr Dalton? Is this girl bothering you?"

Amelia felt annoyed and restrained herself from scoffing and rolling her eyes. She reminded herself that she came here for Lana and should not let herself get away with anger. She looked at Fitz again with half pleading eyes, hoping he would let her get her way.

"No. Everything is fine here. She is my guest. Could you please prepare a room for her? Pass the key to me later."

Amelia was taken aback hearing that. The office manager nodded and walked away.

"Follow me." Fitz gestured to her, and she ran after him.

They entered the lift, which was operated by the access security card Fitz was holding. Once they reached the 10th floor and the lift door opened, Fitz extended his arm, allowing her to pass through first. She held her breath when her body passed his as if she was afraid she could damage his suit. Nevertheless, there was a sense of achievement when she managed to pass through with no touching.

Fitz took her to one of the rooms in the corner with a double door. He knocked on the door gently and called Charlie's name before the door flew open.

"Yes, Fitz?"

Charlie did not notice her presence initially, perhaps because she was shorter and looked filthy. He probably thought she was just one of the apartment cleaners.

"Oh, Amelia?" His eyes grew wider when he finally recognised her.

"Hi, Charlie." She flinched. "Sorry for suddenly turning up, I came here as soon as I received your call. Is Lana getting better?"

Charlie was still recovering from his shock, so he stammered. "Yes. I mean no!" He put his hand up to his eyes with a deep sigh. "She looks pale, but she's sleeping now. "

"May I come in?"

Charlie nodded and moved back to let her in.

As she had guessed, it was a big spacious room with luxurious furniture filling it. She was taken to an enormous bedroom, and her eyes caught her sister's figure laid motionless on the king-size bed in the room. Slowly she approached the bed, took a closer look at her sister, and touched her forehead while carefully making sure that her filthy body did not touch the bed. Lana's eyes were half opened, recognising the different touch that she felt from her small hand.

"Liz...?"

Amelia broke a fond smile on her lips. She felt relieved at least her sister could still recognise her.

"Hi there."

"What are you...?"

She stopped her sister from trying to get up. "It's fine. I'm just checking up on you."

Lana did not seem to have enough energy to speak further. Her eyes were closed again. Amelia turned her head to find Charlie and Fitz standing about a metre away from the foot of the bed watching them. She noticed that Charlie's face looked worried. She felt pity for that guy, but at the same time, she felt her heart swelling, knowing that this man seemed to care for her sister's wellbeing.

"I suppose you're busy," she said while approaching the two men. "I understand that this is supposed to be your business trip."

Charlie nodded weakly. "Yes, there is a couple of meetings today. Lana is supposed to have a shopping day with Clare. I want her to have fun too."

"She will be fine." Amelia tried to give her best reassuring smile. "Leave her to me. I'll take care of her. If anything is urgent, I'll give you a call. Go to your meetings. I believe Lana does not want to hold you back because of this."

Charlie seemed hesitant and unsure, shifting his eyes to both her and Fitz. Amelia could see Fitz was getting impatient and strode towards the door.

"I'll wait for you in the lobby, Charlie," he said before disappearing behind the door.

Charlie took a deep sigh. Amelia gave him another reassuring smile.

"Alright. You have my number, do you?"

She nodded. And soon afterwards, after informing her what time Lana had her last paracetamol, Charlie also disappeared behind the door.

Amelia checked on her sister again and touched her forehead. It was slightly warm, but she knew her sister was still breathing evenly and sleeping soundly. The first thing in her mind was to get herself freshened up. She found Lana's clothes in the wardrobe and went to shower.

The warm shower made her feel how tired she was after the long drive. She noticed her sister was half awake and offered her a drink. She also took a towel and put a cold compress on her forehead. While changing the towel, she was eventually dozed off on her sister's side.

When she was awake, time showed 5 pm. She checked on her sister again, who was still sleeping soundly. Her tummy started to grumble, realising that she had not had her lunch. She took the room service menu and shook her head exasperatedly, looking at the premium price shown on the menu for a bowl of porridge. However, she could not go out as she did not have the keys to the room. She was about to order her food when suddenly the door opened, and Charlie came in.

"How is she?"

"She's alright. I think her fever starts to come down."

Charlie took a sigh of relief. "Her face's colour also seems to be coming back. Oh, did you give her a cold compress?"

Amelia nodded. "Our family's little trick when someone gets a fever."

"We're going to have dinner soon. I think this time we will just go to the restaurant downstairs. Please join us. I believe you haven't had anything since you arrived."

Amelia had to admit that she was starving. Still, the thought of having a meal in a luxurious restaurant in this place made her feel uneasy. Of course, she preferred to have a Whopper from Hungry Jack's, but refusing the dinner offer would not be nice either.

She slowly nodded. "Alright. What time?"

Charlie looked at his watch. "In one hour, I think. Clare complained that she was bored, and luckily we finished our meeting early."

"Sure. I'll join you once I feed Lana. I'll order a porridge for her now."

"Great! I'll order for her. By the way, I wonder whether you would like me to get another room for you."

Amelia felt awkward with the question. Her presence was to help Lana, but she realised that this room was supposedly for Lana *and* Charlie.

"If you don't mind, let me sleep in this room with Lana." She had thought about this before, and she felt this was the best solution. "And I think you shouldn't sleep here. I'm afraid you'll get sick too."

"I'm not worried about getting sick. But you're probably right. Perhaps she would be better to have you closer to her."

"I'm sorry that I have to chase you out of your room."

Charlie chuckled. "Don't worry about that. I don't have lots of stuff here anyway. I'm relieved that you've come here. I appreciate that. Fitz told me that you drove all the way from Melbourne to here?"

Amelia only nodded. Charlie shook his head in disbelief.

"I hope you're not the one who's getting sick. You must be exhausted."

"I had a little nap earlier, and it helps. Don't' worry. I may have been born with a physical defect, but I seldom get sick".

Her words were meant for a tease, but she felt guilty afterwards when he winced. Then he excused himself to get the food order for Lana and reminded her to join them for dinner.

The food order came 15 minutes afterwards and at the right time when Lana was awake and could eat more than half of the bowl before consuming another paracetamol. Charlie came in when Lana was eating. Amelia noticed that he had changed his business suit to a shirt and a pair of jeans. His face was glowing when he saw Lana was awake and looked better. He approached her and gave her a peck.

"I'm taking Amelia for dinner in the restaurant downstairs," said Charlie.

"That's a great idea!" Lana smiled excitedly. "You're going, aren't you, Liz?"

Amelia nodded reluctantly. She could not say no anyway. She believed her sister could see that she was not really keen.

"Please promise me that you will enjoy the dinner, Liz," pleaded Lana. "I believe the food must be fantastic."

"Of course," mumbled Amelia, while taking her sight away from the lovebird, slightly blushed with the affections exchanged between her sister and her boyfriend.

After Lana went to sleep again, she and Charlie went downstairs together. When they entered the restaurant, she noticed Clare looked bewildered to see her presence.

Again, she felt out of place. It was a luxurious dining restaurant. She noticed that most ladies were dressed elegantly with expensive jewellery and accessories. Clare even looked glamorous and sexy with her Tosca sack tube dress that pressed her curvy body. She had tied her hair up nicely, which showed off the diamond necklace on her swan-like neck. It was a full bold make-up on her face and arched eyebrows. Her full lips were also highlighted with bright red colour. Amelia believed that Clare must be dressing up her best for Fitz tonight.

Amelia was wearing a dress, too, because most of Lana's clothes were dresses. However, she believed she must be very plain compared to other people and looked like she was sinking in her dress. She was shorter and skinnier than Lana, and she had a flat chest compared to Lana's curvy body. She has chosen a black knee-length A-skirt dress with tiny red flowers on the bottom. Since it was a sleeveless dress, again, her little left limb was on display.

"I can't believe that you're here, Amelia." Those were the first words that came out from Clare's mouth when she was seated down. "I thought Charlie was joking when he said that you drove all the way from Melbourne to here."

"I did."

Clare looked at her in disbelief. "You must be joking. You drove 12 hours with one hand on the steering wheel?"

Amelia held her smile. "Many people drive with one hand although they have two hands, Clare. You don't drive, do you? I suppose you always have a chauffeur to drive you around?"

Charlie laughed. "You're right, Amelia. I even sometimes have a habit of just holding the steering wheel with one hand."

Amelia knew it would be a long night with such opening mocking words from Clare. She hoped she could run away, but she was starving too. She could not wait to finish her dinner and made an excuse to accompany Lana back in her room soon.

"Have you eaten in a French restaurant before, Amelia?" Clare gave her a smug smile.

Here it goes again, Amelia thought. She shook her head.

"Would you like me to order for you?" asked Charlie.

"That would be great. Thank you. Anything with chicken will do." She had to admit she did not understand any single French word on the menu.

She closed the menu book and kept silent while watching all her companions start ordering. She promised herself that she would just be a listener tonight. Inadvertently her eyes were observing Clare and Fitz, who sat opposite of her and Charlie. She could see how Clare spoke in a flirtatious way towards Fitz. On the other hand, Fitz seemed to ignore her and looked impassive. She wondered whether he had a bad mood towards his girlfriend. But the next words from Charlie made her realise that Clare and Fitz were not a couple as she had thought.

"Stop bothering him, Clare. Fitz is not your boyfriend."

Clare was laughing instead, seemingly unaffected by the admonishment.

"How is Georgie, Fitz? I believe she must have grown up now," echoed Clare while batting her eyelashes at him.

Fitz did not look at her. Amelia found he was staring at her instead because she sat exactly at his opposite. She was taken aback, but when she returned his look, he averted his eyes.

"She's alright," he replied. "She would complete her university this year."

"Will she handle one of the Dalton businesses afterwards?"

"That's the plan."

"Which business, if I may know? Well, whatever it is, I believe she will handle it well. She is a smart girl. She must be graduating with cum laude. I never see such an accomplished girl like her."

Fitz lifted his wine glass and sipped it briefly before he responded. "I have to admit that Georgie is indeed one of the most accomplished women that I ever knew. I don't see many of my acquaintances as accomplished as her."

Amelia could feel a sense of pride from that comment, which made her curious and open her mouth without thinking.

"You must have a great deal definition of an accomplished woman, I suppose," she mouthed, directed at Fitz. She heard a light chuckle from Charlie.

"Of course." Clare echoed in. "Perhaps it's not something common for your circle, Amelia." She smiled smugly. "A woman from our circle is most appropriately called accomplished because she is not only clever but also talented in many areas. Georgie is a smart girl in terms of academics, and she is talented too. She can play almost any musical instrument and speaks many languages."

She stole a flirting glance towards Fitz again before continuing, "So, at least, an accomplished woman has to be a graduate from a prestigious university, has a good career and comes from a strong educational background family. Naturally, that also means she has a good financial background too."

"On top of all, an accomplished woman should be someone who ceaselessly improves her knowledge through an extensive reading," added Fitz solemnly.

Amelia listened attentively and thought what a high standard Fitz has set for a person. His comment on her on the first day they met suddenly resonated in her mind. *She's not good enough for me.* Somehow it made her upset. She looked away as her eyes pricked with tears again. She did not understand why she had to feel this way. Why did his opinion have to affect her so much?

"So, what do you do again, Amelia?" quizzed Clare.

Amelia was startled by the question. For a moment, she thought whether she had told any of them about her job before. She presumed Lana had told them.

"I am a community officer," she replied.

"And a kitchen helper?" Clare raised an eyebrow with a scornful smile on her lips.

"Lana told me that you are also a taekwondo instructor," added Charlie.

Amelia nodded. "That's right."

"I think we have a good example of an accomplished woman here," complimented Charlie while smiling meaningfully at her.

Clare made a light scoff. "You did not graduate from university, did you?"

"No."

"And Lana did not either?"

"Both of us completed our vocational study and training." Amelia did not want to add on the reason because they did not have enough money. They could take a government loan to go to university, which she encouraged Lana to do because she had a better academic brain than her. However, they decided to enter the workforce as soon as possible since their parents depended on them for a living. She planned to keep encouraging her sister to take further studies, if possible, to advance her career in teaching.

She pondered the meaning of the questions. She noticed how Clare raised her eyebrow towards her brother. This must have something to do with Charlie's choice of girlfriend. Amelia tried to think carefully about saying something positive about her sister.

"Why do you need to do multiple jobs?" Fitz's deep baritone voice interjected. Amelia turned to him and found his eyes staring at her sternly.

"Because my parents are retired," she replied with a lifted chin. She wondered whether Lana had mentioned anything to Charlie about their father's business failure. If her sister had not told Charlie, she would not be embarrassed to tell them now. "Leah is still in school," she added. Inwardly, she complimented herself for not mentioning her mother's high spending appetite.

"Are Lana's and your income from full-time jobs not enough to support the family?"

"Unfortunately, my father's business was insolvent a few years ago. We are currently in debt agreement to pay back all the creditors."

Amelia could feel, rather than look, that Charlie, who was sitting beside her, shifted uncomfortably. Then, from the corner of her eyes, Clare spread another condescending sneer on her face.

"How long have you been doing all these to repay the debts?"

"Perhaps for the last five years since I completed my study."

"So, does Lana also do other jobs apart from her full-time job?"

"No, she does not." Charlie quickly jumped in. "Otherwise, we don't have time to have dates." He chuckled. Amelia wondered whether he did that to stop Fitz from asking more questions.

"Unfortunately, my sister is not physically trained as much as I do. She's generally healthy, but she can't overwork herself, or she will fall sick easily," explained Amelia.

"And when do you think you can repay all the debts?"

Charlie cleared his throat loudly, which Amelia could sense as his effort to stop Fitz from asking questions. However, Fitz seemed unaffected by it.

"If my calculation is correct, perhaps I can do it in five years."

"You're not considering declaring bankruptcy?"

"That will damage my father's reputation and credibility as a businessman."

"He's retired anyway."

"That's not how he would like to end it. And I agree. You're a businessman too, Fitz. Perhaps you don't feel it right now, but could you imagine if one day you lose everything and are forced to enter voluntary bankruptcy?"

"I don't think that will ever happen," Clare interrupted. "I think you have no idea at all about Dalton Enterprise, Amelia." She turned her eyes to her brother and continued, "Like I said earlier, choosing a life partner with a strong educational and financial background is important." She lifted her chin with a superior smile towards Amelia. "I suppose your father is not a university graduate, either."

Amelia tried to hide her scoff by lowering her head. "No, he is not." She turned her head back again and blurted the questions that popped into her mind. "How about the person's character? Isn't a good manner, personality and character also important traits of a person?"

"Absolutely," Fitz responded firmly.

Clare laughed to scorn. "Of course, that comes naturally from someone with good education and comes from the good breed."

"Really?" Amelia smirked. "I disagree."

"Do you have proof?" Clare lifted her chin, challenging her.

Amelia almost wanted to laugh out loud. "Good question, Clare. I suppose you have recovered from the attack that we had a month ago. You looked petrified at that time. I believe you still remember who has helped you."

"Well, don't you see the generosity that we have extended to your sister now?"

Amelia's jaw half dropped in shock. Her anger started to flare up. "So you are trying to replace a simple good manner with this generosity?"

"I do not think we owe you anything, especially since the attack was something you have pl...."

"Clare!"

Amelia was startled, and she almost jumped from her seat. Charlie's loud voice cut off his sister abruptly. His face turned pale and angry.

"What??" Clare scowled at her brother. "Fitz said..."

"Nothing is confirmed yet." This time Fitz interjected with his deep, firm, baritone voice.

Amelia wondered about the exchange between these three people. She could feel that something was not right, and they were hiding something from her. She wondered what it was and whether it would affect Lana. She knew her sister was a peace-loving person in general, and she believed Lana would not like the commotion that she had just initiated.

For a second, there was an awkward silence between them. She heard a deep sigh from where Charlie was sitting.

"Look, Amelia. I want to apologise if we offend you in any way," he said softly.

"I'm just teasing all of you," teased Amelia, hoping it would melt away the situation. She felt relieved when Charlie broke a weak smile, but Clare put a grumbling face, and Fitz gave her a flinty stare.

The rest of the dinner became stiff and was only inserted with small talk between Fitz and Charlie about their meeting tomorrow.

When the dinner ended, Amelia made an excuse to leave to see Lana soon, while the rest said they would be sitting in the lounge for some drinks. She entered the lift and pressed the button to Lana's room level with a deep sigh. She could not wait to leave this place.

Her wish was not immediately granted, but she was relieved when Lana was recovering the following day, and she drove back to Melbourne in the evening despite Lana's insistence on staying. This was perhaps the first time she did not listen to her sister.

CHAPTER FOUR

An Accusation

Another month had passed, and Amelia could see how Lana was more deeply in love with Charlie. Charlie had invited their family for a simple belated housewarming celebration. His parents were coming from England for this special occasion.

Amelia understood that Lana would be nervous about meeting Charlie's parents. She could only suggest her sister be herself, and everything would be alright. But deep inside her heart, she knew that Lana was worried about what Charlie's parents would think about her 'disabled' sister.

Amelia almost suggested the idea of not turning up with the excuse she had to work. But on the other hand, Lana warned her that she MUST turn up to accompany her. She could not deny her sister's request. Furthermore, as one of Charlie's closest neighbours, Sharon was invited too. She looked forward to seeing her friend, especially after hearing that Sharon was engaged with someone.

Sharon shared this news a couple of weeks ago through personal messages. She even shared a picture of her fiancé. He was not a handsome guy, not according to Amelia's opinion. He was a tall and skinny guy, with a long face and long nose. He looked nice, but Amelia wondered about his personality. She always thought Sharon had an angelic character, like Lana. However, she had to admit that Sharon was not as beautiful as Lana. Sharon had dark straight hair and downturn eyes. She was as tall as her, but she was pretty plain and simple in her appearance, although she came from a well-off family. But at least Sharon had a perfect physical body, unlike her. She always thought Sharon deserved a good man to be at her side.

She kept her promise to attend Charlie's housewarming party. She rushed back home to freshen up before going to the party and changed into a dress. As a result, she forgot to wear her prosthetic hand as she had planned. She almost wanted to turn her car back home. However, she thought she should not be bothered by what people might say. She knew for sure that Lana would not blame her if she did not wear it. Her mother and Leah may have different opinions about this, though.

She arrived one hour late. Charlie seemed to have invited many guests, and her late presence would go unnoticed anyway. She looked around to find anyone familiar and smiled when she saw Sharon with a man on her side, which she guessed was Colin, her fiancé. He looked slightly different from the picture without his glasses, but Amelia was sure her guess was correct from his tall skinny feature.

"Hi, Liz! Finally, you're here." Sharon welcomed her warmly, looking excited to see her. "Let me introduce you to Colin. Colin, this is Lizzy, my best friend."

Colin nodded his head and smiled at her, but Amelia could notice that his eyes grew wider in shock when he saw her little left limb. She was wearing a short sleeve dark blue dress tonight, which made her little left limb displayed. Colin did not hide his astonishment at what he saw. His face even slowly turned into a disgusted look that reminded Amelia of Clare's first reaction when she saw her little limb.

Amelia was used to such a reaction. She glanced at her best friend and gave her a smile reassuring her that she was okay. Sharon felt uneasy, though.

"Lizzy has had this since she was born. But she is the most independent person that I have ever known. She is a taekwondo instructor, you know," uttered Sharon as if hoping it would change Colin's perspective on her best friend in this instant.

Colin forced a nervous smile. "Oh yeah, that's wonderful. Mrs De Boyville is a charitable person. She is a benefactor of an organisation that helps kids with disabilities."

Amelia raised her eyebrow. She wondered who Colin meant. He spoke as if he had just complimented the most extraordinary woman in his life. Amelia wondered whether Sharon should be jealous or not.

"Mrs De Boyville is Colin's employer," explained Sharon.

Amelia made an inaudible "Ahh.." mouth shaped and nodded.

"Yes, Mrs De Boyville has been generous to me. She gave me a good role in her company, and I am honoured to be her trusted person. I believe you've heard De Boyville's company before."

Amelia shook her head. "Is it in Melbourne?" she doubted.

"It's actually from the UK, but it's also Australia wide. Haven't you ever heard it before? The corporation worked in various fields, including winery, FMCG manufacturing...."

Blah..blah..blah...Amelia could not listen to him anymore. Colin loved to talk and not only talked but boasted. She wondered how Sharon could stand this guy. She felt Sharon deserved a better one.

Fortunately, Colin's attention was taken by another guest whom he claimed he knew. Thus, she and Sharon had an opportunity to be alone and talk as she expected.

"How do you know him again?" quizzed Amelia curiously.

"He's one of my dad's acquaintances," answered Sharon timidly while sipping her drink.

"What makes you like him?"

Sharon took a sigh. "He's nice. I found him sometimes funny too. But, I know he could be quite annoying for some people."

Amelia looked at her friend for a while, trying to read her expression whether she was happy with her choice. She knew Sharon was not a fussy person and was quite easily content. Perhaps someone like Colin was good enough for her, and Amelia did not wish to comment about it. She did not even dare to find someone for herself.

"Congratulations, by the way," she breathed while taking a glass of champagne and raising the glass to Sharon's.

"You have to attend my wedding. It will be in Adelaide."

"Oh? Are you moving to Adelaide?"

"Yes, because that's where Colin will be based. He will manage one of De Boyville's businesses in Adelaide."

"When is the wedding? Let me save the date."

"In Spring. In October."

Their conversation was severed as Colin came back to claim Sharon to introduce her to some of the guests that Colin knew. She would not be surprised if Colin knew many people here. Charlie must have invited people from his business network and high-class social circle.

She looked at her surroundings again and spotted her mum and dad talking with another old couple. From their looks, Amelia did not believe that those people were Charlie's parents because there was no resemblance. She looked around again to find Lana and Charlie with a couple who now she believed were Charlie's parents. Fitz and Clare were also standing next to them. Lana talked with Charlie's mother politely, while Charlie's mother's lips kept moving as if she was lecturing Lana.

She was hesitant to approach them. Perhaps it was better not to turn up at their nose at all, so they did not need to know what Lana's sister looked like. However, she was too late as Charlie spotted her immediately. He waved at her and signalled her to approach them. It seemed she could not run away anymore.

"Hi, Amelia. I am glad you have finally come. Let me introduce you to my mum and dad. Mum, Dad, this is Amelia, Lana's sister."

Amelia gave her best smile while rubbing her wet nervous hands on her dress. "Hi, nice to meet you, Mr and Mrs Bentley."

As she would expect, the old pair gave her an astonished look as their eyes landed on her little left limb. At that moment, she cursed inwardly that she had forgotten her prosthetic hand. Instead, Lana gave her an assuring smile which made her feel upset for potentially embarrassing her sister.

"Amelia was born like that, Mum," snickered Clare as she noticed her parents' reaction. "I told you Lana has a disabled sister."

"Amelia is not disabled. How could you say that?" Charlie defended her. "She is the most independent person I ever met, much more independent than you, Clare."

Clare scoffed and looked away.

Seeing that his parents seemed to disagree with his opinion, Charlie tried to melt the situation by taking Lana away for a dance. Fortunately, his parents were also taken away by one of their acquaintances. Amelia quietly took a sigh of relief that she could escape from the tension.

She just wanted to find someplace quiet while filing up her tummy. She took some of the canapes and found a spot outside the house just behind the pillar. As she stood facing the swimming pool, she saw Leah talking with some young boys around her age near the pool. She had to admit that her sister managed to spread her charm again, joking around with her new friends. Undoubtedly, that was one of her sister's talents that she must envy. Regardless she could not change the fact that she was not physically perfect like her sister.

Suddenly she heard a voice that sounded familiar to her; her mother. She was unsure whom her mother was speaking to, but she rolled her eyes, wishing she could stop that conversation.

"I always know my Lana is the best. Soon she would bring our family back to where we were."

Amelia took a peep over her shoulder to see it was Sharon's mother that her mother was speaking to. *Right, of course*, she thought. Perhaps in this party, Sharon's mother was the only person with whom her mother was familiar with, and she would be boastful to.

Once she finished her little snack, she decided to approach the bar and get something to drink. She needed some, especially after what she had just heard. She ordered a glass of wine and drank it at once. She was ready to go back to her 'hiding' place when someone landed precisely in front of her. She held her breath, recognising the person.

"May I have a dance with you?"

She could not believe her ears. Fitz stood in front of her asking for a dance?

She was probably the most unattractive girl at this party, and perhaps the only one that had not been asked for a dance that night. She did not care and never bothered. Now, being asked instead, she wondered whether she had drunk too much.

She blinked a couple of times, thinking that probably this was just because of her drink. But as if hypnotised, she took the hand offered to her and quietly followed Fitz motioning her to the dance floor.

It was a slow song, not an upbeat one. That meant they had to stand close and touch each other's hands. With her little left limb that could not reach Fitz's tall shoulder, she left it down instead, and Fitz took the small of her back.

She could hear her heart pounding and her head spinning. She wondered whether it was the effect of drinking a glass of wine at once instead of sipping it. His earthy masculine scent overtook her senses, which she had to admit she liked. *This guy smells so good*, she thought. She never smelled any other guy as good as this. Perhaps because most of her male friends so far were not from wealthy circles like Fitz. *So, this is probably the smell of a rich guy,* she giggled in her mind.

"Are you well?"

Amelia wondered if she had actually giggled instead.

"Yes, I'm good. Thanks for asking. And how are you, Fitz?"

"I'm good, thank you."

There was a silent pause for a moment. Amelia took that opportunity to glance at her surroundings. As she expected, some eyes looked at them curiously, including Clare, who looked furious. That made her think about the intention of Fitz asking her for a dance. Many eligible girls at the party must be dying to dance with him.

"Is your sister still seeing Gerald?" he asked.

"Not that I know of."

"Are you seeing him? It seems that you had a good chat with him last time."

Amelia swallowed and wondered where this question was going. "That was the last time I saw him."

"I wonder what he has told you."

Amelia was even more intrigued. "You mean on what he told me about your history with him?"

Fitz nodded slightly.

"Whatever your history with him, it's not my business," she answered tactfully.

They went into silence again. For the outsider, it looked like they enjoyed the romantic music that played along with their slow dance. Amelia almost forgot to breathe, realising how close they were at that moment. Fitz was much taller than her, and her head was only at Fitz's lips level. She could feel his breathing blowing her hair softly.

"May I ask something? On the night of the attack, what prompted you to come back and check on us?"

Amelia pondered on the question. She braced herself to look up to see him.

"Because I felt something wasn't right."

He stared down at her with his glassy eyes. "Why did you feel that way?"

Amelia sensed that he did not believe her.

"Those three big guys walked past by my sisters and me. Looking at their faces straight over to us, I turned my head to see where they were going. It looked to me they were following you. And I was right. I saw them attacking you."

"I believe those people were only targeting me," he muttered. His deep voice was calm and even. But Amelia could sense it meant something else.

Their eyes met again, and Amelia felt her body getting tense. She felt something was not right. Suddenly the conversation at the dinner in Sydney when she was teasing Clare for being ungrateful came into her mind. Clare almost said something to her, which was then cut off by both Charlie and Fitz. She tried to link all this conversation with Fitz's question earlier about her relationship with Gerald.

An answer struck her mind that made her gasp. She snatched her hand away and stopped dancing despite the music was still playing, and the couples around them were still swinging. Their abrupt movement invited curious glances around them.

"You think that the attack was plotted by Gerald... and us?" She was bewildered. He gave her an equally steely look with a lips upturn with contempt. She was furious.

"That night, I only wanted to help," she hissed in an effort to control her anger. "My sisters were also in danger. And is this what we get in return? What's wrong with all of you, rich people?"

Fitz did not immediately respond to it. Instead, he glanced at their surroundings. The song had ended, and they knew it would be awkward for them to stand stiffly in the middle of the dance floor. So he took her arm gently and motioned her outside, behind the pillar where Amelia had called her favourite 'hiding' spot earlier.

Amelia understood what he tried to do and quietly followed him without resistance. She still remembered where they were. If they were somewhere else, she was sure she would not hesitate to start a fight; a real fight.

"You sounded like Gerald. I believe you learn those words from him," whispered Fitz to her ear as they were walking.

Amelia's eyes grew wider in disbelief. Though Fitz's stiff expression still did not change, she perceived those words as sarcasm. "I do not need to learn from Gerald to say those words. The evidence is right before my eyes. We came back to help you, which put all of us in danger. But you're accusing us instead now?"

As they had found their quiet corner to talk, she turned around and faced him with a lifted chin.

"Listen to me, Fitz. Whatever your history with Gerald, it doesn't mean that everyone that he meets would be your enemy too."

"Those attackers have admitted to the police that Gerald hired them as a way of pleasing his girlfriend whom he met at the bar," gloated Fitz with curled lips.

Amelia was stunned. "So, are you going to press charges? Are the police going to capture him?"

Fitz did not reply. He averted his eyes instead. Amelia did not expect the reaction and looked at him, confused.

"What those attackers said did not mean anything," hissed Amelia. "They could make up whatever story they like. If you think that Gerald and I or my sisters plotted the attack, then why did we come back and help you?"

Again Fitz did not reply and only looked at her expressionless. Amelia hoped that was a sign that her reasoning made sense to him and may alter his false accusation.

She quietly took a deep breath. "Whatever your theory about this, please keep Lana away from this. Her feeling towards Charlie is genuine."

With that, she walked away, ready to leave that party. She did not care if any of her family scolded her later at home for leaving the party without a word. Her heart was in turmoil after the accusation Fitz threw at her and her sisters. After all, it was not a great night for her and especially for Lana.

She could not believe that things were getting worse than she thought. Lana was already humiliated enough by having a disabled sister presented, and now Leah's involvement with Gerald made things worse. Lana could potentially lose her chance of happiness because of this.

She thought whether Fitz's accusation could be true, whether Leah was aware of the planned attack. Her body shivered with worry, and her mind was set. First, she had to make sure Leah stayed away from that person called Gerald.

CHAPTER FIVE

A Broken Heart

It was another busy day for Amelia. She went to her full-time work as usual and continued with her duty as a taekwondo instructor. She reached home when the time was already showing 10 pm. After work, she felt tired and could not wait to have a warm shower, but it did not stop her from checking the mailbox.

A couple of letters were addressed to her father, which made her sigh as those letters were from the bank, debt collectors, creditors and even some law firms. All must be related to her father's business close down and the unpaid debts. Now she was the one who took care of most of her father's business settlement. Somehow, it became her responsibility. Any related matters to the business close down only brought her father back to old, painful and devastating memories.

She could not blame her father. It was a painful memory not only to him but to each of his family. Her father was beating himself too much for what happened. What she did not understand was why his father had lost the fighting spirit within him. He was the father who had been fighting for her, encouraging and trusting her when she did not have confidence in herself since she was born with her little left limb. But this time, her father seemed to want to run away. Amelia sometimes thought perhaps it was now her turn who needed to fight for him.

One of the letters was different from the others, making a smile break on her lips. It was a wedding invitation. She knew it must be from Sharon, who had texted her specifically about this.

The wedding would be held in a beautiful winery estate in Adelaide. It was also one of the businesses that Colin was handling as a General Manager for De Boyville. Initially, Sharon wanted to ask her as the bridesmaid, but she was hesitant, knowing Colin's reaction. However, Amelia had given assurance to her friend that she would be happy to be there as a guest only. She also promised that she would attend it with her prosthetic hand, so none of Colin's relatives and friends would freak out seeing her.

When she entered the house and turned on the light, she was startled to find her father sitting in the corner of the living room, staring blankly at the floor. She wondered for how long her father had been there sitting in the dark.

"Dad?"

Mr Bettney looked up at her and smiled. Amelia was relieved that at least her dad was responding.

"Another mess again, Liz," he smiled bitterly.

Amelia furrowed her brow while slowly approaching him. "What do you mean, Dad?"

Mr Bettney took a deep sigh. "It's Lana. Charlie left her."

Amelia held her breath. The news that she had been dreading to hear was finally here.

She had forgotten how many weeks ago Charlie's housewarming had been. She had left the party with turmoil in her heart after Fitz's accusation of her involvement with Gerald in planning the attack outside the pub. None of those conversations she had shared with Lana, and she was sure Lana was even unaware that she was dancing with Fitz that night. But, as far as she remembered, everyone came back home with a high spirit. Lana was a bit down as it was not a smooth meeting with Charlie's parents. But afterwards, her sister's enthusiasm returned, and she even told her when Charlie's parents returned to the UK.

Nothing between the lovers seemed odd. Last week, Lana mentioned that Charlie flew to London with Fitz and Clare for some business matters. Lana seemed sad that she had to be separated from her boyfriend, but Amelia believed they had been keeping in touch. She did not understand why they broke up.

"Your mum was excited thinking that Lana would end up with Charlie and bring our family back to where we were. I was excited too. But don't get me wrong, Liz. I'm not selling your sister for the sake of money." Her father's voice faltered. "I think he is a nice guy, and they seem to love each other. But I was probably wrong."

Amelia quietly took a sigh too. It was a piece of sad news. Lana must have been devastated, but it seemed the breakup was affecting not only Lana but almost their whole family.

"Your mum was hysterical, blaming all of us for what happened," sniffled Mr Bettney. "She blamed me for bringing all of us down. She blamed you for showing up at Charlie's party."

Amelia bit her lips. From her father's description, she could vividly visualise the image of her unhappy mother. Her chest became tight.

"It's not your fault, Liz." Her father looked at her with a soft smile. She always had that encouraging smile when she felt upset over her little limb.

Amelia nodded, returning the smile with her own. "It's not your fault either, Dad."

Mr Bettney released a soft laugh, and Amelia knew it was a sad laugh.

"Where is Lana?" She looked around, noticing that the house was calm. Even though it was already late on a Friday night, she knew Leah would typically still be awake watching TV at this time.

"She's with Leah. Leah took her together with some friends to the city, I heard. To cheer her up."

Amelia checked her mobile phone. Lana would inform her if she was going out with Leah. She had not had a chance to check her message since she had finished work. Her guess was correct as Lana sent her a message informing their whereabouts and asked her whether she could join in. She replied and grabbed her bag again.

"I'll get them home. " She looked at her dad, who was still not moving from his seat. She planted a kiss on his forehead. "Go to sleep, Dad. Please don't overthink this. Lana will be fine. All of us will be fine."

Her dad stretched his arm and gave her a brief warm hug while nodding his head. Then, she went out, leaving the light on.

Her drive through the quiet street to the city took only about 20 minutes. However, the pub where Lana and Leah were, was still lively when she entered the place. Unfortunately, the light in the pub was quite dim, but she managed to spot her sisters sitting on one side of the bar.

Lana was sitting alone, quietly sipping her drink. On the other hand, Leah was laughing excitedly, dancing around in the arms of a man. A man that Amelia did not expect to see. She was supposed to make sure Leah was not seeing this man. But she was too late.

"Hi, Liz! Finally, you're here!" Leah welcomed her with a luminous smile. Looking at her erratic behaviour, Amelia was sure her sister must have been drinking a lot. Her eyes landed on the table, and she counted how many empty glasses there were, including those within Lana's reach. Lana probably had drunk a lot too. But instead of being like Leah, Lana was into a quiet mode when she was drunk.

"Hi, Liz. How are you?" Gerald gave her his charming grin, to which she was hesitant to respond.

"Good, thank you," she muttered flatly. She looked at Lana, who seemed unaware of her presence, staring blankly at her glass while sipping from it.

"Poor Lana. And damn that Charlie!" yelled Gerald with a laugh, followed by Leah. "As I told you before, he is not serious with your sister. They are just bastard snobbish rich people!"

Amelia wished Lana did not hear that. She winced and ignored the crazy couple, thinking she would deal with them later. She approached Lana and took the glass from her hand. Her action did make Lana finally pay attention to her surroundings and become aware of her presence.

"Hi, Liz." Lana broke a weak smile. "Glad you can join us. Please sit down and have a drink."

Amelia followed her wish and quietly took the seat next to her sister.

"I heard about you and Charlie. What happened?"

Lana took a sigh before she answered, "For three days, he did not reply to any of my messages and calls. I knew something was not right. And today, I received this message."

Lana showed her the message on her mobile phone. *We'd better not see each other anymore. I wish you the best. Goodbye.*

Amelia felt her blood boiling. *What a coward!* Her eyes were back to Lana, who again sipped her drink.

"Did he say something before? Perhaps about his parent's opinion on you?"

Lana shook her head. "Not exactly. He knows that his parents are not approving of us 100% yet, but he said they only need more time to get to know me better."

"And did they mention their concern about my hand?"

Lana's eyes flew widely opened. "No! And I won't let them!"

Amelia felt proud to see the flame in her sister's eyes again. It was the same burning fire that she used to see whenever her sister defended her from anyone who tried to mock her because of her little limb.

"You know me, Liz. I won't let anyone mocking at you, even though that person is Charlie and his family. If that is the reason he leaves me, I'm even more relieved that he goes away!"

Amelia knew Lana would say that, but it still did not remove her guilt that she could potentially be the reason for the breakup.

The huge laughter from behind made her turn her head. She watched Leah and Gerald drank, laughed and danced like they were enjoying the time of their life. She knew she had to do something with them.

She was confused about who to believe. It looked like Gerald's words now had been proven by Lana's breakup with Charlie. However, somehow deep inside, she was not comfortable with Gerald either. Fitz's accusation of Gerald's plan in organising the attack did haunt her. Fitz was probably correct, but she was scared if Leah had been aware of the attack too. Now with the breakup, perhaps it did not matter anymore. But she still strongly felt that they should stay away from Gerald. She could not trust someone who could organise such an evil plan to hurt others.

"Let's get you home." Slowly she took Lana's arm and made sure she could stand. Luckily she could, though Amelia knew that Lana was not herself anymore. If there was a bad guy around, she could be easily taken advantage of. Lana leaned on her while walking towards Leah and Gerald.

"Come on, Leah. Let's go home," she ordered her sister.

Leah turned around and looked disappointed that her fun time was over.

"I can take her home later," offered Gerald.

Amelia did not want to give him a chance. "No, thank you. She's coming home with me." She gave a grim look to Leah, which made her sister obey. She knew Gerald looked unhappy with her cold attitude toward him, but she did not give him a damn.

Reluctantly Leah said goodbye to Gerald and then helped her sister to carry Lana. After they stepped out of the bar, Amelia briefly turned to her back, ensuring no one followed them. She knew she had offended Gerald. If what Fitz said about him was correct, she could expect Gerald to do the same to them too, which meant she had to be aware. Nevertheless, she felt relieved when they reached her car and got into it.

"Why are you still seeing him?" quizzed Amelia while driving. Leah sat next to her while Lana was sleeping in the back seat.

"It was a coincidence that we met earlier. I'm not exactly seeing him. Anyway, since Lana has now broken up with Charlie, it doesn't matter anymore whether I'm seeing Gerald or not. I know you don't want me to see him because Charlie does not like him," answered Leah.

"It doesn't matter whether Lana is still with Charlie or not. I don't think he's a good guy."

"He's cute."

Amelia rolled her eyes.

"Look what Charlie has done to Lana. Charlie and Fitz are real snobs. I was happy that Gerald managed to get those guys to give them a lesson."

Amelia's heart almost stopped; what she was scared of seemed real. She could not take her eyes off the street because she was driving, but from the corner of her eyes, she could see Leah gasping and her hand flew to her mouth, realising the words she had just spat out.

"Gerald planned on the attack on Fitz and Charlie that night," muttered Amelia as comprehension down to her. "And you knew it!"

"I did not!" Leah shouted in a whisper. "That night, he only said that he would give them a lesson. I did not exactly understand what he meant."

"But you realised it after the attack, and you did not say anything."

"Of course, I would not say anything! It would get all of us into trouble. And Lana was with Charlie at that time."

Amelia grunted in frustration. "Yet, now knowing what he had done, you are still seeing him?"

Leah shrugged. "Well, no one got hurt in the attack anyway."

Amelia almost wanted to slam the brake and smack her sister in anger. But she remembered that Lana was still sleeping in the back seat. She did not wish to wake her up and know what they were quarrelling about. Her right hand was clutching tightly on the steering wheel in an effort to control her rage.

"How could you say that? Those attackers almost hurt you and Lana, too, if I did not stop them. If Gerald could plan such an evil thing, how could you trust him?"

Leah did not retort back, and it gave Amelia time to control her frustration further while focusing on her driving. There was only silence for the rest of the journey, and Amelia hoped her last words could shake Leah to her senses.

They carefully took Lana to the bedroom upstairs, which Amelia shared with. Meanwhile, Leah had been fortunate to have her own room.

Amelia sat on the edge of the bed for a moment while observing her sister. After Leah's confession earlier, her head was even more in a mess. Fitz's accusation was correct that Gerald planned on the attack, and they were dragged into this. Even though now Lana was not with Charlie anymore, this could be one of the reasons Charlie broke the relationship. Fitz must have shared his suspicion with Charlie.

Amelia was startled when her hand was softly touched. She did not realise that Lana was half awake and saw her presence there.

"I will be fine, Liz," Lana mumbled with a weak smile on her face. Amelia took her hand and squeezed it as if giving her strength. "I thought he's the one. I was so happy with him. I even have given myself to him...."And a tear rolled down her cheek. Lana wiped it, then turned her body around and sobbed.

Amelia buried her head in her hand. Her tears were also threatening to roll down. Her heart suddenly felt heavy, and her chest was tight. She knew Lana was never into any man before. Losing her virginity to the man she loved probably was not wrong, but losing it to someone who did not appreciate her must be hurtful.

She went to the shower room and cried, too. Cried for Lana and her broken heart, for the misfortune that had befallen their family since the failure of her father's business, and for herself for feeling so useless unable to protect her loved ones.

CHAPTER SIX
A Moment of Weakness

Amelia was unsure how many times she had been sneezing for the past weeks. It was spring, and it was also hayfever time in Melbourne. She was not immune to hayfever, but she had never had it this bad as far as she remembered. Consuming antihistamine did not seem to work entirely on her this time. Her eyes and nose were watery, but what annoyed her, every time her body shook vigorously because of the sneeze, she felt worn out.

She threw her sight to the scenery around on her way to Barossa Valley. It was a beautiful winery estate in South Australia, about 40 minutes away from Adelaide, where Sharon's wedding would be held. It had been ten hours of driving right after she completed her taekwondo teaching session. She enjoyed her long drive as usual, but she had to admit she felt weary too.

Lana had offered to get her a flight ticket instead, but she refused. She still preferred to drive no matter how far her destination was. She enjoyed the scenery displayed in front of her throughout her journey; the farms, the river, the bridge, the growing spring yellow wildflower, and even the little town that she would pass by and sometimes stop by along the way. For her, that was the best entertainment that she could appreciate rather than sitting idly on the plane.

She had hoped Lana would join in the trip. However, her sister refused. Sharon's invitation was extended to any of her family. Her mother was too embarrassed to attend the wedding, especially after Lana's breakup with Charlie. Her dad preferred to be in his solitude in the library. Leah still had school, while Lana did not want to skip her work. Although Amelia planned to head back to Melbourne straight after the wedding, Lana preferred to keep herself busy with work, preparing for the upcoming exam.

Despite Lana's refusal to join her, Amelia felt she could leave her sister with peace of mind. The season had changed from autumn to winter and now spring, and Lana's breakup with Charlie was almost six months ago. The breakup did affect her sister, but she had to admit Lana was holding up pretty well. Her sister was not interested in any social gathering at the moment or even trying to meet a new guy. She needed more time to heal her heart wound. That was why Amelia thought this trip could help her forget the past, but Lana preferred to bury herself with work instead.

Amelia took a deep sigh whenever she remembered Lana and Charlie. Her heart was heavy remembering what happened, but perhaps things sometimes were not meant to be.

She looked at the time as the sun started rising. She had been driving for the whole night with little sleep. As she had estimated, she would reach her destination in another two hours. Then she would have a couple of hours to sleep before joining Sharon's wedding ceremony in the afternoon. Her body yearned to rest on the bed soon. Perhaps this was the first time she felt this way after a long journey. Her energy seemed to have been drained.

As she entered her accommodation, which Sharon had already arranged and booked, she had to admit that Sharon had chosen a beautiful place for her wedding. She had not been to this area before, and despite her fatigue, she felt excited at the same time. Though the wind was still slightly chilly, the clear sky and sunshine made the atmosphere peaceful and serene.

Sharon booked a room for her in a small guesthouse accommodation not far from the actual wedding place, only a five-minute drive away. She was the one who requested to be booked here instead of in the winery accommodation itself. She did not want Colin to think that she was trying to take advantage of Sharon's hospitality. Anyway, she did not need a big room to sleep in since she came alone.

After her warm shower, she managed to rest for a while though it was not enough. Luckily she put her alarm on. Otherwise, she felt it was hard to get up. She got herself dressed up for the wedding, put on her makeup, and did not forget to wear her prosthetic hand. She giggled when imagining Colin's horror face if she came with her little limb instead. In half an hour, she left wearing a V-neckline long sleeve dark green wide skirt dress and a pair of short heel shoes that allowed her to move her legs freely.

She arrived at the right time when the ceremony was about to start. She looked around to find familiar faces among the guests, mostly Sharon's family and some of her parents' acquaintances. The rest, she guessed, would be Colin's side of family and friends.

The matrimonial ceremony was held outdoors, in the backyard of the winery. Amelia admired the beautiful set-up of the wedding with colourful soft champagne and pink roses decorating the wedding arches. She slowly walked to get to her seat in one of the rows when she noticed a tall, familiar figure standing not far from her. She held her breath, recognising the person approaching her and greeting her.

Amelia did not expect him to greet her first. "Hi, Fitz. How are you?" She did not expect to see him here. She frowned, wondered how Fitz had any relation with Sharon apart from knowing her as Charlie's neighbour.

"I am from the groom's side," said Fitz as if he could read her mind.

"Oh? You're Colin's relative?"

He shook his head. "No. But he works for my aunt Catherine."

"De Boyville?"

He nodded affirmatively. "I was not planning to attend the wedding. However, I happen to be in town. My aunt wants to see me, and she asks me to come for the wedding."

"Right." Amelia nodded. Now she could link the connection.

"Are you staying in the winery accommodation too?" he quizzed.

Amelia felt that he was scrutinising her look. Was her appearance so poor that even he thought she did not deserve to be in such a luxurious place as here? Moreover, her attire was mainly from the Target department store, unlike him or other guests who seemed to be wearing some international boutique designer products.

"No, I am staying in the nearby guesthouse."

Their conversation had to stop as the ceremony was about to start. Fitz excused himself and walked toward a lady whom Amelia estimated perhaps slightly older than her mother. She guessed that lady must be his aunt, who was also Colin's employer.

Mrs De Boyville looked glamorous in her expensive dress and blinking jewellery. She had a sharp nose, square chin and stern eyes with dark brown wavey hair. Somehow, Amelia found the similarity between her and Fitz.

The wedding ceremony was beautiful, quirky and touching, even though Amelia still felt Colin was not a pleasant man. Sharon looked glowing, and she wanted to be happy for her. She only prayed that Colin would be the right man for her best friend. Sharon also looked beautiful in her mermaid tail wedding gown and full-face makeup, which improved her downturn eyes and overall look.

It was also a lucky day for Sharon and Colin. Although the sky was clear and sunny earlier, the cloud started coming in when the ceremony was over. So the guests moved slowly to the reception area, which fortunately was indoor. Amelia was seated at a table with some of Sharon's parent's friends, whom she knew as her neighbour before her family moved out from the suburbs. But most of them did not recognise her anymore.

When the guests started to move around and dance, Amelia took the opportunity to congratulate the bride and groom.

"I'm so glad you are here, Liz," thanked Sharon while their cheeks met.

"You look beautiful," complimented Amelia. "Congratulation, Colin." She turned to Colin and shook his hand. Colin seemed taken aback by the firmness of her handshake. "Please take care of her. If not, I'm not going to be easy with you."

Colin chuckled nervously, which made Amelia smile in satisfaction for intimidating him.

"Will you still be here tomorrow?" asked Sharon.

"I will drive back to Melbourne early tomorrow morning," answered Amelia. She could catch a glimpse of disappointment on her friend's face.

"I hope you can stay for another day. I want to show you my new house."

"I'm sorry, Sharon. Not tomorrow. But I promise I will revisit you. By the way, aren't you going for your honeymoon tonight?"

Sharon shook her head. "We will fly off tomorrow late night. Colin still has a meeting with Mrs De Boyville in the morning." Her eyes glanced to her husband, who coincidentally was talking to his employer. "I suppose you are surprised too to find out that Fitz is Mrs De Boyville's nephew," observed Sharon as they were also seeing Fitz talking with his aunt and Colin.

"Yes," Amelia nodded, and without realising it, she took a sigh.

"You don't look happy to see him."

"Seeing him only reminded me of Lana's breakup with Charlie. You know, he's Charlie's best friend."

Sharon smiled. "I know. But you don't have a right to dislike him just because of his connection with your sister's ex-boyfriend."

Amelia chuckled. "Yeah, of course, I know that, Sharon. Anyway, I'm not going to see him frequently."

"But I find him staring at you a lot."

Amelia frowned, then she laughed. She did not understand what her friend meant. Since today was her friend's special day, she did not want to take more of her time while many other guests seemed to queue up to congratulate the bride and the groom.

"I'm happy for you, Sharon," she whispered while giving her best friend a tight hug. She missed their moments together before she was too busy struggling with her family's dire financial situation. Now Sharon even lived further away from Melbourne. Sometimes people tend to take things for granted when their close friends and family live nearby until they are gone.

She walked towards the bar afterwards, ordering a glass of wine. She looked at her watch and thought of disappearing from the party quietly. It would be good for her to have a couple more hours of sleep before another long drive. While enjoying her wine, she stood behind the pillar at the outside alfresco.

Suddenly she heard some conversation from behind the pillar.

"How's thing going, Fitz? Is Georgie keeping well?"

A deep baritone voice that sounded familiar answered. She was sure that must be Fitz's voice.

"Yes, aunt. Georgie is finishing her study soon, and afterwards, she will manage the foundation left behind by Mum. She always wants to be involved in charity work."

"That's good. It is important to show your kindness to the less fortunate people than you. I heard you just helped your friend too. That Bentley?"

"Yes, aunt."

"I heard you saved him from a girl who ensnared him for his money?"

Amelia's heart skipped a bit. She wondered whether 'the girl' they meant here was her Lana. But Lana was not after Charlie's money!

"They are just not suitable for each other."

"And that girl is still Sharon's friend?"

"Yes, aunt. But she's not here tonight."

Amelia held her breath and closed her eyes as if scared of being seen. She finished her wine and looked at her surrounding for a moment, thinking where she could find herself out from this place. Her hand was shaking in anger from the conversation she had just heard.

For a moment, she felt lost. She did not know where to go. She just kept walking and walking further away from the wedding reception towards the grass backyard. It was dark outside. However, she saw some lighting from a couple of small villas a few metres away. Her head was heavy, and her surrounding seemed to spinning. She wondered whether this was because of a glass of wine that she had consumed. She always knew she was a good drinker. How could she start to get drunk only after one glass?

She kept walking towards the lights. Her blood was boiling with fury. How could Fitz do this? Why? What had Lana done to him, that he was so cruel to her, separating Charlie from her? Was this because Fitz was still thinking about their connection with Gerald? But he had no evidence at all about the attack. He could not simply believe just because they knew Gerald by chance, they would do such a thing! And what did he say? Lana was after Charlie's money?

She buried her face in her hands. This was what she had been afraid of before. Their financial disadvantage only made people think their family was more material-oriented. She believed it would never be in Lana's mind to ask Charlie for help to get out of her father's financial debt. They knew it was something that was out of the question! Her father was too proud, and even they were too proud to ask. She had promised that she would never stop working until her father repaid all his debts. Even that meant until she died! She would not even ask for anyone's help. But people did not know her intention. They would only see from the outer side and judge. That was what Fitz exactly did to their family too.

She took a breath, a heavy one. She looked up to the sky for a moment and felt a drop of water on her face. It started drizzling. She hurried towards the light for a shelter but froze when she saw a familiar tall figure entering one of the villas.

It was Fitz. She was sure it was Fitz. She quietly followed behind him. He opened his villa door and went in. Before the door was fully shut, she held it open and quietly entered it.

He seemed not to realise that someone was behind him. That made her even more confident to walk in and let the door fully close. She observed him for a moment while he loosened his tie and took off his blazer with his back still on her. When he turned around, his posture stiffened.

Amelia smiled smugly as if she had just successfully cornered her enemy.

"Amelia?" He gave her a dubious look before he recovered quickly to his impassiveness. "What are you doing here? Are you well?"

Amelia stepped forward, followed by a step backward from him. She smirked in triumph that her presence intimidated him. She kept walking towards him until they were just an arm's length away. With him being much taller than her, she lifted her chin to see him eye to eye.

"I am well, thank you," she sneered. "But my sister is not."

Fitz furrowed his brow. "Your sister? Lana?"

She nodded. "I just heard your conversation with your aunt. You intentionally took Charlie to England to separate him from Lana. Is this true?" Her inquiry tone was in a hiss and sharp manner.

"That's true," he replied outrightly without wavering. "I did everything in my power to separate him from your sister."

Amelia clenched her fist. Her anger flared up to her head, she could not figure out what to do or form any word. Her body was shaking, ready to burst out, releasing her anguish. She lifted her leg swiftly and gave him a hard kick on his chest.

Fitz stumbled back and landed on the sofa behind him. He was astonished by the attack and quickly regained his balance as she moved forward again.

"How could you?!" she roared fiercely. "Why had Lana done to you that you did such a cruel thing to her?"

"Nothing. They are not just suitable for each other," he replied with a calm tone while stepping backward, maintaining their distance.

"Why do you have to think that way? They love each other!"

She threw her front kick, and this time he seemed prepared and deflected her kick while moving sideways. At that moment, Amelia thought that he was probably trained in self-defence as well. She did not remember how he fought when they were attacked outside the pub last time. She felt even more challenged than she thought. She was always ready to fight for her loved ones, even if it had to be a real fight.

"Is this because of the attack outside the pub? Because of your stupid theory that we planned it with Gerald? Did you plant that idea to Charlie?"

"Nope."

"Then what? Because Lana has a disabled sister like me?"

Fitz took a sigh before shaking his head. "Nope. Nothing to do with that."

Amelia was not sure whether she wanted to believe him. His collected manner made her feel more irritated. She could feel that his eyes briefly looked at her left prosthetic hand, which made her even more infuriated.

"Is it because of our family's financial disadvantage? You think that Lana is after Charlie's money?"

Fitz did not immediately reply but gave her a cold stare instead. Amelia held her breath, realising that was the answer.

"Lana would never, never be interested in anyone's money." She gritted her teeth. "Her feelings towards Charlie are genuine."

His lips were upturned with contempt. "It was suggested, though."

She narrowed her eyes. "What was suggested?"

"Your mother said it to Sharon's mum at Charlie's housewarming party. The union of them would bring your family a better financial position."

Amelia held her breath again. She could not believe her mother's words at the party were heard by him. She hated the fact that the last person who should not hear it instead heard it.

"Does Charlie have any objection?" She cocked her head with a flare of anger from her nostril.

"I just want to protect him," he replied curtly.

She scoffed. "I think you are meddling with other people's lives too much." And without even thinking that she was wearing a dress, she threw her kick again.

She missed it as Fitz was prepared. He turned around and suddenly was behind her. She threw her back kick which he deflected. His body swirled to her back and strangled her shoulder with his sturdy arm. She used her elbow to strike his rib, which he managed to avoid and consequently, she was free from him. She swung her left arm with her prosthetic hand to knock him out, but he blocked it, grabbed it, used her momentum against her, and she was flung to the floor. As a result, her prosthetic hand was shifted out from her hand and dangling inside her long-sleeved dress.

She looked up to see his guilt-ridden face realising what he had done. Being pitied for her condition only fueled her anger more. She rose and lashed her kick again, which he managed to deflect. Before she had a chance to flick her sidekick, he moved quicker than her and was suddenly behind her. This time he wrapped her both arms and lifted her petite body, which made her feet fly from the ground, and she could not extend her kick.

Now she realised that he was much stronger than her, and she did not understand where all her usual strength had gone. Her kicks became aimless, and he pushed her hard to the wall, which made her unable to move. She used all her remaining power to struggle, but she knew she did not have it anymore. Finally, she groaned in frustration, feeling his warm chest tightly behind her and his heavy breathing behind her neck, pinning her body hard to the wall.

Unaware of how her body had been locked tightly by his, she was still unwilling to admit the defeat. She breathed heavily and went still for a moment, which probably made him think that he had wrapped her too tight, making it difficult for her to breathe. When she felt his arm around her start loosening up, she took the chance to struggle out. However, as she managed to twirl her body around to face him again, her right wrist and left forearm were also grabbed and pinned hard to the wall. Her groan reverberated again as she admitted her strength was not up to his level.

There was only the sound of their heavy breathing as they were panting, realising how much power duel they exerted. She started to feel her head heavy, spinning and slowly bow down. Then, with her vision getting blurry, she only felt a warm breath touching her cheek. She was unaware of how close their faces were until her lips were brushed softly.

Her eyes closed as she felt the tingling sensation on her lips, caressing every part of it, tempting her to open it and want to feel it more. Her both arms were released, and her petite body was lifted into his embrace. She felt warm enwrapped in his sturdy arm and against his broad chest. She had never felt such a warm embrace before as far as she could remember except at the time when her father cuddled her when she fell sick as a little girl. His earthly masculinity took over all her senses, making her feel even more comfortable and secure.

Her soft moan shook both of them back to reality. She felt bereft when she was abruptly dropped and cold air splashed on her face. She slowly opened her eyes, finding herself standing in front of him again. He gave her a bewildered look that she had never seen in his stiff demeanour before. He looked mortified.

Amelia was not even sure what had just happened. She did not recognise where she was now, she felt she was not supposed to be here. This was not her room. She even was not sure why she was here in the first place. Weren't they fighting before? She remembered she was furious earlier, knowing that he was the cause of Lana and Charlie's breakup. But how exactly did the fight end?

Staying in the room made her feel suffocated and yearned for fresh air. She walked tipsily toward the door. Once she was outside, the cold air and the sound of rain and thunder greeted her. It was a hell of a storm. She wondered how she would get herself into the car without getting wet. She chuckled, knowing she had to get wet anyway. It did not matter anymore since Sharon's wedding party was over.

She kept walking towards the rain absentmindedly, which soaked her body, and she began shivering. She saw a couple of lights ahead of her, which she believed would bring her to the car parking area. When the lights started to get dim, she wanted to scream to anyone on the other side to let the lights on. But before her voice came out, her mouth was too dry, and her vision became black. Her body could not support her anymore, and she collapsed to the ground.

CHAPTER SEVEN
An Unexpected Attention

It was only darkness in her vision with a painful drum beat thrummed inside her head. Her body was uncomfortably warm, and she wished she could push away the blanket that covered her body. However, her hand and feet froze as well, which made her body shiver uncontrollably. She groaned in pain and curled herself further under the blanket.

She tried to open her eyes but felt too weak as the drumbeat in her head was getting louder. The pain was excruciating. She tried to recall what happened, what made her so powerless like now. However, the more she tried to squeeze her brain, her headache got worse.

She heard some voices as if someone was whispering in her ears. The sound was too loud for her, and she wanted to scream, telling them to stop. She did not recognise those voices. When she tried to close her ears with her hands, she was horrified to see her little left limb. No palm, no fingers; it was a missing limb, unlike her other hand. She cried, but her voice was lost in her throat, making her feel confused and lonely.

An arm wrapped around her as if trying to soothe her. She felt a warmth of safety under the embrace and curled further into it. Under the embrace, her shivering slowly subsided, and a familiar earthly masculine scent overtook her. She wondered from where she had sniffed this scent before. It did not belong to her dad, the only man in her life. Her headache slowly subsided, and she felt at peace. A deep lull of sleep washed over her, and she let herself succumb to it.

The next moment she was awake, she knew she was no longer in that warm and secure embrace. The masculine scent that she somehow missed had gone away. Fatigue still overtook her, but at least the loud drumbeat on her head had gone. She felt she had a little energy to at least open her eyes.

The first thing her eyes laid on was a full-length light grey curtain covering the window. A ray of sunshine peeped through it, indicating it was daylight. She felt the comfort of a pillow on her cheek and the comfy bed where she laid down now. It made her frown, wondering where she was. This definitely was not her tiny bed in her house. If she rolled from one side to another, she was sure she would not fall as the bed was much bigger than her own.

She gathered all her strength to get herself up and sit down. Her surroundings confirmed her guess that she was not in her room. The room she was in now had luxurious furniture, a high ceiling, a full wall glass window, and heavy drapes. She did not recognise this room, and she was sure she had never been here before. But somehow, despite the foreign stuff surrounding her, she felt she was in a safe place.

It took all her strength again to get herself down from the bed, reach the window curtain and pull it to the side. The bright light from outside made her eyes squint for a moment. When her vision slowly reappeared in the next minute, she started to figure out where she was as she saw a field of grapevines outside.

It is a winery place, she thought. Slowly her memory started to reappear. Sharon's wedding. Barossa Valley. Her fight with Fitz over Charlie and Lana's breakup. And the storm. She gasped to realise that she was still in this place instead of back in Melbourne. But she did not understand one thing. This was not her room accommodation in the guesthouse. This was probably the accommodation in the winery where Sharon's wedding was held. How could she end up in here? There was no way she would be able to afford this place.

Her thought was severed as the room door opened. She was startled and looked at the door where a lady, whom she guessed around her mother's age, appeared with a tray of food in her hand. The lady was startled as well to see her, but slowly her lips broke into a friendly smile.

"You're awake. That's wonderful," exclaimed the lady as she walked in and put her tray on the bedside table.

Amelia looked at her with furrowed brows. She did not recognise this lady. Instead, the lady seemed to have known her for quite a while. The lady stood in front of her still with a warm smile on her face. She seemed to understand that her head was now filled with so many questions.

"You are sick, my dear. Have a seat and have your breakfast. I have made some porridge for you. I hope you like it. My name is Tess, by the way."

Tess approached her and pulled her arm softly, gesturing her to go back to the bed. She was too weak and confused to reject the offer as her body yearned to touch the bed again, feeling another fatigue overtaking her. Tess helped to organise some European pillows behind her head before sitting at the edge of the bed, taking the bowl on the tray, and feeding her.

Amelia was startled. "Thank you. But I think I can do it."

Tess let her take the bowl. Amelia squeezed it between her little left limb and her chest, scooped the porridge with the spoon in her right hand.

"It seems your strength has come back, which is good. I had to make sure that at least some of the food had entered your mouth for the last three days. You were too weak even to open your eyes."

"Three days?" Amelia could not believe her hearing. She had been in this place for three days? "Isn't this the place where Sharon had her wedding?" she blurted out the question.

"Yes, this is the place where Miss Lucas, sorry Mrs Webster, had her wedding."

Hearing Sharon was addressed as Mrs Webster reminded Amelia that Colin's last name was Webster. Tess had formally called Sharon. She would guess that Tess must be working here. But did she hear it correctly? She had been here for three days? She was supposed to stay for one night and left immediately after the wedding. How could she still be here?

"Mrs Webster must be relieved too to know you're recovering," added Tess.

"Where is she?"

"Mrs Webster has left for her honeymoon," replied Tess while standing up from her seat. "it was such a horrible storm after the wedding. So many fallen trees were blocking the road. But Mrs Webster managed to get to the airport on time. Actually, she was reluctant to go knowing you were sick."

Amelia tried to recall things that happened after the wedding. She did remember that she had confronted Fitz over Charlie and Lana's breakup. She remembered they were fighting, and she was losing her strength as Fitz managed to subdue her. However, what happened afterwards, she could not precisely remember. Something was missing, and everything was blurry. In her effort to squeeze her brain further, the drumbeat on her head came back. Her hand moved to her head instinctively, and she closed her eyes tightly.

"Oh, my dear. Are you alright? Please don't exhaust yourself more. You are not fully recovering yet," shrieked Tess while removing the porridge bowl from her hand and putting it on the table.

Amelia did not want to give in to the pain. She slowly opened her eyes. Even though the pain did not go away entirely, and her head was still heavy, at least she was still sitting upright and conscious. She panted briefly before the pain began to subside.

"Why am I here?" Her voice was harsh, her mouth dry. "I am not supposed to stay here. I thought my accommodation was in the guesthouse ...."

"That's right. But you fainted outside the villa here when the storm came. Your luggage from the guesthouse has been retrieved. They are here," explained Tess while pointing at the wardrobe. Amelia recognised her dark blue travel bag that she had carried for this journey, lying on the table beside the cabinet. A couple of her clothes were also hung up.

"I... fainted?"

"Yes, you had a high fever and were shivering badly. Mrs Webster wanted to bring you to the hospital, but the storm was horrible. It was not safe at all to be on the road. However, we managed to get a GP to come over to examine you the next day. Since your fever started to subside, the GP felt it was safe to treat you here."

Amelia still could not comprehend fully. She could not remember any single thing that Tess had told her. It seemed her only option was to believe the story and get herself recovered soon so she could leave this place. She wondered whether Sharon may have informed her family in Melbourne since she had not returned yet. Her family must be worried about her. Her eyes started to wander around, trying to spot the whereabouts of her mobile phone.

"Oh, you must be looking for your mobile phone," said Tess as if she could read her mind. Tess walked to her bag, took the mentioned object out, and passed it. "I think Mrs Webster has informed your family in Melbourne about your condition."

"Thank you," said Amelia softly and started to open her mobile phone screen. A couple of missed calls from Lana and a hundred messages which she believed were coming from her work. She could not believe that she was so sick that she was oblivious to what had happened.

"I will leave you for now. But if you need me, please feel free to call me from this phone." Tess pointed at the phone set on the bedside table. "Just dial number one, and I will attend to you. Please don't forget to finish your food. You need more energy. Also, I have prepared paracetamol on your food tray if you need it. The GP did not prescribe any medicine. He said you are overtired, and you only need rest."

Amelia nodded weakly, but she managed to give her gratitude smile to the person who had taken care of her these past few days. Sharon must have instructed her specifically to look after her. She felt terrible that she had come to the wedding and became a burden instead. But, at least, she was glad that Sharon still went ahead with her honeymoon.

She looked at the time shown on her mobile phone. It was already 11 am. If Sharon now was in Europe, it must be late night there. She did not want to disturb her. She would give Lana a call first, at least to give peace of mind to her sister that she was alright and would be back soon. But before she dialled Lana's number, she received an unexpected incoming call. She gasped that it was from Sharon.

"Liz, oh God! I'm glad you're finally awake." Sharon's voice sounded relieved. "Tess texted me, and immediately I called. I've been waiting for any progress news about you."

Amelia took a sigh. "I'm sorry to make you worried and not enjoying your honeymoon. How are you?"

"I'm excellent. Don't worry about my honeymoon. Yes, I am worried about you. But I know you're in good hands. I feel bad that I can not be there for you."

"Don't be silly. I'm fine now. Which part of Europe are you now?"

"London. It's magnificent here. I will send you some photos later. But Liz, oh God!" Amelia could hear Sharon take another deep breath. "I was so worried when Fitz found you fainted in the middle of the storm."

"Fitz?" Her heart skipped a beat as the name was mentioned. Fitz who found her? She remembered the fight they had, but she could not remember what had happened afterwards. How did she end up fainting in the middle of the storm, and Fitz find her?

"Yes, Fitz found you. I have informed Lana too. She was freaking out and almost flew over to Adelaide. But I managed to assure her that you would be in good hands. But please don't blame me, Liz. Lana did not know that I had left you for my honeymoon. I wanted to postpone the trip, but Colin...." Amelia could hear a deep sigh. "He insisted on going, or we would never have a chance to go at all. And Fitz assured me that you would be taken care of. I...." Another deep breath. "I have a feeling I can trust him. Oh..." Sharon grunted. "You must hate me by now."

"How could I hate you?" Amelia said softly, but she was lying. Her head started spinning as she tried to unpuzzle the pieces of stories that Sharon had given her. Fitz's name was mentioned a couple of times, making her confused. She did not understand how Sharon could trust Fitz to take care of her. But she did not want to blame her friend either. She did not wish Sharon to be trapped between their friendship and her new husband.

"Look, Tess is fantastic. She has worked there for so many years. Fitz specifically organised that Tess could be devoted to taking care of you. That was the reason I could go with peace of mind. I promise I will make this up to you," added Sharon.

"Don't be silly." Amelia chuckled. "You don't owe me anything. I'm the one who troubled you. I should be thankful that you organised everything to make sure I'm alright."

"I did not organise anything. Look, Colin is probably the manager in that estate, but I'm just his wife. I don't interfere with his work. Fitz owns the place, so he has more authority over the people there."

Amelia closed her eyes as she heard Fitz's name mentioned again. "I thought this place belongs to his aunt?"

"No. Actually, that place belongs to the Dalton family. I'll explain to you later." Sharon's voice turned into a whisper. "I think Colin is awake and probably looking for me. I have to go now. Look, I'm so relieved you're fine. Please text me as much as you can, alright? Every day! Until I know you're back to Melbourne."

"Yes, of course."

And the call was hung up. Amelia felt her head spinning again. She was happy to speak with her friend, but on the other hand, knowing the truth made her headache come back. She recalled again the fight that she had with Fitz and how she had kicked him hard out of her anger. Though in the end she was defeated, she felt so stupid that she ended up fainted instead and had to receive his help. There was a missing piece on what happened, but she could not figure it out. The more she tried to recall it, the drumbeat came back in her head.

Slowly she sank in on the bed. At least it relieved her pain a bit. Her eyes were looking at the high ceiling, and she admired the beautiful and detailed classical modern interior in that room for a moment. *It must be expensive to live in this accommodation*, she thought. Sharon's words resonated again in her head that Fitz organised everything to take care of her and that he was the one who owned this place.

She did not understand why Fitz had to be so nice towards her. He had admitted that he separated Lana and Charlie because he thought their family was after Charlie's money. Supposedly he thought their family was that low and materialistic; why should he bother to ensure she was being taken care of when she fainted? He never expressed his gratitude to her after she helped him on the attack outside the pub. Instead, he accused her of plotting the attack with Gerald.

Her head started spinning again, which made her succumb back to her sleep. The next time she was awake, it was almost dark. She jumped out of her bed, feeling that her headache had gone and felt she had more strength. Her food tray had been changed with new food, and her tummy started grumbling. She knew if she wanted to recover soon and leave this place, she needed to fill up her belly. She did not want to depend on Fitz's generous hospitality anymore.

She munched her food while being multi-tasked placing back all her clothes and stuff into her travel bag. While changing to her new t-shirt and jeans as well as a jumper, she suddenly remembered that she had brought her prosthetic hand and was glad to find it kept nicely inside her bag. She took some of the biscuits and paracetamol on the tray into her bag before dashing out of the room.

She was taken aback when seeing another room apart from the one she was leaving. While descending the stairs, there was a déjà vu feeling looking at the spacious high cathedral ceiling in the living room. Her memory started to come back, and she remembered that this was where she fought with Fitz. She gasped, realising that this villa was the place where Fitz stayed. For the past three days, that could mean she had been sleeping in the accommodation that was supposedly for Fitz. As much as he wanted to help her as he had promised to Sharon, he could just put her in another place. The thought suddenly made her confused, and she wondered whether she was thinking this too much.

She paced towards the door. Before her hand reached the handle, she was startled when it swung open. The person who entered was equally astonished as her.

She did not expect to see him. From the stories that Sharon gave her, she was under the impression that Fitz had left her under Tess' care. Now finding him entering the villa as if he also stayed here, she was bewildered. For the past three days, that could mean that she had been under the same roof as him. He could be sleeping in the other bedroom.

"Are you leaving?"

His deep baritone voice shook her from her shocks. She nodded and tried to remind herself to remain composed. There was a spark of anger in her heart seeing him again. However, knowing that he had been ensuring her recovery, she did not want to be ungrateful.

"Thanks for your help. I feel much better now. I think it's time for me to leave."

There was a glimpse of concern in his eyes. "Are you going to drive back now?"

She nodded again firmly. "Yes. I heard the storm had stopped a few days ago. I suppose most of the roads are clear by now."

"But you are still recovering."

"I'm alright. I can drive back."

For a moment, there was only silence between them as their eyes locked. Amelia clenched her travel bag tightly and found that his eyes seemed more tender than usual. There was something different in the way he looked at her, which made her heart beat faster. She wondered whether he might feel guilty for what he had done to Lana and Charlie, and that was his guilt-ridden look.

She was about to pass through him, thinking that he would move sideways for her. However, he did not move. Instead, she could feel the heat of his intense gaze at her while his face moved closer to her until his warm breath fanned on her cheek. Something struck in her memory, but she was not sure what.

It was a good ten seconds how they were standing close to each other before he straightened his back and finally slid away.

"Take care."

She forced a faint smile and continued her pace. After a couple of steps away, she turned her head to see him still standing in the doorway. She wondered what in that man's thoughts. His behaviour was different from what she had known him before.

While she walked to the car parking area to retrieve her car, she felt she had just remembered something. The brief closeness that she had just encountered with him earlier somehow flashed something in her memory. Suddenly she felt a familiarity with that proximity. A familiar masculine scent that she had also in her dream.

She gasped and breathed heavily afterwards while shoving her hair. Her heart pounded fast as she remembered vividly now what exactly happened after their fight. She could not believe that it had happened and now she wondered whether it was just a dream. Everything seemed real, and she did not understand why it could happen.

They had a kiss.

CHAPTER EIGHT
A Forgiveness

Amelia scrolled her mobile phone screen and smiled to see all the beautiful scenery pictures sent by Sharon. It had been four weeks after the wedding, and Sharon even had come back from her three weeks honeymoon. She had been keeping in contact with her best friend over a chat message, and she could see how happy her friend was with her new life.

Sharon was surprised when she informed her that she left Barossa Valley the night after she was awake. Her friend reprimanded her and could not believe that she still had the strength to drive for twelve hours back to Melbourne and continue to work straight afterwards. Sharon even called her insane.

One thing that bothered her was how she would repay the accommodation cost during her stay there. Sharon was reluctant to reveal the amount and only advised her to thank Fitz. She did, and even Fitz knew when she left. Clouded by her vanity, recalling how Fitz thought their family was fortune hunter, she looked up on google the pricing and sent a cheque for half the amount. A note was slipped along with the cheque indicating that she would pay the other half of it in three months. *Damn!* The cost per night of that place was at least her one week's job as a kitchen helper. This only added another pile of debts that she had to take care of anyway.

The more she recalled what happened at Sharon's wedding before she fainted, she felt even more embarrassed. Her behaviour was horrible, in fact. She was drunk. Definitely, she was drunk. She was furious, knowing the involvement of Fitz in breaking Lana and Charlie, but still, it did not give her a right to confront and even attack him. And the kiss. She could not believe it had happened. It was only one glass of wine, and she was so easily kissing a man. How dare she even kiss this guy! He must have felt disgusted with the kiss itself.

Luckily when she reached home, none of her family mentioned or asked in detail about what happened in Adelaide. This was the first time she felt jovial about Charlie and Lana's breakup. Because it meant she had no reason to bump into Fitz anymore.

She had just finished her shift when she saw Sharon's message. She had been busy again with her work and routine since she returned. This was the first night in the weekend that she finished her shift and reached home early. A visualisation of crouching on the sofa and relaxing, possibly chatting with Lana or her dad, or watching some night show on the TV was already in her mind.

Most of the living room and kitchen lights were still on when she entered the house. There were some noises from the kitchen, and Lana was in there, placing the dirty dishes into the dishwasher.

Lana did pester her about what happened in Adelaide and why she fell sick, but she only told her briefly that she fainted and was taken care of by the lady who worked for Colin. She had not told her about her nasty meeting with Fitz on why Charlie left. She thought to keep that to herself, avoiding Lana's heart wound even further. Perhaps it was better if Charlie left Lana for another girl rather than accusing her of loving him for his money.

"Hey there," Lana greeted her with a smile. "I'm glad to see you back early tonight. Do you want a cup of warm milk and cookies?"

"Sure. If Santa can get it, why not me?" she replied with a laugh.

"Of course. You are our Santa. Without you, we won't even get any Christmas present every year,"

Lana put a mug of warm milk, and Amelia then put the chocolate powder in it. She loved chocolate milk rather than plain one. Then she took an oat cookie on the table and took a bite.

"Did you make this?" she asked.

Lana took a seat opposite her and nodded while holding her mug. "I'm thinking of making some for my students."

Lana always liked to bake cookies for them, her students, or even her friends. Amelia sometimes wondered whether Lana could make it as a business.

For a moment, there was silence between them while both of them enjoyed the food.

"Liz, I want to tell you something." Lana's soft voice broke the quietude.

Amelia looked up at her sister with a frown, waiting.

"I met Charlie yesterday. He's back in Melbourne."

Amelia had some cookies in her mouth, and for a second, she was stunned and forgot to move her jaw, chewing her cookies. Lana looked hesitant to continue speaking because of her reaction. She quickly recomposed herself and drank her milk.

She could not believe that she would hear this. Wasn't it just a few days ago she felt grateful for her sister's breakup?

"Are you seeing him again?" she asked carefully.

Lana shook her head. "No. Not yet. I mean, I don't know." She took a deep sigh as she rubbed her temple. "He apologised for the breakup. He said he cannot forget me, and he wants to start it over."

"Did he say why he wanted a breakup?"

"He said he was influenced easily by his family and friends. They were against our relationship. "

The word 'friends' mentioned made the flash of Fitz and his haughtiness come into Amelia's mind. Her anger started to flare up again, recalling the moment Fitz said he intentionally separated Charlie and Lana.

"Did he say why they were against your relationship?"

Lana reached and squeezed her hand gently. "It's nothing to do with you, Liz."

"Alright. Then what was the reason?" She wondered, after what Charlie had done to hurt her sister, he would have a gut telling the truth.

"Because they thought I was after a financial advantage over this relationship."

Amelia held her breath. That was what Fitz told her too.

"So he thinks you're a materialistic girl."

"His family does think that way."

"And he listens to them. So it means he also thinks that way."

Lana took a sigh. "I was hurt when I heard that too, Liz. I am still hurt."

"I don't understand." Amelia stared at her mug while thinking. "Now he's asking you back. So does it mean he still thinks that you're after his money, but this time he can close his eyes and accept it? So he's happy for you to be his girlfriend and use his money?"

Lana shook her head weakly. "I don't know."

It was her turn taking a deep sigh that resonated faintly in the quietness in the kitchen. She believed her mother probably was in her bed watching from her iPad. Leah perhaps too, and her dad buried himself in his study room. She felt relieved that only two of them were here having this conversation.

"You have sacrificed a lot, Liz. I did think that if I ended up with him, it would help relieve your burden and dad's financial debt."

Amelia glared at her sister. "You cannot expect him that!"

"I know, it's not fair for him. I got rid of the idea because I did not want to be disappointed if he could not help. That was also not the reason I wanted to be with him. But he left." Lana's tears started to roll down her cheeks. "I was disappointed. And knowing now he left because his family influenced him to make such a decision makes me doubt him. What if in the future, because whatever his family's words against me, he will not stand up for me?"

Quietly Amelia felt proud of what her sister was thinking. She was glad to know that her sister was not entirely blinded by love.

"It's only a matter of whether you will give him another chance or not," she said softly.

Lana slowly wiped her tears and smiled sadly. "Yes. I want to give him another chance. But I'm scared."

Amelia reached out to her and cuddled her. "I'm so proud of you. You know how to respect and appreciate yourself. That's the important thing. If you want to know whether he deserves you, then you have to make him work harder to win you back."

Lana chuckled. "Yeah, you're right. He asked to see me tomorrow, but I said no."

"That's a good start."

They laughed together and stayed in their cuddled position until they decided to go to bed.

Amelia could not immediately sleep that night, though her body was weary. Likewise, Lana could not sleep as well as she tossed back and forth on her bed.

The following day was the first Sunday that Amelia did not need to go to work. She was thinking of going through the settlement regarding her dad's business financial debt. She heard the doorbell ring and her mum shouted, asking anyone to open the door. She knew Lana was probably doing her work in her room, dad was in the library, and Leah must be in her room playing on the Ipad. Her mum was probably cooking in the kitchen, so it was left to her to get up from the sofa and answer the door.

She held her breath when she saw the uninvited guest.

"Hi, Amelia. How are you?"

Charlie smiled at her nervously. He was wearing a white suit with a colourful flower bouquet in his hand. Amelia did not return the smile and looked sharply at the man who had hurt her sister. She had to admit most of the flowers in the bouquet were Lana's favourite; the yellow tulips.

"Hi," she greeted back curtly.

"Is Lana available?" He winced, realising the cold manner he received.

Amelia did not immediately answer it. Instead, she turned her head around to see her mother approaching them with excitement.

"Oh, Charlie!" Mrs Bettney exclaimed. "What a surprise to see you here. Please come in! I'll call Lana to come down soon."

Amelia rolled her eyes. She hoped she could prevent that. Lana had told her yesterday that she did not want to see Charlie yet. Reluctantly she let the door open wider and let Charlie come in. A few minutes later, Lana descended from upstairs with a sombre look.

Perhaps Charlie had expected it, but he was saved by Mrs Bettney's excitement to welcome him.

"Have a seat, Charlie. Lana, have a seat here too! Liz, please prepare some drinks for Charlie."

Amelia almost wanted to scoff, but she closed the door behind Charlie and followed her mother's instructions. Soon after, her mum's enthusiasm was even fuelled further when Leah came downstairs and joined in the conversation. Her dad came out of the library with a frown. He approached her first in the kitchen while she was preparing the drink.

"What is he doing here?" whispered Mr Bettney.

"Not sure. Perhaps throwing some money to mum's face to let him marry Lana off," chuckled Amelia. Her dad gifted her with a sharp look.

"Do you think Lana would just accept him back after he left her without words?"

Lana shrugged her shoulder. "Don't worry, dad. I had this conversation with her last night. She knows what to do to make sure she won't get hurt anymore."

"Are you saying that this is not the first time they've met since the breakup?"

Amelia nodded.

"Did he say why he left?"

Amelia did not answer it, and she was glad that Leah's erupted laughter distracted them. She did not want to let her dad know that the reason was related to his failed business and debt. It would only add to his stress. Her dad was much more peaceful, humorous, and fun when nothing related to his failed business was mentioned.

She went back to the lounge with a tray of food that she carried single-handed, making Charlie's eyes shift to her. It helped him to escape from listening to the prattle of her mother's nonsense.

"I understand that you take a couple of casual jobs apart from your full-time job, Amelia," he remarked. "Do you work as a server?"

"Yes, I do," she replied.

"I can see how proficient you are from the way you carry the tray," he smiled. "I'm sorry I never ask this before, but where do you do your casual work?"

Amelia wondered about the sudden interest in her work life, whether because he tried to win Lana's heart.

"A couple of places. There is this chef who I've known for a while, and we work well along together. I help him to prepare food, et cetera. I only help as a server if it's really needed. I guess it's a bit scary for some people to see someone like me serving their food."

"May I know where your chef friend is working?"

"I don't know whether you've heard it before. He's the owner of an Italian restaurant Sofia."

Charlie's face glowed. "Yeah, I know that restaurant. I heard good things about it. In fact, Georgie is planning to get them to cater for her upcoming charity event."

Amelia raised her eyebrow. "Georgie?" That name seemed to ring a bell to her.

"Yes, Georgie is Fitz's sister. She is a lovely girl. She is graduating from university and will take over some of Dalton's charity foundations. This will be her first charity event, and she's thrilled and nervous about it. She's also a talented person. She can speak many languages and plays many musical instruments, such as the piano. I will call her a wonderful talented pianist."

As he talked about Georgie with enthusiasm, it invited curious glances among Lana, her mother and Leah. Amelia now remembered that Clare also talked about Georgie when they had dinner in Sydney. Clare seemed to hold Georgie in high regard and even complimented her as an accomplished woman. Amelia also remembered how Fitz talked about his sister with a complete sense of pride. She thought whether Georgie was the sister Gerald mentioned that he had a relationship with.

While Amelia suppressed her laugh, her eyes could not hide her amusement. Charlie seemed to realise that he had talked too much about another woman, which was probably not a good idea if he wanted to win Lana's heart.

"I always treat Georgie like my own sister," he added nervously.

Amelia still tried to hide her laugh. Her dad finally joined them in the lounge as a polite gesture, making Charlie even more nervous. But she had to salute his courage to open his mouth again while gazing at Lana affectionately.

"Would you excuse Lana and me? I would like to take her out for lunch."

Mrs Bettney replied excitedly. "Of course."

"I'm sorry, but I can't. I have work to do," interjected Lana, which made her mother frown. Charlie looked disappointed.

"Come on, my dear Lana. You can do the work later. This is Charlie here. Surely you miss him too. It's been a while since the last time you saw him."

Lana blushed, but Amelia could see a determination on her sister's face that she would not give in to her mother's request. "No, I can't. I don't want to end up working till late later. I could get sick instead. My body is not trained to work hard like Lizzy, unfortunately. "

"I understand," Charlie conceded before Mrs Bettney opened her mouth again. "Would you mind having a walk with me for a while? Just for a while, perhaps to a nearby park." His eyes were pleading.

Lana took a sigh. "Yeah, sure. Can Lizzy come along too?"

Amelia raised her eyebrow, looking at her sister, confused.

"Sure," replied Charlie.

All of them rose together from the seat. While Charlie was saying goodbye to her family, Amelia approached her sister and whispered in her ear.

"Why do you need me to be a chaperone? We're not in olden times."

Lana laughed softly. "I don't want to give him too much hope now. Please come along."

Amelia did not protest anymore. Anyway, it was just a couple of minutes. They went to the nearby park, walked side by side together. Though she felt like a third wheel, she found the walk was refreshing too. She let Lana and Charlie be involved in their conversation while enjoying the park scenery with a couple of little children playing in the playground.

Amelia looked at her watch half an hour later. She could not bear it anymore because she had many things to do related to her father's financial debt settlement. She approached the couple, somehow signalling Charlie that it was time for him to leave.

"Nice to see you again, Amelia," said Charlie in all his politeness. "I just mentioned to Lana that it would be great if she could come to the upcoming charity event that Georgie is organising. You could come along too."

Amelia exchanged glances with her sister, who seemed did not want to answer it. "When is that?" she asked.

"The plan is next month."

"And they are going to use Sofia as the catering?"

"Yeah, I think so."

"Well, we'll see. We will let you know if we can come."

There's a slight disappointment spread on Charlie's face, but he still smiled. "Sure. I really hope both of you can come. It's going to be an enjoyable event, I suppose. Clare and my family will be there too to support the event. They are also looking forward to seeing all of you again." He looked at Lana meaningfully while saying those words.

After saying goodbye, Charlie took his leave, leaving the sisters behind in the park.

"Are you interested in coming to the event?" asked Amelia after Charlie disappeared from their sight.

"I don't know." Lana shook her head while motioning her to begin their stroll back to the house. "I suppose for such an event, you will be asked to work too? "

Amelia nodded. That meant she would not be able to come if she needed to work. But in her mind, she had another plan. She had to make sure that she would not accept the job related to that event. She would not know what to do if she saw Fitz there too. The thought made her shudder inwardly.

CHAPTER NINE

A Revelation

Another month had passed, and Amelia noticed that Lana and Charlie were meeting more often. Still, they were never be left alone together, which made her feel amused.

When Charlie asked Lana out almost every weekend, Lana always brought along one of her family. Amelia was not available most of the time due to her casual job. Leah mainly became the third wheel, especially if they went to an expensive restaurant. One time Lana brought her mother, and they ended up shopping, and naturally, her mother was thrilled. And lastly, Lana also got her dad, who was reluctant initially, but obediently followed when they had brunch. She only shook her head, wondering what her sister was up to.

"Are you testing him?" she asked one night when she got home from work and managed to catch up with her sister, who hadn't gone to bed.

"Sort of. "

"But why in this way? What is your intention?.."

"To make him realise what he's signing up for if he still wants to be with me. A union of two persons is also a union of two families. So if I could accept his family for what they are, he also has to learn to accept our family for what they are."

"Do you mean our family who is poor, loud and materialistic?" Amelia grinned. "Oh, and also disabled!"

Lana laughed. "That's what we are!"

"How about if that scares him away?"

"Then that means we're not meant to be. And that's for the best."

Amelia felt her heart swell with pride at her sister. "Will you be okay?" she asked softly.

Lana reached out to her hand and squeezed it. "I'll be fine, Liz. I went through this, remember?"

Lana was right, and Amelia was glad to see how strong her sister could be despite from the outside, people may see her as a soft and weak girl. Sometimes going through pain in life could make you more resilient, though sometimes it could break you down too.

It was another busy weekend. Amelia glanced at her watch while preparing her bag for her next work shift. It was an event in a winery restaurant in Yarra Valley, about two hours' drive from their home. She was about to drop her bag into her tiny car when Lana appeared at the door.

"Are you going to work, Liz?" asked Lana. Amelia looked up to her sister, who looked glowingly graceful with her cream halter neck dress, and most of her hair lifted with some strands behind her ears. "Aren't you going to work at the charity event in Yarra Valley?"

Amelia frowned. "How do you know?"

"That's the event that Charlie told us about, remember? It's Fitz's sister's charity event. He keeps asking me to come. So I finally agree. I think that you will be there too, though I know most of the time you'll be working. So I insist that I will join you in your car."

The mention of Fitz's name made her breath catch in her throat. She was supposed to avoid accepting this job but absentmindedly signed up for it because the pay was higher than usual.

"Oh, great!" she grunted in frustration, which baffled her sister.

"Why? Why do you look so upset?"

Amelia quietly sighed. Until now, she never told Lana about the incident between her and Fitz at Sharon's wedding. She could not tell her, even now. She knew she just had to keep it to herself.

"It's okay. Nothing." She waved off her hand. "So, are you coming?"

Lana nodded and entered her small car. Although she was anxious at the prospect of seeing Fitz again, Amelia enjoyed the driving, especially with Lana as her companion. They talked about many things along the way, mainly about how far Lana and Charlie's relationship was now.

"Are you nervous about meeting Charlie's parents and Clare again?"

"A bit. But I don't want to give a damn about it. I just want to show them who I am."

Amelia smiled. She felt proud of how her sister handled this.

"I have not seen Fitz for a while. I wonder how he is," added Lana, which made Amelia's heart skip a beat. "In the past, he normally joined us occasionally when I hung out with Charlie. But this time, no."

"Perhaps he is away," murmured Amelia.

"Yeah, I heard he's swamped with work. I suppose he will be in the event today, though. It's his sister's event. I heard they are close."

Amelia kept quiet and did not reply to that statement hoping the conversation about Fitz could stop there. She was lucky as their car started approaching the venue. She dropped her sister off at the main gate, and Charlie enthusiastically welcomed her. Meanwhile, she sneaked into the kitchen from the back door. Before the meal preparation, there was a short briefing for all the kitchen staff, and she reached precisely on time.

While listening to the briefing, her eyes caught a familiar figure who stood at the very end of the line. Her eyes widened, recognising that person. It was Gerald! He was dressing up as one of the servers. It had been a while since the last time they met. She never knew and never bothered to learn what Gerald did as a job. From her previous conversation with Leah, she hoped Leah also had cut off their contacts.

She wondered what Gerald was doing here, knowing his history with Fitz's sister and the attack he plotted against Fitz and Charlie. When the briefing was over, she was determined to find out, but the chef pulled her to begin her work.

For the next hours before the meal serving, Amelia was busily occupied. At the time of her break, she was reminded again of Gerald. From the shift timetable hung up on the wall, Gerald was also on his break at the same time as her. This would be the right time to find him and find out what he was doing here.

She went out of the kitchen to end up in the backyard of the winery. It was daylight saving time, so the sun was still shining brightly even though the time already showed 8 pm. Her eyes were scanning around to find her subject, but she only saw a couple of other servers and kitchen helpers who were also having their break nearby. She decided to navigate further, but carefully not too close to the reception place where the event was held. The reception was in a room surrounded by a full wall glass window, so it would not be nice if some of the workers appeared in the guests' view.

She walked further to a field area behind the building's wall, hidden from the reception area and away from the kitchen back door. With high curiosity, she walked in that direction to check. When she heard a commotion from the site, her chest tightened. She heard a woman's screaming in the middle of that commotion.

She was bewildered by what she saw. It was in fact, Gerald, the person that she was looking for. A girl was struggling to free herself from under his arm, while Gerald's hand was covering her mouth to keep her quiet

It was a disgusting view in Amelia's eyes. Her fury started to flare up seeing such a scene. She grabbed the back of Gerald's shirt and pulled him hard. Gerald did not expect that. He fell, and the girl was freed from his arm.

When he turned around, Amelia could see the astonishment on his face realising who had pulled him down. He rose with his fierce eyes.

"Stay away from my business," he hissed angrily.

"Stay away from her," responded Amelia with an equally fierce look.

"You will regret this." Once he said that, he lurched forward with a pocket knife in his hand. Amelia tried to back down as much as possible while maintaining her balance. But, at the same time, he kept furiously swinging the knife at her.

After a couple of attempts to avoid the slice of the knife, Amelia stumbled back due to the uneven ground of the grass field. Gerald took the opportunity to stab in her direction as she rolled sideways. She tried to stand up, but Gerald was quicker than she thought as he swung the blade again, which managed to slice her right cheek. Amelia gasped, but as she did not feel so much pain, she assumed it was only a little scratch. She struck back with a roundhouse kick which was spot on, smashing Gerald's face and knocking him down.

Two big men with tuxedos suddenly came forward and grabbed him. She saw the girl that Gerald was with, come behind the men.

"Get him out of here!" yelled the girl furiously.

"You have to listen to me, Georgie. I Love you, you know I do! Don't listen to your brother! He always wants to separate us," shouted Gerald while his body was dragged away.

Amelia was panting, between relief and curiosity. She wondered where those men took Gerald away. But at the same time, she was relieved that Gerald was gone. She hoped she did not need to see him again.

She felt something rolling on her cheek, and when her hand touched it, it was her blood. It was still a tolerable pain, but she must look horrible.

"You're wounded. Let me take you inside and treat you," said the girl while approaching her and gasped when she looked at her left little limb. "Oh, you must be Amelia!"

She frowned, wondering how the girl knew her name.

"You're Lana's sister! I'm Georgie," exclaimed the girl with a broad smile on her face, perhaps the first smile that she had since the frightening incident that she had just encountered. "We just talked about you. Let's go inside, and let me treat your wound. I can't thank you enough for saving me from that scoundrel."

The girl's name rang a bell in her head. So that was the reason Gerald was so desperately trying to get this girl. She was Fitz's sister, the girl that Gerald claimed he had forgotten in pursuing Leah. *Well, obviously, he had not forgotten her*, Amelia scoffed, thinking how dangerous Gerald was. She had to keep reminding herself to ensure Leah was not seeing him anymore.

"Thank you, but I'm fine." She took out a handkerchief from her pocket to wipe the blood on her cheek. "It's just a little scratch. Unfortunately, I have to go back to work."

Georgie looked at her bewildered. "Back to work? No, forget about the work. I'll speak with the kitchen captain later. Please come inside."

"I don't think it's a good idea. Your guests will be frightened. I need to go back to work anyway." She turned around, but Georgie's hand on her arm put her to a halt.

"Promise me that I will see you again after the event. Please don't go away without telling me."

Amelia did not expect that Georgie would be pretty persistent. She expected a wealthy born, elegant girl like her would simply get someone else to organise something on her behalf if she wanted to show gratitude to a worker like herself. She wondered whether it was because she was related to Lana, hence Charlie.

"Alright. But promise me too that you will not tell Lana about my wound," warned Amelia.

Georgie smiled and nodded her head vigorously. "I promise."

She went back to the kitchen and kept pressing her cheek wound with the hope it would stop bleeding. Her effort was not fruitless as the bleeding stopped. The chef looked at her with a raised eyebrow, but the kitchen captain seemed to have received instruction from Georgie. No one questioned how she got the wound. The kitchen captain took her to the first aid area, treated her wound and at the time she looked in the mirror, she had a band-aid stuck to her cheek. She smiled, at least she knew the scratch was merely an inch long.

She went back to focusing on her work while reflecting on what had just happened. She wondered what happened between Gerald and Georgie in the past, which also spread the hatred between Fitz and even Charlie. She could not trust Gerald either, especially knowing of his capability to plot an attack against Fitz and Charlie and now even trying to kidnap Georgie. In addition, she was worried about how Leah could potentially be entangled in this.

When her shift finished, she took her mobile phone to call Leah. She dashed out to the quiet backyard. The sky was already dark, with the sounds of grasshoppers filling the air. She was too engrossed in her thoughts and did not pay attention to a tall figure leaning against the wall near the door. Her head turned to it twice when she sensed there was someone.

Fitz was still in his black tuxedo with his tie already loosened up, unbuttoned collar and both hands in his pockets. He reminded her of college schoolboys that she usually saw gathering in the train station after school hours. He seemed to be waiting for her and straightened himself when she finally turned around. She held her breath as his umber eyes stared at her.

"Thank you for helping Georgie earlier." His voice sounded crisply in the tranquillity of the night. "She told me what happened."

Amelia swallowed thickly as she tried to appease her apprehension. She had sworn to avoid him today, but it seemed impossible now.

"It's alright. I would do the same for any woman in distress. I hate to see violence against women," she replied honestly.

"I would like to apologise that I have accused you of conspiring with Gerald in plotting the attack outside the pub last time."

She admitted his apology seemed genuine. However, there was still a spark of annoyance in her heart, remembering how he threw the accusation last time. She even thought it was one of the reasons for Lana & Charlie's breakup. But everything was only a past now.

"Gerald was my and Charlie's old pals," he continued while taking a heavy sigh. Amelia could sense that he might want to share something with her. She decided to stay on her spot, which was about an arm's length away from him.

"But his behaviour was getting out of control towards the completion of our university. As one of my closest friends, there were occasions when he and Georgie got to know each other. Looking up to him as her brother's friend, Georgie trusted him. Until he took advantage of her trust. He tricked her into giving him money for all his gambling habits. I tried to protect my sister, so I tried to reason her out to stay away from him. He was not happy, definitely."

He took another deep sigh, and his face turned grievous. Amelia's eyebrow knitted while watching him, and she guessed that something awful had happened.

"One day, Georgie did not come home for more than a day. I started to worry. After a frantic search, I found her in a holiday house, sleeping on the bed."

He closed his eyes and shoved his hair with his fingers. At that moment, Amelia seemed to see a vulnerable side of him that she had never seen before.

"She was unconscious without any layer of clothes on her. Gerald was beside her with a bottle of beer in his hand. And there was a camera with a tripod recording them. She was only 16 at that time."

Amelia's mouth half opened in shock. She felt sick to the stomach. Her body shivered, imagining if such a thing happened to any girl and wishing she would have given Gerald a more brutal kick earlier.

"I scrapped the camera and its recording. But he claimed he still had a copy. I am never sure whether I should believe him or not. That was why

I did not press for any charges from the last attack. I wanted to protect Georgie."

Amelia pursed her lips. Now everything started to make sense. She wondered, too, why Fitz did not press any charges if he had evidence that the two men hired by Gerald confessed to his plan. Gerald took advantage as much as he could to get away from his wrongdoing.

"After what happened today, Georgie convinces me that Gerald does not have any more copies of the video. Otherwise, he would not come here so desperately trying to kidnap her. Probably she's right."

"She's a smart girl," remarked Amelia. "She's probably right. I had a feeling Gerald was under the influence of drugs or perhaps alcohol when he was here. I was surprised too when I saw him as one of the servers for the event today. He must be desperate to meet Georgie and to get more money."

He nodded his head, agreeing with what she said.

"I'm grateful that you were there at the right time before he tried to take her away," he said again while giving her a tender look that made her cheek warm. She then realised that they had been standing too close. She slowly shifted her body backwards and avoided his gaze.

"Georgie is grateful for what you did. She has asked me to make sure that you are not leaving without telling her. I think she can't wait to have a friendship with you."

The word 'friendship' made her heart feel warm. Amelia did not mind at all making friends with anyone, regardless of their social status, with money or without. She could see Georgie's genuine intention to get to know her better. She looked at Fitz for a moment and wondered what had run through in that guy's mind.

As far as she could remember, from the moment they were introduced, not many words were spoken between them until she helped him during the attack. Since then, there was only an exchange of harsh words between them, starting from his accusation over the attack plan, Charlie and Lana's breakup, which she felt embarrassed recalling it because they even had a physical fight. Though he helped her while she fell sick after Sharon's wedding, there was only coldness in his behaviour towards her. She also perceived him as proud and arrogant, which she understood was typical of a man of his position and wealthy background.

But it did not mean they could not be friends. Especially now, Lana and Charlie started to get back together again, and now she was Georgie's saviour from Gerald's kidnapping attempt. There would be more possibilities for them to bump into each other more often. She did not see any reason why they could not be civil to each other.

She chuckled at the thought and smiled. "I'm more than happy to be her friend. She's a sweet girl. But how about you?" She smiled mischievously, wishing it could melt the stiffness between them. "Do you mind if I become her friend? Do you mind if we become friends too?"

He looked puzzled, which made her slightly nervous. Did she say something wrong? It was meant to be a tease.

"Well, you know. We had some misunderstandings. Gerald was one of the causes. I still blamed you for Lana & Charlie's break-up, though. But I think they are back together again now. I understand you only care about Charlie, and that was why you separated them. I think we're getting used to receiving judgement from people on how an advantageous marriage would be beneficial to our current financial difficulties, especially if that comes from the people from your circle. But at the end of the day, it's about them."

She did not realise that he had stepped closer to her while she was talking. When she looked up, she had to raise her head to find his eyes gazing intensely at her. She was breathless, realising how close they were standing.

"I don't want to be your friend," he said softly, his voice barely above a whisper.

She was taken aback. Her heart was like being stabbed. She pursed her lips and clenched her fist. Her eyes even hurt, and tears threaten to roll down. She did not understand why she had to feel this way. She knew she was never good enough for him. He even said it before.

She turned her face away, trying to hide her anguish but was startled when her cheek was touched softly. She was paralyzed, unable to move while his fingers were caressing her cheek, which was scratched earlier with Gerald's blade.

"I wish we could be more than friends."

At that moment, she probably forgot to breathe. His fingers slowly travelled to her chin and lifted her face gently. He lowered his head and sealed her lips softly with his.

There was a feeling of déjà vu when her senses were filled with his masculinity. She had this before but in a different place. While letting her lips moulded in his, she suddenly remembered the same feeling she had the last time they met. And now she understood that the kiss they had that night in Barossa Valley was not because she was drunk. But because he initiated it.

CHAPTER TEN
The Harsh Truth

Amelia stared blankly at the dark road ahead while listening to a piece of smooth music from the car radio. She threw a glance to her side, where Lana was sleeping soundly on the seat beside her. Her eyes were back on the road again, but her mind was muddled with what had happened earlier.

They were on the way back from Georgie's charity event to their home. Lana kept her promise that she did not want to be left alone with Charlie. Charlie had offered to drive her home and even offered her to stay overnight instead. Georgie also extended the same offer to her. But she tried to decline the offer as polite as possible, using her work schedule tomorrow as an excuse. Lana joined in using the same reason, which seemed to work as both Charlie and Georgie gave up. While the conversation was going on, she quietly stole a glance at Fitz, who was unmoved from his spot. His eyes gazed away as if not interested in the conversation. He was back to his usual wooden manner, despite the fact that it was just a couple of minutes ago they were into a deep kiss.

It was the voices of Lana and Charlie from the distance which startled them. Abruptly he dropped her chin and took a step away from her, which made her somehow feel dejected. She believed none of them was suspicious of their sudden shift before their arrival. Lana was surprised to see the wound on her cheek, which she replied as a minor accident in the kitchen. She glanced at Georgie, who seemed to understand that she made up the story to avoid talking about Gerald.

Her head was in a mess. She did not understand what had just happened. It was already two kisses from him. What was he trying to do? She believed she was not the type of girl who would be an interest to a man like him, especially with her birth defect. They had such a big gap, not only financially but also in terms of family, educational background and social circle. On the other hand, she felt Lana, who was not only graceful and beautiful in her physical look but also in her personality, deserved a prince charming like Charlie.

She was confused. Was he in love with her? How could that be? After so many unpleasant exchanges of words and encounters that they had. Was he playing her? Well, he was a rich wealthy guy, he could get any other woman that he wanted. Perhaps he found her intriguing, and he wanted to play her. She could not believe Fitz was such a man unless she was completely wrong.

Perhaps Fitz was cold and distant, looked arrogant. However, she witnessed the way he spoke tenderly and affectionately to his sister, one side of him that she only found recently. When he talked with Charlie, sometimes he spoke with stiff authority, but she could see that he cared for his friend and acted as his big brother. If he was such a playboy, then he would probably be like Gerald. But his manner and behaviour were different, like the earth and sky compared to Gerald. And if he was a scoundrel, would she also have trusted Charlie because both men were best friends?

From the first time she met Charlie, she knew he was friendly, polite and charming. She understood why Lana could fall in love with him. The only fault he had made so far was his lack of principle, which caused Lana to be brokenhearted. She hoped Charlie would learn from his mistake.

What did the kiss mean, then? Amelia took a deep breath. She never imagined she would even experience a kiss, as she strongly believed too that she was not going to end up in a romantic relationship with any man throughout her life. But now, she could not deny that she was thrilled with the kisses they shared. How far they could go if Charlie and Lana did not find them, she would not even dare to imagine.

She stole another glance at Lana, who was still sleeping peacefully, before fixing her eyes back to the road. She wanted to get away from her messy thoughts and forget what had just happened. It was probably nothing for Fitz himself. He was perhaps the one who was drunk and did not realise what he had done. She would not want to embarrass him by questioning his kiss. Maybe she would just drop the subject and never mention it anymore as if nothing happened. She did not wish the awkwardness between them would affect Lana and Charlie's attempt to reunite. Not for the second time she jeopardised her sister's chance for happiness.

Her car reached home when the time already showed two o'clock in the morning. She could not sleep that night as she tossed herself to her bed. Her mind was still playing the moment Fitz was kissing her, in Sharon's wedding and tonight. The tingling sensation of the kiss made her heart tremble, but at the same time, she tried to dismiss the feeling as if it was not real. Assuming that all that happened was just a mishap became her resolution before she finally drifted to sleep.

She woke up the next morning feeling sleepy. She practically only had a good sleep for a few hours. The noises from Leah and her mother's voices from downstairs made her give up her slumber. She took her mobile phone and sent a text message to one of the casual job's managers that she was supposed to do today, to cancel the job.

As her tummy started grumbling, she dragged her feet to see all her family were in the kitchen and the meal table, having their breakfast in a lively manner. Even Lana looked fresh in her flowery dress with hair tied up in a ponytail.

"You look tired, Liz. Are you alright?" Lana asked while pouring milk into her mug.

"I'm alright. Yeah, I'm just tired. I don't think I can go to work today," she muttered, which made her sister and her father's eyebrow arch. They knew it was unusual for her to reject a weekend casual shift because of the higher hourly rate offered.

Her father was puzzled. "Are you sick?"

She shook her head while getting herself seated. "Nope, I'm fine. I'm just thinking of taking a break today."

Her answer only gave another surprising look from Lana and Mr Bettney.

Suddenly their house doorbell rang, and her mother excitedly went to the door to open it. Amelia wondered whether it was Charlie in his early morning attempt to ask Lana out again. He had done it almost every weekend since he came back to Melbourne to win Lana's heart. But the guests who appeared from the door were beyond her expectation, and she smiled happily, welcoming them.

The guests were their uncle Gardiner and aunt Marie, her mother's brother and his wife. They live in Perth, and their visit was a pleasant surprise. Uncle Gardiner and aunt Marie were already in their retirement. Still, as a successful businessman, uncle Gardiner enjoyed his retirement in a relaxing way without any concern over finances as he had enough for both of them. Their three kids were already grown up, had decent careers and own families. Two of them were in Perth with them, and uncle Gardiner and aunt Marie were at the stage enjoying their time with their little grandchildren. Meanwhile, one of them married a man from England and lived in a town in the UK which Amelia was not sure exactly where.

Apparently, her mother already knew about her brother and his wife's coming, but she forgot to inform the rest of her family.

"What a pleasant surprise to see you here, uncle, aunt," greeted Lana. "Did you just arrive this morning?"

They nodded. "We came straight from the airport. Our luggage is still in the car," replied aunt Marie.

"Both of you must be tired," commented Amelia. "Where are you going to stay?"

She believed their house was too small to receive guests. She knew her uncle and aunt would not demand hospitality from them.

"In the city. The usual hotel," replied uncle Gardiner. "I have some conferences to attend next week here in Melbourne. So I think it's a good time to visit you guys as well. We are going to be here for about a week."

"That's fantastic!" exclaimed Mrs Bettney. "You should have dinner with us every day. So many things for us to catch up!"

For the next hour, the conversation was dominated by Mrs Bettney informing of her new recipe and her excitement over the possibility of a marital relationship between Lana and Charlie. However, when Mrs Bettney mentioned that Charlie was actually from the UK, aunt Marie brought the conversation in a different direction.

"I want to visit Elena in August while escaping from the winter here." Elena was their youngest child who married an English man. "But I want to visit my hometown Derby as well, before going to Elena's place in Nottingham. That means we need to drive from the nearest international airport, which I think is Manchester. It's going to be a long drive, and you know I don't drive, and your uncle is getting older." She looked at Amelia expectantly. "I hope you can join us and drive for us, Liz."

Amelia did not expect the suggestion, and she repressed her smile as she noticed her aunt exchanged a look with Lana and her father.

"That would be a wonderful idea," grinned Mr Bettney. "Lizzy loves road trips. And this would be a good time for you to take a break, Liz.

Didn't you just say that you would like to take a break? You have not taken any holiday trip for the last couple of years."

"Thank you for the offer, but I cannot afford to go for a holiday trip at the moment, especially to Europe," responded Amelia tactfully.

"Since you're doing us such a great favour by accompanying us, please let us pay for your trip," added uncle Gardiner.

Somehow Amelia had expected this financial offer, but she was uncomfortable taking it. "Thank you, but I can't."

"Oh, come on, Liz." Lana reached her and squeezed her shoulder affectionately. "You know you will love this."

"Why no one offers me to go?" complained Leah.

"You still have school, silly!" Mr Bettney scowled at Leah. "And you don't even have a driver license yet!"

"Why don't you go, Lana?" Amelia looked at her sister with a teasing smile.

"Well, Lana perhaps doesn't need one. Soon she would go there as Mrs Bentley," joked Leah.

Lana gave her little sister a reprimanded glare, then looked back to Amelia tenderly. "You know I am not a big fan of road trips. This job is perfect for you. Come on, what are you waiting for? Don't you want to do a favour for your favourite uncle and aunt?"

Amelia laughed softly. She knew her family were conspiring this and making sure she would not be able to reject the offer. She glanced at her mother, who raised an eyebrow at her.

"Unfortunately, I'm not a good driver too. Otherwise, I would propose myself for such an exciting holiday trip," smirked Mrs Bettney.

"Alright, let me think about it." Amelia raised her hand as a sign of giving up and hoping the subject would be dropped. Her uncle and aunt seemed satisfied with her answer for now.

Their conversation then went in a different direction again as Leah laughed loudly while looking at her mobile phone screen.

"You will not believe this, Lana!" She rushed towards Lana and showed her mobile phone screen. "Isn't that Fitz, Charlie's best friend? He was red-handed caught kissing a girl!"

Amelia held her breath while looking at Leah with high curiosity. Still, she tried to calm herself, not reacting impulsively to show it. Lana looked at Leah's mobile phone screen with a furrowed brow, seemed unsure of what she saw.

"I don't expect such a stiff guy could kiss a girl!" Leah laughed again. "I wonder what the girl looks like. Unfortunately, the picture is blurry."

"What news are you reading, Leah?" Amelia hesitantly asked.

"It's from Facebook. Don't you know that he is the most eligible bachelor in the UK? Well, I guess here too. He's much wealthier than Charlie, with hundred generations of wealth. He is probably as famous as Prince William!"

"Who is this guy?" queried Aunt Marie curiously.

"Fitz Dalton," answered Lana. "He is Charlie's best friend. We know him from Charlie."

"Ah..." Aunt Marie seemed to have a light bulb moment. "I heard about his charity foundation before."

Amelia felt her heart pound as Fitz's name was mentioned. As she would expect, Leah came over to her as well to show her finding. She took a deep breath as if preparing herself before seeing the picture. It was blurry like Leah said, but she was familiar with Fitz's tall, broad shoulder figure. The picture must be taken from their kiss last night. She wondered how a paparazzi could be there too. She had no idea that Fitz had been the centre of social media attention. She was not a social media follower, unlike Leah. Quietly she took a relieved breath realising that the picture was not clear enough to show her face. Unless someone knew both of them well, the girl in the picture would not be guessed as her. The picture was also taken from her right-hand side; hence it did not show her little left limb.

"The girl has curly brunette hair like you, Liz," commented Leah. Amelia's heart skipped a beat. She caught a glance from Lana, which made her shift her eyes to the newspaper that her father was reading.

"It is just a piece of gossip news, Leah. That picture even is too blurry. I am not even sure it is Fitz," said Lana while pouring tea to uncle Gardiner and aunt Marie to dismiss the conversation. It worked as Leah slowly moved to the sofa in the living room while she kept reading from her mobile phone screen.

The rest of the afternoon was filled with a lot of other conversations surrounding their family. As the fatigue started to sink in, Uncle Gardiner and Aunt Marie finally bid them goodbye. They wished to rest at the hotel accommodation they had booked in the city. The liveliness in the house slowly dissipated as Lana excused herself to catch up on some work, Mr Bettney retreated again to his library, Leah went to her room with her iPad, and Mrs Bettney went to try a new recipe in the kitchen.

Amelia took the opportunity as well to get herself alone. She decided to get some fresh air by taking a stroll in the nearby park. She wore her jumper and put the hoody on as the cold wind started to blow forcefully, making some leaves fly around. Her eyes were wandering in the park, seeing people who were still diligently doing their exercise, had a jog and a stroll like herself. Unfortunately, today's weather was cloudy, which did not invite many young kids to play on the playground.

Her mind was back to the news on herself and Fitz, which made her anxious. The picture of her and Fitz on social media was upsetting for her. She wondered whether this would bring something negative for a man like Fitz with his position and social status. He might think that she had trapped him like last time he accused her of plotting the attack with Gerald against him and Charlie. He had apologised, though, for his baseless and false accusation. But the fact such a thought slipped into his mind made her worried that he could have a similar idea about that kissing picture. But, did she need to care? She took a heavy sigh. She just did not wish this would affect Lana and Charlie's potential reconciliation and happiness.

As her mind was muddled, she was not fully on her guard. When her awareness of her surroundings was back, she realised someone was walking quite close behind her. She did not want to think negatively as this place was a frequently visited park by most locals. The person behind her could be just another passer-by. However, she could sense that the person was getting closer to her. Her gut instinct made her braced herself to turn around and be ready to strike, but she caught her breath as she recognised who had been following her.

"Sorry, I did not mean to frighten you."

She took a relieved sigh. The person was exactly the one that had been occupying her mind. She did not expect Fitz Dalton would appear in front of her instantly right now. She noticed that he was dressed up casually, unlike what she usually saw from him. He was in his jumper, too, with the hoody on his head. Still, she could see his attire was a classy one suited to his class.

He took a heavy breath as they were facing each other within arm's length. His face looked grave and agitated.

"I saw you came out of your house. So I decided to follow you here." He looked to his surroundings briefly before turning to her again. "Perhaps you have seen the picture that is currently circulating on social media. I did not expect someone would see us and take a snap."

"Yeah, Leah showed me the picture. I'm not into social media," she muttered. She would have expected him to come to her to talk about this. She looked to their surroundings as she understood now that he was concerned there would be another paparazzi around who might take another snap of their picture without their knowledge. But as far as her eyes could see, there was no one holding a camera or mobile phone directed at them.

For a moment, she was only watching him pacing back and forth with his eyes staring down at his feet. It made her wonder what was on his mind now. It seemed it was the first time she saw him unsettled like this. His breath was heavy, and when he lifted his face, she saw a stressful look.

"This is insane." His voice finally was heard, sounded hoarse and troubled. "I have been struggling in vain with my feelings towards you, Amelia. But I can't repress it anymore. I ardently admire you. I like you."

Amelia's jaw dropped as her breath caught in her throat. She could not believe what she had just heard.

The wind had blown out his hoody, and he shoved his tousled hair, rubbing the back of his neck, looking frustrated. He interpreted her reaction with a bitter chuckle.

"I know this is insane. This is not something that someone from my background will do rationally. We come from different backgrounds and social circles. Surely you know that your family's financial situation and your own circumstances will make our relationship...." He swallowed thickly while his eyes shifted to her little left limb. "I would say impossible. This is against my family's expectations and even my own better judgement. But I have come to feel for you a strong feeling, which despite my struggle against it, it only makes me suffer."

As he spoke while pacing back and forth anxiously, the colour on her face drained. His voice became like an echo hovering over her.

Those words were supposed to be expected. She was fully aware of that too, and she did not need to be reminded about it at all. Still, those words stung. A spark of rage was ignited within her, while at the same time, looking at how miserable he looked, she felt pity too. It must be hard for someone in his high-class social background and position to be trapped in his feelings towards someone like her, who was not only penniless but even had a physical defect. It must be humiliating for him. He did not even dare to look at her as if the feeling that he declared a minute ago was disgraceful.

Amelia stood frozen with a dazed look at the green grass beneath her. Then, after what seemed like an eternity of silence between them, she took a deep breath to prepare herself to speak.

"I am sorry for your struggle." Her voice sounded weak to her. She gathered again her strength to speak louder. "I don't know that our encounters have caused you pain. Believe me, it was unconsciously done." She took a deep breath, wishing it could fill her lung, lighten the heaviness in her heart as her tears were threatening to roll down. However, her effort was fruitless. "I believe this is only a short infatuation." Her voice started to falter, and crack, mixed with the tears that she desperately tried to hold off. "I will do my best not to cross into your path again as much as I don't want this affecting Lana and Charlie's relationship."

He raised his hand and shook his head in exasperation. "You don't understand".

She scoffed and looked away, wishing he could not see her eyes that were already welled in tears. "Oh yeah, I understand you perfectly." She gritted her teeth while saying those words and clenched her fist to control her emotion. She took a glimpse of him for the last time and could see his astonishment at her words. She could not stand to be there any longer.

She turned her body around and walked away as briskly as she could without looking back anymore. Her brisk walk eventually turned into a jog, then a sprint. The cold breeze touched her face, which was already wet with her tears. She just wanted to run as fast as she could until all the heaviness in her heart went away. But she knew regardless of how fast she ran, his stinging words were still echoing loudly in her head.

She never expected this, not from any man, because she never imagined anyone would make such a declaration to her. She knew she had been a constant shame to her family, especially to her mother and sometimes her younger sister. Though Lana and her father kept telling her there was nothing to be embarrassed about her physical defect, deep down, she knew even they felt pity for her. And now, when someone did fall in love with her, she was partly flattered. However, the feeling was forbidden because it would only bring shame to him.

She stopped running when she was out of breath. She stood for a moment, looking down on the grass path while letting her tears keep rolling down her cheek. Her heart was still heavy and hurt, and when she took a deep breath, nothing changed. Her body slowly bent down and quivered as she let herself down to her feet. The dam of tears that she had been trying to hold finally broke down. She was sobbing in that position until she had no more tears.

CHAPTER ELEVEN
Another Rescue

The night wind blew stronger and colder as Amelia zipped up her jumper and put on her hoodie. She stepped out of the restaurant building where she had just finished her late-night shift as a kitchen helper. Time showed it was almost midnight. The quietness of the street and the flying amber leaves accompanied her brisk walk to her car.

She started her car engine and came out of the driveway carefully. The weariness of her body reminded her to stay alert while driving. An accident was not the thing that she wanted to encounter at this moment. She already had too much in her mind right now.

It was over a month ago since she had that conversation with Fitz in the park. The good thing from that meeting was there were no more pictures of them on social media. Like any other gossip news, the story about a young multi-millionaire kissing a girl disappeared without traces. She believed that was what Fitz exactly wished too, as much as he wanted to ensure his feelings towards her go away. And she promised herself that she would help him to achieve it.

Fortunately, despite Lana spending more time with Charlie, no occasion required her to be present, potentially bringing Fitz into the picture. Instead, Lana informed her that Fitz had been away overseas for business, which she believed was a way for him to forget what happened between them. Likewise, she buried herself with work, taking more shifts, to ensure that there was no breathing space for her to think about him.

However, the image of him was still haunting her mind. The wound of their last conversation still felt fresh in her heart. She wondered why his words could bring such pain to her. Even from the first day they met, though it was by accident she heard it, he said she was not good enough for him, she had a brief meltdown which she did not understand why. She used to hear mocking words about her, especially when she was at school. It hurt at first, but eventually, her heart was numb, and she did not even bother anymore. From the beginning, it was impossible to be more than friends with someone like him. In fact, It never crossed her mind.

Unsure of how many deep sighs she took for the past month, she hoped it would one day chase away the heaviness in her heart. She did not know how long she would be like this, and only expected time would heal her heart. The upcoming Europe trip with uncle Gardiner and aunt Marie was something she looked forward to. Even though she had not given a firm answer, she was sure she needed this trip badly to get away.

She pulled up her car and entered the house driveway before switching off the engine. As she stepped out of the car and took her stuff, she heard the sound of rushing steps from the house door. Lana appeared and ran toward her with a panting breath. Her gut feeling told her something was not right.

"Lana? What happened?"

"Liz, we have to go to the hospital." Lana's voice was hushed but filled with panic. Her eyes briefly turned back to the house as if worried someone from the house could hear them. "Leah is in the hospital."

Amelia held her breath. The word hospital always brought a negative connotation.

"What happened?"

"Charlie just called me. He initially wanted to come here to pick me up. But I heard your car came in, so I told him we would go together. I haven't told mum and dad. I don't want to make them worried. Let's get into the car."

Amelia was still perplexed, but as Lana rushed to the passenger seat beside the driver seat, she also hopped in soon without further ado.

"Leah has not come back home, and I started to worry," explained Lana while the car started rolling. "Suddenly, Charlie called and informed me that Leah is in the hospital. He hasn't told me what happened, so I think we just get there first and find out what happened."

Amelia nodded without protest and focused on her driving. Once they found the off-street parking outside the hospital, they surged into the emergency room. Charlie had waited for them in the waiting area. His face looked anxious; however his congenial smile still appeared while opening wide his arms letting Lana crush herself into them.

"Shhh...she's alright. I have told you on the phone, she's alright." Charlie soothed her before looking up to see Amelia. "Hi, Amelia. You must just come back from work."

Amelia nodded while her eyes were looking around to see the hecticness in the hospital despite the wee hours. A glimpse of a tall figure that looked familiar to her made her body stiff. It was only his back, covered in a long dark jacket, but Amelia could discern that it was Fitz. He rushed out from the emergency door, which somehow made her feel dejected. She tried to focus her mind back on Leah, thinking that it was for the best since they were not meant to see each other. However, her critical thinking made her wonder what exactly he was doing here. Didn't it mean that Fitz also knew what happened to Leah if Charlie was here too?

"What happened?" She immediately queried Charlie.

Charlie took a deep breath while looking at both of them hesitantly. "She was drugged." Lana gasped, which prompted him to hug her tighter. "She was with Gerald."

Amelia's heart stopped, and she forgot to breathe. Hearing Gerald's name made her blood boil with anger. She should have known this could happen. She was too preoccupied with her own heart matters that she forgot to warn Leah about Gerald again, especially after Gerald's crazy attempt to kidnap Georgie. How could she forgive herself for letting this thing happen?

"I should have warned her...," she hissed while pacing around in rage. "Especially after that night...."

Lana narrowed her eyes at her. "What do you mean, Liz?"

She hadn't told Lana anything because of too many things in her mind. First, she felt she did not have the right to tell Lana about Gerald and Georgie's history since it was pertaining to Fitz's family reputation.

"I believe Fitz does not mind if you tell Lana about Gerald," said Charlie reading her dubious expression. "I should have told her too."

Lana looked at both of them, still puzzled.

"Gerald also drugged Georgie last time," began Charlie which made Lana's hand fly to her mouth in shock. "That was the reason I told you to stay away from Gerald when the first time Leah met him at the pub. He took a video of him raping Georgie. He threatened Fitz to give him money. Otherwise, he could distribute the video out."

"Fitz told me he managed to discard the video," Amelia continued. "Yeah, but Gerald kept saying he still had a copy."

Charlie took a sigh. "Yes, that's correct. Gerald was revengeful toward Fitz because he separated him from Georgie. Fitz did that because Gerald used all Georgie's money for his gambling habit."

Lana would probably slide down if it was not because Charlie was holding her up. She clutched Charlie's arm tighter until her fingers turned white. "But...what he did to Georgie was motivated by money. Leah does not have anything."

"He must have done it to take revenge on me." Amelia's nails were biting into her palm. "Remember in Yarra Valley when I had a scratch on my face that I told you about the little kitchen accident? It was actually because I ruined his attempt to kidnap Georgie."

Lana gave her an incredulous stare. "Why didn't you tell me, Liz?"

Amelia squeezed her eyes shut and groaned. She knew she had to be blamed for what happened. She could not bring herself to tell Lana about the kidnapping because of what happened afterwards that night, her kiss with Fitz and many other things that occurred after.

"Let us have a look at Leah." Charlie's voice interjected as if trying to mediate between the sisters. "The doctor said her condition is stable. So she should be fine."

Amelia nodded and followed after Lana gifted her a glare. That was an indication that her sister would drill her once she had a chance. At this moment, she only wanted to ensure that Leah was safe and deal with it later.

They entered the hospital ward, where Leah was sleeping soundly with the oxygen meter on her finger. Her little sister slept blissfully as if she was oblivious to what happened. Amelia felt relieved that there was no sign of physical abuse or injury on her sister's face.

"How do you find her?" she whispered, afraid of waking Leah up. But, unfortunately, her voice did wake her sister up. Leah was struggling to open her eyes, but she managed to open them after a couple of blinks. Even though she looked sluggish, her lips broke a weak smile, which brought a relieved breath to both her older sisters.

"How do you feel, Leah?" Lana reached out to her other hand and squeezed it gently.

"What happened?" Leah asked weakly.

"Do you remember what happened?" Amelia asked carefully.

Leah closed her eyes briefly before opening them up again with a frown. "I was with Gerald. He gave me a drink. I felt dizzy afterwards, and I think he took me somewhere. I was not sure where. But I heard some noises before everything went black. I think I saw someone that I knew. " Her eyes shifted to Charlie with a knitted brow. "Your friend. Fitz."

Amelia's body went stiff as her muscles became rigid. Now she understood why she saw Fitz earlier. He was the one who found Leah!

"That's correct." Charlie nodded his head. "It was Fitz who found you and stopped Gerald from doing anything further to harm you, Leah."

"What was he trying to do?" asked Leah, but her question was left in the air as she was too weak and succumbed to her sleep again.

Charlie squeezed Lana's shoulder, reassuring her that Leah was alright and gestured them to leave the room.

"Fitz managed to stop Gerald before he even started," uttered Charlie once they were outside in the waiting room.

"How did he know?" asked Amelia. Her gaze flitted around the room but Charlie. "How did he know that Gerald would plan this?"

"I think Fitz knew Gerald too well. He hired someone to keep watching him. Especially after Gerald's attempt to kidnap Georgie."

"Oh, we must thank him," exclaimed Lana. "We owe him."

"And how about Gerald?" Amelia asked again, still with her unfocused gaze. "What did he do with Gerald?"

"He's in custody now. We have ensured no one could bail him," answered Charlie firmly. "Fitz said he's going to press the charges against him."

Amelia tilted her head towards Charlie with widening eyes. "This could drag down his family's reputation."

As if he had expected her reaction, Charlie answered firmly. "He is ready for that. He told me himself that even Georgie is more than ready to face him in court. After what he tried to do today to Leah, he must stop Gerald from going further. I fully support him too."

"If we press the charges, you and your family's reputation could get dragged too," Amelia breathed heavily. She stared at both her sister and Charlie. Lana returned her look with concern, realising the meaning of her words.

Charlie again replied calmly. "I am fully aware of that too. But I agree with Fitz. We cannot let Gerald go any further. He could do this to anyone else in the future, or even come back to us, to you, Lana, Georgie, Leah or even Clare. I will not be in peace until I am sure he is punished for what he has done. So, regardless your family will press charges or not, Fitz and Georgie will go ahead."

Silence fell upon them as there was only breathlessness in Amelia. She could sense that her sister was looking at her, alarmed as she was speechless. But she raised her hand and shook her head, assuring her that she was alright.

That night, it was decided that she was the one to stay back in the hospital accompanying Leah. The task of filling in Lana with the background of Gerald's story was left to Charlie as he was the one who took Lana home. Amelia sat on the sofa in the room where Leah was sleeping and thinking about their earlier conversation.

She did not understand. Why did Fitz do this? After Georgie's kidnapping attempt, he could just leave Gerald alone since he knew by then that Gerald had nothing further to blackmail him. Instead, he hired a professional to keep watch on Gerald, and consequently, Leah was saved. Now with more substantial evidence of Gerald's criminal conduct, it was more likely they would successfully press the charges and get him punished. But that also meant they needed more proof apart from this incident alone, and that meant Georgie's past would be disturbed too. Wouldn't that be painful for them, becoming the centre of social media attention that would expose their horrible past?

She could not fathom why he did this. He was embarrassed for being trapped having feelings towards her. Instead, in his effort to catch Gerald, he got involved again with her and her family. He must have felt responsible for how he indirectly had caused Gerald to enter their life. But wouldn't this bring too much risk to him, his sister and his family's reputation? How could he avoid her if now they were entangled in this case together?

She took a deep breath, wishing the air could fill her lungs, easing the tightness in her chest and the quivering inside her. Before she realised it, tears started rolling down. Slowly she shut her eyes, letting herself drift to sleep with dry tears on her cheeks.

CHAPTER TWELVE

A Journey

Amelia placed her luggage onto the overhead compartment above her seat and tried to squeeze it between other luggage belonging to other passengers. Once finally she successfully did it, she took the window seat beside her aunt Marie. The pilot's announcement echoed, welcoming all the plane passengers and wishing them a good journey ahead. Amelia could not believe that this was the first time, perhaps in her life, that she was looking forward to this long-haul flight trip.

Without a doubt, she was looking forward to her Europe trip with her aunt Marie and uncle Gardiner. Initially, thinking that she had to take a minimum of 22 hours of flight discouraged her. She never enjoyed a flight trip, perhaps a short interstate trip would be fine, but she preferred a road trip. Clearly, this time she had no other choice. Naturally, she looked forward to the road trip within Europe itself, but strangely, she also looked forward to these 22 hours flights.

Looking back on what happened in the previous months before this trip, she knew the reason why. Leah's incident with Gerald was one of the reasons. It was a huge relief and triumph when they won the case, and Gerald received a punishment of 25 years in prison. She hoped he could be punished more severely. They have presented substantial shreds of evidence and witnesses from the direct victims, including Georgie and Leah.

Amelia had to admit how proud she was of her younger sister. The incident changed Leah completely into someone she would not expect for her age. Leah was upset when she knew what Gerald had almost done to her. Initially, she was scared to stand up in court as a witness. There was a hint of embarrassment, realising how easily she was being taken advantage of. Her mother did not make things better by worrying about losing her reputation and damaging their relationship with Charlie's family.

However, Leah's perspective changed, partially contributed by Lana's gentle advice and persuasion. Another reason was that Georgie did not hesitate to stand in court as a victim and witness, despite placing her family's good reputation to the test. As expected, the Dalton family became the centre of media attention throughout the hearing. However, Georgie presented herself very well as a vulnerable woman with strong resilience in facing the scrutinization. Amelia's heart even swelled with pride watching her, let alone Fitz as her brother. The various media news covering the hearing process revealed that Fitz and Georgie's parents have long passed away. They were the heir of various multi-business and charity organisations that belonged to the family. De Boyville's name was also mentioned many times in the news as one of their closest acquaintances.

Throughout the hearing, Charlie had been on Lana's side, giving support as he had promised. Even there was one time, Charlie's parents and Clare attended the hearing, which attracted media attention. Amelia noticed that Clare took the opportunity to be as close as possible to Fitz, as if she was there as his girlfriend. On the other hand, she tried to hide away from him as much as possible by getting Leah as her shield.

The only close encounter they had, which was unavoidable, when the favourable outcome was announced. There was a feeling of weightlessness watching the security lead Gerald away after the verdict. Georgie bounced to her feet, and her eyes danced with sparkle when she came up to Leah for a massive tight hug, sharing their joy, for justice had been on their side. It would not change the past, but it gave unlimited hope for their future.

That was the only moment that Amelia had a chance to see Fitz closer. However, she intentionally hid behind Lana and Leah while looking away as if not realising his presence. The next minute, she quietly watched him leaving the courtroom with Clare leaning on his left arm while Georgie took his right arm.

On that victorious day, Charlie's parents also extended an invitation for a celebration dinner and invited all their family. Amelia made an excuse not to attend it due to her usual weekday night shift work. She believed Fitz would be there, and it would be best if they did not see each other. Lana was disappointed, but her sister did not push her as she was in her euphoria.

That night Lana came back with a beautiful, elegant diamond engagement ring on her finger. Lana could not wait to show it to her. Lana and her family even waited until she returned from work that night to break the news. She was surprised that all her family was still awake and in lively conversation when she reached home. It was another joyful news to complete their day.

"Ooh, Liz....I've never been so happy in my life," beamed Lana while giving her a tight hug.

"You deserve it, Lana," whispered Amelia. It was the truth, as she would not let Lana go for someone less than Charlie.

"Oh, you have to be my maid of honour."

Amelia was taken aback. She never thought about that. "I don't think it's a good idea."

Lana gave her a reprimanded look. "Why? Because of your hand?"

"Leah could be one of your bridesmaids. I could help you with the wedding preparation from the background."

"You can't do this to my wedding!"

Their mother interrupted and gave Lana a lecture about how important it was to honour Charlie's family wishes. Amelia laughed inwardly because perhaps this was the first time in her life that she agreed with her mum.

When their mother talked about getting a dress and suit for their family, Lana suddenly said something that startled them

"I have told Charlie that I want a prenup agreement."

Amelia's mouth fell open. It was Lana this time who gave her a mischievous grin. Her mother looked horrified while her father smiled proudly at his eldest daughter. Leah was utterly lost.

"You're a fool!" scolded Mrs Bettney. "What would happen if he leaves you for other women? You will be left with nothing!"

Amelia cocked and shook her head, almost at the same time as Lana's deep sigh.

"Mum, if now you already have that thought, do you think I should marry him then?" challenged Lana.

Her mother was speechless. Lana smiled triumphantly.

"I do this for the sake of all of us. I love him for who he is, regardless of his wealth. As much as I don't care what other people say, we don't need help from him to settle dad's business debt. Like Lizzy, I will work as hard as I can to repay it. I don't want to owe him any single cent."

"That's true," continued Amelia. "So far, it is almost 50% of dad's business debt has been settled. And don't worry, mum, I'm going to be a spinster anyway. All my income will help to support our family and settle the remaining debts."

"That's unfair for you," murmured Mr Bettney. But he knew that was probably the truth that would not change. Amelia squeezed his shoulder while giving him a soft kiss on his forehead.

Despite her mum still grumbling about the prenup topic, they went to bed afterwards. Amelia did not expect Lana to have such courage, but she was quietly proud of her sister's decision. When she lied down, she started counting the days until she would depart and begin her journey to Europe. It was only two weeks away.

And here she was now on the plane, the beginning of her long-awaited overseas holiday. She enjoyed her long haul flight by simply relaxing, watching the on-air entertainment, sleeping and chatting with her aunt and uncle.

Aunt Marie and Uncle Gardiner were the loveliest couples she had ever met, and she could not help comparing them with her parents, who always quarrelled. Her mother could be unreasonable, and her father lost patience with her mother's silliness. But on the other hand, her aunt and uncle were only showing affection between them. It was only a subtle one, but from the way they looked at or addressed each other respectfully, it meant more than that, and sometimes she could feel the warmth shining out from it. She felt a similar atmosphere as well with Lana and Charlie. She was thrilled for her sister, and she hoped that their relationship was stronger than ever after what had happened.

Their flight stopped in Dubai for two hours, and they took the opportunity to stretch their legs at the airport. It was still an exhausting trip, but it seemed her aunt and uncle could sleep well on the plane. She had to admit she did not have a great sleep, but because her mind was away from all the trouble that had passed, she did not feel tired.

They reached Manchester International airport late afternoon, but the daylight still welcomed them because it was summer. They collected a hired car, and here was the moment she had been waiting for. A road trip! Luckily Derby was not far, as she did not think she could drive for longer than two hours. She was glad to see similar enthusiasm from her travel companions even though they were worn out too. But it did not stop them from enjoying the warm weather, the lovely scenery throughout the journey and the remaining yellow wildflowers that still spread out along the road.

Derby was a small county village with plenty of cottages and villas in the neighbourhood. Amelia slowly drove the car to the town centre, following the direction given by the car GPS while observing the people and the shops on the street. It was a lively town, but it was not crowded. People seemed relaxed while enjoying the weather. She spotted more older people as well as some young couples too. She kept following the GPS direction until they reached the accommodation place they had booked, about five kilometres away from the town centre. It was a simple bed and breakfast accommodation, an old farm holiday cottage in a hilly place overlooking the town centre. After pulling her car, Amelia took a deep breath and closed her eyes, enjoying the fresh summer air.

She paid attention to the cottage and the beautifully manicured garden surrounding it. She looked at the town centre direction and could see some of the shops they had passed earlier. However, when she turned to the other side of the hill, she gasped and almost could not believe what she had seen.

It was the most beautiful, magnificent estate she would have ever seen in her life. The building itself was a well maintained grand mansion with a highly detailed European architecture. Though Melbourne also had some Victorian and heritage-listed buildings like the Werribee mansion or Flinders Street Station, this mansion was much larger in a quadrangle layout, a large middle courtyard, and a sky scrapping water fountain. It was probably still ten kilometres away from them, but the green pasture in between made it look prominent from where she was standing. Aunt Marie and Uncle Gardiner joined behind her.

"Beautiful, isn't it?" murmured Aunt Marie.

"It's ...." Amelia could not form any word to describe it as she was mesmerised.

"I know that place belongs to the Daltons," added Aunt Marie.

Amelia turned her head to her aunt with widening eyes. "Dalton?"

"Yes, Charlie's friend, isn't he? I believe you know him. Especially after the court hearing that you attended together with them?" echoed Uncle Gardiner.

"The same Dalton?" she repeated, still unsure about her hearing. It was a silly question. Knowing his background, she should not be surprised if his family owned such a grand estate. It was just after trying to forget the past and thinking she came here to forget it easily, she was haunted again by his name.

"I believe it is the same Dalton," asserted Aunt Marie while gesturing for them to enter the accommodation's reception office. "Let us ask the people who work here. They must know better."

"Perhaps we don't need to ask." Amelia swallowed nervously while following her aunt and her uncle to collect their luggage from the car. "We are not going there, are we?"

"We could actually," stated uncle Gardiner. "And I believe you are interested in going there too, my dear Marie? "

Aunt Marie nodded. "Yes, it is on our itinerary list."

Amelia cursed under her breath that she never bothered to check on the itinerary for this journey. She had let aunt Marie plan everything. However, she would have no idea that such a grand estate belonged to Dalton anyway.

"I don't think we can simply enter a privately owned estate like that. I suppose we may only take a couple of snaps from the garden." Amelia still tried to reason it out.

"Oh, that estate is now the most expensive boutique hotel accommodation in England. Though I don't think we can afford to stay there, I heard we can book a tour to see the inside. I heard the interior is splendid," commented Aunt Marie.

Amelia's shoulder went down, and her brow wrinkled, realising that it seemed she could not avoid this. Perhaps she was thinking too far. Fitz was a busy businessman. That estate belonged to his family, but it did not mean he would be there. The chance of their meeting would be very slim.

They were welcomed warmly by the cottage owner, who also served them tea and homemade English scones while processing their check-in. They were seated in the lounge, enjoying a refreshment, overlooking the same breathtaking building from the window. Amelia had to admit she was also curious to see what the inside of that building looked like.

"Are we allowed to pay a visit to that estate?" Uncle Gardiner broke the question. The cottage owner lady named Monique approached them with a beaming face when she heard the question.

"Of course. I would recommend you do it as soon as possible before this weekend. There is an annual masquerade ball that will be held on the estate. It's going to be spectacular! Only those who are invited can attend. They are mostly close family and friends of the Dalton family."

Amelia almost choked from her tea. She swallowed thickly. How could she not think about this? Sharon did mention her plan to go to England as well, to attend a masquerade ball. However, she never shared in detail the itinerary and location. Her friend had mentioned it was an annual event that De Boyville would invite Colin and his family. How could this be such a coincidence?

Amelia remembered Lana also mentioned this, but Charlie regrettably declined the invite due to another business commitment. Again, she never bothered to check the detail because she did not want to hear anything related to Dalton.

"Wow, that sounds fun!" exclaimed aunt Marie. "We can visit the place tomorrow. I suppose the place is always open to the public?"

"Yes, but not all of the area of the building is accessible to the public. The centre wing is closed for private use only. The right wing is for hotel accommodation, but only selected guests or people who could have an opportunity to stay there. While the left-wing is the one open for the tour because that's where most of the collections and the library are," explained Monique enthusiastically. "For the masquerade ball, sometimes some of the guests do not have the opportunity to stay in Pemberley. So, we, the surrounding cottages, have the opportunity to accommodate them. It has been our annual thing."

"So, that estate is called Pemberley?" murmured Amelia.

"Yes. It belongs to the Dalton family for generations. I know the current Daltons very well, too, Fitz and Georgie. They are such lovely young people, very humbled and down to earth like their parents."

"Amelia also knows them personally," echoed Aunt Marie while gesturing to her niece.

"Oh, really? This young lady knows the Daltons well, too?" wondered Monique while throwing a glance at Amelia before her eyes travelled to Amelia's little left limb.

Amelia shifted uncomfortably. She presumed Monique would not believe that the Daltons were connected to someone disabled like her. "Their best friend is my sister's fiancé," she muttered. "I don't know them that well."

Monique did not respond, but her eyes were still lingering on her for a moment before she handed out the room keys.

"So, you'll be staying for three nights only? You're not coming to the ball?" queried Monique while tilting her head.

"No, no, we are not invited," replied Amelia quickly. "We even have no idea about the ball. We solely here because aunt Marie used to live here when she was little."

"Oh, that's a shame. Otherwise, you could meet Fitz and Georgie. Usually, they would be here one to two days before the event."

Amelia let out a deliberately quiet exhale. So that means after she left this town, the Daltons would just arrive. It seemed since the first time she heard about Dalton's name again, she finally felt a lightness in her limbs.

They turned in early that night after such an exhausting long journey. However, on the first night in the other part of the world, the jet lag started creeping in. Amelia managed to lie down and drifted to sleep for a couple of hours before waking up and feeling vigorous when the clock still showed four A.M. She chose to stay in bed, closed her eyes again and tried to do a meditation, hoping she could get more sleep. But her meditation only worked for half an hour. Afterwards, she gave up.

She grabbed her mobile phone and saw a couple of messages from Lana, Sharon and some from her work. Sharon sent a message informing her that she was flying to the UK. She just found out from Lana, that apparently, they were going to the same destination.

Right, she huffed. Based on Sharon's arrival date, she would already move to another town as planned. Sharon's arrival was the day before the event. She was disappointed that she could not meet her friend but could not allow any chance that she would bump into Fitz.

When the morning sun started peeping in from her room window, she decided it was safe enough for her to have a jog outside. She believed her aunt and uncle must still be sleeping in bed. Still, her body ached for some activities that she usually did as an early riser. She changed into her track pants and jumper, tiptoed and descended the stairs to the reception area. A young teenage boy was at the reception table, whom she guessed as Monique's son since they shared the same nose and long shape face.

"Good morning," she greeted.

"Good morning," the boy replied.

"I would like to ask whether Can I have a walk as far as Pemberley? Or no trespassers allowed?"

"Yes, definitely you can. No boundary fence separates the two properties."

"Thank you."

She went out of the cottage, inhaling the fresh air of the flower fragrance from the garden in the front yard deeply.

As the morning crisp air touched her face, she felt light and free. She began her jog with a steady pace towards the green pasture heading in the direction of Pemberley. Paying a visit to the estate garden would be one of her plans because she believed it would not be her aunt and uncle's interest due to the summer heat, which was not suitable for their age. Therefore, she thought to do it on her own this morning while the sun was not at full blast yet.

She probably had jogged for about five kilometres when she reached the edge of Pemberley's garden, which was technically the borderline between the estate and other property. She jogged through the aisle of the beautifully high manicured shrub while inhaling the fresh morning air and the smell of the grass and trees. She had not spotted any single soul so far, which urged her to close her eyes, feeling the breeze on her face and being immersed in her 'flying' moment. The warmth of the morning sun touched her face while she kept running without realising that she was reaching the end of the shrub row. In a fleeting moment, suddenly, her body bumped into someone's chest, which came from the other side of the shrub.

Calling it a normal bumping was probably an understatement. It was a hard collide, which made her release a soft grunt and flinch. She squeezed her eyes shut in pain.

The collide caused both of them to lose balance. She was wrapped in that person's arm before both of them plummetted to the grass, and her body was crushed underneath. Something familiar struck her senses, a masculine scent that was always dear to her heart. When she opened her eyes, her breathing was suspended for a split second. He was the last person she would wish to see here, and now he was just on top of her!

A sudden coldness hit her core. From all the cursing words that she had known all her life, all of them were echoing in her head at the same time. How could this happen? Was she just dreaming?

A shock was also written on his face. They were staring at each other for a moment, unable to move from their position while still trying to catch their breath. His face was just an inch away from her as his breath was on her cheek.

Their proximity brought her mind to the previous intimate kisses that they shared, the warmth and secure feeling that she liked very much under his embrace. How much she longed for that moment again, but the reality always kicked in, reminding her that it would be impossible. She could not have him. And now he was just an inch away from her. His deep umber eyes looked at her initially with disbelief, but slowly, it was replaced with a tender gaze. It was something she had always dreamt of seeing from him.

Her eyes traced the heavy stubble on his jaw, but her vision was blurry as his face got closer to her. She closed her eyes to feel the prick of his stubble on her cheek. His lips caressed her corner lips while his fingertips skimmed on her jawline before moving to her forehead fringe.

"Amelia..."

His low pitched husky voice slapped her back into the present. Her eyes flew open, realising that she was supposed to stay away from him! He resented her, and her appearance only made him in agony! She wriggled her body which made him roll to the side. She practically scampered to get up.

"What are you doing here??" Fitz chastised, full of disdain. It was not pleasant to her ear, which made her wince. She wished she could be invisible at this moment.

"I mean..." he stammered. "I don't expect to see you here."

"Neither do I." She was flustered and surprised to hear her shaky voice. "I absolutely had no idea that this place related to you. I have been informed that you will not be here until the masquerade ball. Believe me, I did not mean to disturb you at all." While she was speaking, she took backward steps further away from him while he instead stepped towards her. Only when he stalled did she also stop too.

"Right." He held his hand up while his eyes were still lingering on her. She found his expression was getting calmer. "Where are you staying?"

"The nearby cottage," she replied still with her shaky voice. She hated it and tried to take a deep breath to recompose herself. "Now I know you're here, I'll make sure I will not cross your path anymore. So forgive me and have a good day!" Without waiting for his reply, she whirled her body and dashed away. She even did not dare to look back anymore.

The sprint took her away further for about three kilometres from Pemberley ground. All her energy and breath were drained, and she continued her journey with a brisk walk. She still had a racing heartbeat with the rendezvous. This was totally not something she had ever planned for her holiday. Why was it so difficult to get rid of him from her mind that even he haunted her on this trip? He must be thinking that she was stalking him! So embarrassing! She went there with the belief he would not be there, as much as she was curious to see the estate up close. She must think of a way to avoid the tour to Pemberley planned by Aunt Marie this afternoon.

She entered the cottage with a weighted heart and mind, in contrast to what she had when she left in the morning. Her aunt and her uncle came out of their room and went down for their breakfast. She excused herself for a shower first and would join them later.

The shower did help her a lot. It made her spirit back. She looked at herself in the mirror for a moment, trying to lift her courage that she could do this, avoiding him as much as possible while enduring the rest of the two nights. She believed it would not be hard as there were many excuses to explore other places. Of course, her aunt and uncle would be disappointed, but it would be better this way.

She came down wearing her beige summer blouse and short jeans. When she entered the cottage meal area, a couple of other guests were also enjoying their breakfast. Her stomach was rolling, either because of hunger or dread, when she spotted her aunt and uncle with the other two persons that she did not expect to see.

Aunt Marie and Uncle Gardiner were holding their teacups. They smiled at her while the two unexpected visitors rose from the chair, welcoming her presence.

"Amelia! It's wonderful to see you here! Such a pleasant surprise!"

Her body went stiff as Georgie flew her arms around her and hugged her tightly before releasing her and squeezing her hand. She looked at Fitz, who also gave her a tight smile and greeted her. He was dressed smartly in his shirt and jeans, already cleanly shaven, in contrast to his appearance this morning. She felt like she just saw two different Fitz.

She was lost, tongue-tied, and unable to form any words or respond for the next couple of minutes. Aunt Marie started to notice her odd behaviour.

"Fitz and Georgie found out that we are staying here, so they pay a visit. When Monique informed them that we're here having breakfast, they come to introduce themselves to us," explained Aunt Marie.

"Yeah, I heard from Lana about your trip," added Georgie. Her blue eyes were sparkling, with a wide grin drawn on her face. "I think it's such a great coincidence. I do not plan to arrive in Derby this early, but I look forward to the event we're organising in Pemberley. Since Fitz has more time, we decided to reach here earlier than planned, which is great because now we get to see you here!"

Amelia was still speechless. She only nodded her head and broke a tentative smile. *Yeah, what a coincidence!* she thought. She glanced at Fitz, who returned her with a steady gaze with his large pupil. She could not fathom why after the encounter this morning, which he seemed to detest, he came here instead?

"Have a seat, Liz." Uncle Gardiner's warm vibrato voice soothed her. "Let us have breakfast, and we can have a chat here. Georgie seems excited to see you."

Amelia understood that her lack of courtesy was not something her uncle or aunt would expect. She tried to calm her racing heartbeat while taking the empty seat between her aunt and Georgie.

"Aunt Marie told me that you are staying here only for three nights," bubbled Georgie. "Please stay until the masquerade ball and join the ball." The girl gave her a half pleading look.

Amelia took a glance at her aunt briefly before answering, "I don't think we can. The purpose of this trip is for Aunt Marie and Uncle Gardiner to see their daughter in Nottingham. So, we have to leave in two nights' time." Her tone emphasized every word clearly, wishing that would give a clear hint to Fitz that she never, never planned to cross his path.

"They have other plans already, Georgie." Finally, Fitz broke his silence. His words made Amelia understand that only Georgie was thrilled to see her. Oh, she wished Georgie could understand the agony that her brother was currently going through. She guessed Fitz was too proud to share with his sister what happened between them.

"Alright." Georgie conceded. "But please join us for lunch and dinner today. I understand that you're planning to visit Pemberley for a tour this afternoon. Pemberley is huge. I think one day tour will not be enough. I can show you not only the left-wing that is usually open to the public, but I can take you to the rest of Pemberley as well," added Georgie without any sign of diminishing enthusiasm in her tone.

Amelia was reluctant to answer, but she could see her aunt and uncle's face beaming with the offer. When her eyes glanced to Fitz to check on his reaction, his unblinking eyes made her heart palpitate.

"Oh, that sounds like a wonderful offer," exclaimed aunt Marie. "Shall we, Liz?"

Amelia bit her dry lips with her head flinched back slightly. Her aunt and uncle exchanged glances before looking back at her, frowning.

"Are you alright, Liz? Are you unwell?" asked her uncle.

The question instead gave her an idea. She rubbed her temple and pretended to be in pain. "Yeah, I'm still tired. I think you should go ahead without me." She could see disappointment mixed with concern from her aunt and uncle.

"Oh, that's a pity," gasped Aunt Marie. "Perhaps we should stay too, dear."

"No!" Amelia quickly interjected. "Please go ahead with whatever you've planned today, aunt. Please don't let me ruin your plan. Let me rest today, and perhaps I can join in again tomorrow."

Her aunt and uncle nodded in agreement hesitantly. Georgie also looked at her with eyebrows drawn together.

"I hope you can have a good rest today, Amelia. But promise me that you will give us a visit to Pemberley before you leave town," she said affectionately.

Amelia tried to give a reassuring smile. "Yes, of course." She stole a glance at Fitz, who gave her rapt attention with his still posture. She presumed he would be relieved that he did not need to spend time with her today.

Aunt Marie and Uncle Gardiner left with Georgie and Fitz's car immediately after the breakfast service was over. With a slumping posture, Amelia went to her bedroom, thinking of lying down. However, the more she thought, the more she felt that she was actually perfectly fine and had more than enough energy to enjoy the town. If her aunt and uncle were in Pemberley, there was a slim chance that she would bump into them in the town centre today. Taking a stroll instead of taking the car to the town centre, which was only five kilometres away, would be awesome. At least she could still enjoy her holiday without having to suffer under Fitz's scrutiny.

She put on her sneakers and started the stroll feeling light and free. The only thing that bothered her was that she had lied to her aunt and uncle. She promised herself that she would explain it to them when the time was right. But at this stage, this was for the best.

The walk to the town centre was downhill, so it was quick, smooth and easy for her. She reached the town within 20 minutes, and the weather was on her side too, being lukewarm only. She checked the town map and was convinced that she could finish exploring it within half a day. When she returned to the cottage in the afternoon, she still had plenty of time to lie down on her bed and pretend to be sick when her aunt and uncle returned.

The atmosphere in town on a summer day was lively and not overcrowded. The lovely ambience with a street musician playing some old songs made her movement even more fluid. She visited some shops until she decided to buy a croissant sandwich from one of the cafés and planned to sit by the river while enjoying her lunch. She enjoyed her own time so much that she almost forgot about her lie. But, unfortunately, her state of euphoria was gone within a second the moment her eyes caught a familiar tall figure who also entered the café.

For a couple of seconds, their body froze, staring at each other. A flush crept across her cheek, realising that she was caught red-handed lying about her whereabouts. And from all the people that she wanted to avoid, he again appeared in front of her.

"I suppose you're feeling better now." Fitz's voice broke the silence between them.

Amelia felt a pang of immense guilt hit her.

"Yeah, much better," she sighed. She did not want to give a damn about what he thought if now he knew she was lying this morning to avoid going to Pemberley. He should have known that she did it for him. Averting his gaze, she simply ignored him and walked past him to reach the exit door.

"Don't you want to join your aunt and uncle now in Pemberley?"

She did not expect him to follow her. She again ignored him and accelerated her walk. Wasn't it his wish not to see her anymore? Why did he have to bother even to speak to her? But her feet were halted on the ground as he was suddenly standing in front of her.

"Georgie will be disappointed," Fitz stated. "She is excited to host you at Pemberley."

Amelia took a heavy sigh. She did not want to offend Georgie. That girl had been courteous and pleasant toward her. She was the one who felt terrible for always acting cold towards her. All thanks to her brother.

"And how about you? I believe you detest seeing me on your property," she said sarcastically. "You should have told your sister you can't stand me," she muttered.

"You misunderstood me," he replied with a sombre tone. "I never said that I did not want to see you."

She tilted her head with squished eyebrows. The moment when they had the conversation in the park was still vivid in her mind. It was correct that he did not say he did not want to see her, but all his words implied that meaning clearly.

"I don't understand. I am doing a favour for you here," she grumbled.

She burst to pass through him, but he stopped her by gently grabbing her little left arm. Suddenly she realised that the people around them giggled at them. It only came to her realisation that he was probably a known figure in the area. Her guess was correct when one lady, who looked like a local, greeted him, and he returned politely. The lady smiled at them meaningfully while passing them and sneaked away. With his hand gripping her left arm, he pulled her towards a BMW Ute parked on the opposite street.

"Let's go to Pemberley. They are waiting for you there."

Amelia did not want to create a scene as much as she wanted to push him away. She obediently hopped into his car.

"I thought you would be in Pemberley for the whole day entertaining my aunt and uncle." She glanced at him while his eyes, covered by sunnies, were fixed on the road.

"That was my plan. I excused myself for a short meeting earlier. I think It happened at the right time because I found you then. I plan to visit you in Monique's cottage to check how you are going."

She scoffed. "You could pretend that you did not see me. Just drop me in a cottage, then you don't need to entertain me as your guest on your property."

"Do you want your aunt and uncle to find out that you are lying to them?" He raised his eyebrow with a cocky smile on his lips. She grunted inwardly and looked away. "As I said, I never said I didn't want to see you. You're definitely welcome in Pemberley."

Amelia did not want to argue anymore and went silent for the rest of the journey. She did not understand him.

It was a short drive since Pemberly was only about ten minutes away from the town centre. Fitz parked his car at the lobby entrance, which Amelia assumed was also shared with the hotel guests as well. She noticed the tour coach parked further on the left, and it reminded her of Monique's words that only the left wing opened for the public. There were not many people around, however she could not help to feel the curious glances around them as Fitz placed his hand on her small back, leading her inside. She felt confused and did not understand why he let such a public display on them when he implied it was embarrassing to be seen with her.

What Monique told her again resonated in her ears as they climbed up the middle stairs. The centre wing was kept for private purposes. She had to admit that the interior of the building was truly magnificent. It was breathtaking that even she stood in awe, admiring them. This was her first time and might as well be her last time to be in such a splendid place. And she wanted to register everything in her memory as much as possible and was too embarrassed to take out her mobile phone for a couple of snaps.

She became unaware of her surroundings. She let herself admire the paintings on the ceiling, the detailed architrave, and the art sculpture they passed along the way. She was taken aback to realise that Fitz was behind her, waiting on her patiently without uttering any words but motioning her which path she should take. It was a long corridor full of artistic interiors. She did not bother to ask where they were going until they reached a double door that one of the stewards opened.

It was a cosy lounge room with luxurious vintage European furniture filling it and a marble fireplace. There she found her aunt and uncle chatting comfortably with Georgie.

"Amelia!" Georgie leapt from her seat, approaching her. "I'm so glad you're finally joining in."

"Are you feeling better, my dear?" asked aunt Marie with a concerned look. Amelia swallowed while giving an assurance nod. She glanced at Fitz, who returned her look with twitching lips.

"How do you come together with Fitz?" asked uncle Gardiner.

"I saw her buying lunch after I finished my meeting. Since she felt much better, I offered her a lift here," explained Fitz.

"Oh, thanks for bringing her here, bro," said Georgie. "I almost wanted to bring your aunt and uncle back to the cottage soon because I'm worried you'll be bored alone there."

"That's true, Liz," added aunt Marie. "This place is too huge for us. Georgie and Fitz have been very kind in showing us the centre wing, which is fantastic because not everyone could come in." She smiled cheekily. " I have taken some pictures. Tomorrow we could go for the left-wing with the tour."

"No, I will take you to the left-wing," protested Georgie. "Don't go with the tour. Please come and have breakfast first with us."

They came into the agreement that the next morning, Georgie again would be the host for the tour. Meanwhile, the rest of the afternoon was only filled with chatting about Pemberley and Derbyshire itself. Aunt Marie shared many memories about her childhood in Derbyshire, which was joined with much anticipation by Georgie and occasionally Fitz. Amelia observed the siblings and realised how different the characters shared between them. Fitz was more reserved and based on her memory when they were first introduced, her first impression of him was as a proud man with his stoic and impassive demeanour. On the other hand, Georgie seemed to possess a natural congeniality. Her elegant attire made her look graceful like a queen. Sometimes her childish laughter and joke appeared, which showed how young she was, however did not deter her from talking flexibly with anyone of different ages.

Uncle Gardiner started complaining about his fatigue and jetlag. Aunt Marie then suggested that they go back to the cottage early, despite Georgie's invitation to stay for dinner. Georgie nodded in understanding. All of them left Pemberley together in Fitz's car and were dropped safely back to the cottage.

"I shall see all of you tomorrow morning," said Georgie when they were already in the cottage's reception area. "Don't need to rush yourself. Whenever you're ready for our pickup, just message me or ask Monique to call us. She knows our number."

Amelia stole a glance at Fitz, wondering about his reaction to tomorrow morning's plan set by Georgie. He just showed his impassiveness as usual that she would never understand. They bid goodbye afterwards, and Georgie gave all of them a cuddle and a peck on the cheek as if they had known each other for a while. Fitz followed his sister's gesture with a firm handshake with uncle Gardiner and a cuddle and a peck on the check with aunt Marie, which then left both of them standing awkwardly for a moment. She waved her hand as a goodbye gesture but held her breath as Fitz moved towards her and gave her cheek a peck.

As he lowered his face closer to her, both his hands rested for a second on her shoulders. She could feel his gentle squeeze on her shoulders as he whispered good night. Their eyes locked for a moment before he straightened himself up and stepped back.

She suddenly felt her cheek warm while watching Fitz's car slowly retreating. Her aunt and uncle entered the cottage without paying attention to the sudden colour on her face. They went to their room without any plan for further conversation.

That night she laid down wondering what actually happened between her and Fitz. She did not understand why Fitz still showed her hospitality, despite clearly saying that the relationship between them was impossible. She was resolute that his friendly behaviour was because of her close connection with Charlie, who would be her brother-in-law soon. He must have done it out of respect for his best friend. Furthermore, with the upcoming nuptials between Charlie and Lana, they would have more occasions to see each other. Perhaps now he started to come to terms that he could not be forever avoiding her. At least they should try to be civil to each other. With that resolution in mind, she drifted to sleep afterwards as her eyes were getting heavy.

CHAPTER THIRTEEN

A Walk to Remember

As planned, the next morning, Georgie and Fitz came to pick them up from the cottage once aunt Marie sent a message to Georgie's mobile phone. Amelia was surprised that Aunt Marie even had exchanged numbers with Georgie as if they had been great friends. She had to admit that Georgie and Aunt Marie were clicking well. And Aunt Marie did not even hesitate to enjoy the hospitality offered by the Daltons.

After having such a pleasant breakfast with lovely morning sun and a lavish menu, Georgie invited them to enjoy the beautifully manicured and well-maintained garden of Pemberley. It was a vast garden and definitely was not meant for everyone unless the person was a great walker. Amelia knew that Uncle Gardiner would not bear such a long walk, but Georgie seemed to have taken that into consideration. She had organised two sets of open horse carriages for all of them, so they could enjoy the morning breeze while viewing the scenery.

Aunt Marie squealed in excitement when the carriage arrived and, without hesitation, jumped in, followed by Uncle Gardiner. Georgie joined them on the first carriage. The carriage was just enough for three of them, which only left Amelia and Fitz to take the next carriage. Amelia wanted to protest the arrangement, however she caught a mischievous look from her aunt that made her frown. Aunt Marie and uncle Gardiner gave her a playful grin while waving their hands as their carriage was moving.

Amelia wondered whether her aunt and uncle had sensed something between her and Fitz. She had to find time to speak to them to explain before they thought too far. She was startled when Fitz offered his hand to help her jump into their carriage. She did not immediately take it.

"I prefer to walk," she said as a matter of fact. Though riding a carriage could be fun, she preferred to stroll in the garden since it was still morning and the sun was not glaring at her body.

Fitz lowered his hand. "Right," he muttered under his breath.

"You don't need to accompany me. I believe you're busy. I can have a stroll by myself," she added while whirling her body around and taking her steps.

"I know you can walk by yourself," he remarked from behind her before matching her pace and walking exactly beside her. "I'm not busy. I will not be able to focus on doing anything anyway. Especially now you are here."

She knitted her brow as she heard those words, but her gaze clouded over and went distant, ignoring his presence beside her. She was unsure whether he was being cynical though his voice sounded toneless.

"How is your family?" he broke the silence between them after strolling a couple of minutes. "I believe your parents are excited about Lana's upcoming wedding."

Recalling that he was the one who separated Lana and Charlie because he felt her family was after financial advantage from Charlie, she again wondered whether he was being sarcastic. However, his tone of voice implied a different meaning as if it was a genuine friendly ask.

"Yes, especially my mother." She almost wanted to boast that Lana initiated a prenuptial agreement to show that their family was not as low as he thought. However, the prenuptial agreement was Lana and Charlie's personal matter that she felt she was not in the position to discuss with someone else, even him.

"I think the engagement news came at the right time. Especially after what your family have gone through with the court hearing." She could feel him turning his head to her briefly before looking ahead again. "You were not at the celebration party when the engagement was announced. Charlie could not contain his happiness. He had been so eager to propose but kept waiting the right time."

"I had work to do. Lana told me everything that night anyway after I came back from work."

"How is Leah after what she had gone through in the court hearing? Is she alright?"

"Yes, she's fine." She suddenly remembered that she still owed him gratitude after what he had done to save Leah. "I am sorry that I'm late to say this, but thank you for saving her from Gerald."

He turned his head to her, and their eyes locked for a moment. She saw him smiling, something that was new to her. He had a beautiful smile that made her feel a flutter in her belly. She warded that feeling off quickly.

"I only did what I wish I could do for Georgie." He swallowed and took a deep sigh. "I do not wish Gerald to ruin any other girl's life like what he did to Georgie. I know him too well that he would do anything to take revenge on me. I will not be able to forgive myself if he hurt you or your family." He gripped her arm gently, stopping her walk. In reflex, she looked up to meet his deep umber eyes.

"I ..." he stammered while lowering his gaze and lifting his eyes on her again without blinking. "I want to apologise for what I've said to you before in the park. Those words were not properly said."

She gave him a blank look with a mouth half-opened, and her mind was racing, wondering what he meant.

"Yes, I struggled to fight my feelings toward you. But that day, I wanted to say what I have overcome to conclude that I couldn't hide it anymore. I ardently admire you, Amelia. I like you."

His voice was low and trembling with emotion, and his soft, intense gaze penetrated through her heart and sent a shiver down her spine. She was breathless and lightheaded, with her heartbeat the only thing she could hear.

She did not expect to hear those words again. The first time he said those words he seemed to be resenting it, how every word he said afterwards was like a stab to her heart. He had a huge concern to be with her, not only because of her family's financial disadvantages but also her circumstances, being born with a birth defect.

"I did not mean to say demeaning words about you or your family," he continued with a pinch of regret. "That was a very poorly done declaration. I did not expect you would perceive it that I did not want anything to do with you anymore, while on the other hand, I want to be with you."

She was speechless, and her brain was still fuzzy as his words slowly dawned on her. This time she could feel he meant every word genuinely, and even there was a hint of pleading from his eyes, wishing she would believe him.

"When you walked away, I thought perhaps that was the answer for both of us, that we were not meant to be. You avoided me throughout the court hearing and Charlie's celebration party. But the more my mind rewinds our conversation, I realise I have made a huge mistake that day. I admit there was a pride in me initially that I did not try to make amend, but I cannot get you out of my mind. I am tortured. I cannot live knowing that you think I don't want you. On the contrary, I want to be with you desperately."

"Your pride." With a trembling chin, she smiled sarcastically. "Deep inside your heart, you still have concerns about my circumstances." Her voice was shaking as she tried to control the tears that threatened to roll down. She turned away from him as her muscles quivered, restraining a sudden huge pain in her chest.

"No, not anymore! Oh, Amelia..." He took a deep sigh in frustration. She could feel that he wanted to touch her, but his hands stopped mid-air. "I don't know how to make you believe me." His voice cracked with emotion. "My greatest regret that day was I did not try to stop you when you walked away. I cannot forget you. My mind was already set before we bumped into each other yesterday morning. Once I'm back in Melbourne, I want to pursue you. It is like an answered prayer from heaven that you appear here! I feel I am getting a second chance, and I am not letting it go anymore."

Amelia tensed her body up to keep them from trembling, unable to face him as her tears welled in her eyes. She could feel that he was moving closer behind her as his breathing touched her neck.

This is not happening, she thought. She had to admit that her heart was flooded with warmth with his words, but could this be true? She was fully aware of who he was and who exactly she was, and the big gap between them. She did not want to raise her hopes easily.

After what seemed like an eternity of silence, she was startled when she felt her fingers were touched by his.

"Please forgive me. Please don't tell me you hate me," he whispered. She could feel the warmth of his chest behind her.

She released a soft and bitter laugh. "How could I? You have every reason to fight your feeling towards me."

"Please give me one more chance," he pleaded.

She braced herself to turn around to face him. She held her breath, realising their proximity and how she could feel his breath on her cheek as he tilted his head closer to her. She breathed in his familiar masculine scent, which brought her to the moments that she could not forget, a sweet memory as well as a slight bitterness.

The loud yell calling their names prompted them to shift away, realising that their private moment had gone. Aunt Marie, uncle Gardiner and Georgie had returned from their horse carriage trip. Their carriage stopped not far from them, near the Pemberley back lobby. Amelia took the opportunity as much as possible to calm herself down from the emotion that was still whirling in her mind and her heart while watching them descending from the carriage.

"We did not realise that your carriage was not behind us," said Georgie after she jumped down from the carriage.

"Yeah, Amelia prefers to walk," replied Fitz.

Suddenly uncle Gardiner's mobile phone was ringing, which made Amelia and her aunt exchange a concerned look. They did not expect him to get a phone call while on holiday overseas. Quietly Amelia hoped that the call was not from Australia, informing him something terrible had happened. But when she heard the conversation, she took a relieved breath to hear her uncle's daughter's name mentioned. Uncle Gardiner's face slowly changed with a furrowed brow as the conversation continued. Once the phone was hung up, he shrugged.

"I'm afraid it is not good news, but nothing serious happened," informed him as all his companions looked at him curiously. "It was Eliana. They had a burst water pipe at home, so the house was flooded last night."

"Oh no...." Aunt Marie's hand flew to her mouth.

"They have to temporarily move out from the house until the pipe is fixed. But that means we cannot go to their place tomorrow. So she asked whether we could extend our stay here for a couple of days until everything is fixed and they can move back to the house."

"Alright. I'll call Monique now to see whether we could extend our stay," prompted Amelia while taking out her mobile phone. Georgie's voice stopped her.

"I don't think so. I know starting tomorrow, Monique's cottage is fully booked for my guests coming for the masquerade ball. But you can stay at Pemberley. There are plenty of rooms here in our private wing." Georgie's lips broke into a wide grin with her eyes shimmered with mirth. "And all of you can attend the ball too!"

Amelia's mouth fell open. She could not blame Eliana for her house mishap that caused them to change their itinerary, but staying under the same roof as Fitz and attending his family's big social charity event was not in her holiday plan at all. She made a closed-lip smile without meeting anyone's gaze.

"Oh, thank you for your generous hospitality, Georgie," said Aunt Marie. "But really, we don't want to trouble you. Surely, we could find somewhere else to stay. You must be busy with your guests, don't let us hold you back."

"Not at all!" squealed Georgie. "Look, I don't mean to be happy over the unfortunate incident in your daughter's house, which makes you have to stay longer here. But I'm excited to be your host longer and have all of you at the ball!" Georgie reached aunt Marie's hand while bouncing from toe to toe. "Pleaaaassse, stay," she begged with her half pleading look to Amelia and uncle Gardiner as well.

"That's right." Fitz's deep baritone voice was finally heard. "We have been enjoying your company, and it would be a great honour for us to have you at the ball as well."

Amelia felt dizzy. She did not know what to say. She could see her aunt and uncle's glimmering face, excited by the offer. This holiday was mainly for her aunt and uncle, and she was only accompanying them. She even let her aunt plan the itinerary. But it never crossed her mind that she seemed not to have any power to decide on this trip. She quietly prayed that her aunt and uncle would change their mind, but she knew it would be a very slim chance.

Aunt Marie looked at her husband and her niece, with eyes that sparkled and gleamed, asking for support before saying yes. Amelia did not want to disappoint her. She returned it with a timid smile.

"We're here for a trip, though. We don't have any proper dress for a ball." She looked at her aunt with half guilt-ridden face. She did not mean to spoil her excitement.

"That's a small matter," laughed Georgie while pulling aunt Marie's hand. "We'll go into town right away now. I'll take you to the best dressmaker in town. You'll be surprised that she has an excellent dress collection despite only living in this small town. She is a well-known designer."

Amelia wondered whether they had actually said 'Yes'. But as her aunt and uncle followed Georgie back to Pemberley full of laughter, it would be enough answer to her question. She rolled her eyes, quickly following them, realising only herself and Fitz were still behind.

The rest of the afternoon was mostly filled with shopping. They spent a couple of hours choosing the dress for her aunt and a suit for her uncle. Meanwhile, she made her choice quickly once she spotted a champagne navy classic V-neck gown with its matching low heel party shoes and a navy tulle masquerade mask.

When she tried the dress on, everyone whistled admiringly at her appearance. She tried to keep her eyes on everyone else except Fitz. But somehow, she could feel the intensity of his gaze at her as his eyes landed wholly upon her. It made her heart beat rapidly and her cheek warm. In the past, she would think he was scrutinising her, but this time she interpreted it in a different light, especially after his declaration this morning.

While waiting for aunt Marie's turn to try her dresses on, she browsed through the other selections. She could feel Fitz walking closely behind her. She braced herself to face him, preparing perhaps a small talk. However, when the shop doorbell rang as an indication of a new visitor, her plan was snapped away. The moment she saw who the person was, her heart filled with annoyance straightaway. She should have known that this mean person would be here as well.

"What a surprise to see you here, Amelia. Don't tell me you're here for the ball?" snickered Clare without any attempt to hide her condescending tone. Before Amelia could retort it back, Clare was startled to see Fitz appear behind her.

"Hi, Clare. Did you just arrive?" greeted Fitz with a formal tone.

"Hi, Fitz." Clare looked at her and Fitz with a slack expression. "Are you here with Amelia?"

"Yes, Clare!" Georgie responded, half yelling as she stood further inside while helping aunt Marie get dressed. "Amelia, her aunt and uncle are here for the ball. So we're helping them to get the dress."

Clare's mouth opened for a couple of seconds, but no words were uttered. Amelia tried to repress her bemused smile. Nevertheless, there was a sense of satisfaction in seeing Clare's reaction, which wiped off her usual smug face.

"This is aunt Marie and uncle Gardiner. They are Amelia's aunt and uncle, that means they are Lana's aunt and uncle too," asserted Georgie as if trying to wake Clare up from her shock and remind her of manner.

Aunt Marie and uncle Gardiner approached Clare without reservation to welcome the introduction, but Clare was still unmoved from her spot and gave them a high chin instead.

"Aunt, Uncle, this is Clare. She's Charlie's sister," said Amelia. Aunt Marie and uncle Gardiner seemed to understand when they heard her name and how this snobbish woman could act that way towards them.

"I did hear from Charlie about your trip," said Clare after she recomposed herself. Her eyes squinted at Amelia with a sneer on her lips. "I did not expect you would be here, though."

"Aunt Marie used to live here when she was little. We planned to leave tomorrow, but unfortunately, our itinerary needed to change."

"I suppose you live in the nearby guesthouse *only.*"

Amelia repressed her smirk, noticing the word 'only' sounded disdainful.

"They're going to stay at Pemberley for a couple of days." Fitz's voice was so clear in her ears as he was still standing very close behind her.

"I thought Pemberley is already full."

"That's correct. They will stay in the centre wing with us."

Clare's mouth was half-opened again in disbelief. Although Amelia suppressed her laugh, she started to enjoy this.

"Centre wing is only for your close relatives and family," muttered Clare.

"That's correct. Amelia, her aunt and uncle, are not strangers to us," responded Fitz. His voice tone was even and calm. However, the effect on Clare was beyond words. Her hands flew to her chest as she gasped with bulging eyes. Amelia started to feel pity for her.

Speechless, Clare fidgetted for a moment before she looked at the people in front of her agitatedly.

"I suppose your parents are coming too, Clare," remarked Fitz formally, changing the direction of the topic to ease the tension. "Are they here with you? I believe they would be happy to be introduced to their future daughter in law's uncle and aunt."

"No, they are not coming," snapped Clare. Her voice was slightly shaky in her effort to control her indignation. "Dad has business to attend. I think the introduction is not necessary. Eventually, they will meet at the wedding. I have to leave now. I have to be somewhere else."

"Will we see you tomorrow at the ball, then?" Georgie looked at her with a thoughtful expression.

"Of course," Clare lifted her chin. "I'll see you at the ball." Then she whirled around and disappeared behind the door.

Amelia quietly took a sigh, and felt relieved seeing that snobbish woman left. When she turned around, she found her aunt and uncle smiling at each other meaningfully while shaking their head.

Aunt Marie shrugged her shoulder. "What a pleasant person she is." It was followed by a suppressed laugh from the rest of them.

After the shopping trip, Fitz and Georgie helped them move their luggage from Monique's cottage to Pemberley. Amelia wondered whether she would be able to sleep that night, knowing how she would, not only spend a couple of nights in one of perhaps the most expensive boutique accommodations in England, but also the fact she would be under the same roof with Fitz. After their conversation this morning, she was unsure how she should feel or act in front of him. She kept telling herself that she did not want to raise her hope high too soon. Perhaps it was unfair for Fitz that she felt he might change his mind again. She had not given him a chance yet, and she wasn't sure whether she should.

The first night at Pemberley was supposed to be somewhat exhilarating. But she could not sleep as she expected. The jet lag was mainly the culprit, but being fully aware that now she was staying on Fitz's grand property and being under the same roof with him made her sleepless. She lied down on the king-size bed in the room provided for her, looking at the room's high ceiling with its classic European interior architecture and decoration. It reminded her of the moment when she fell sick in Barossa Valley and stayed in a villa that belonged to the Daltons too. The night before was their first kiss, the first time she tasted the lips of a man, which made her elated but dejected too when he released her from his embrace abruptly. She still could remember his bewildered expression, regretting what he just did. She took a deep heavy breath.

This room was too big for her alone. Fortunately, Georgie had arranged rooms with an interconnecting door between her aunt and uncle's and hers. At least if she wanted to find them, she did not need to get out of her room and potentially get lost in this large estate. She remembered Georgie mentioned that her room and Fitz's were just two doors away, separated by a lounge and the library.

She was startled and got herself up when she heard someone enter her room. It was aunt Marie who entered from the adjacent room door. She was tiptoeing in with her pyjama robe, a bottle of wine and two empty wine glasses in her hand.

"Georgie and Fitz are great hosts," remarked Aunt Marie after she shut the door behind her without any sound. "They even provide us with this beautiful wine in our room." She started opening the wine bottle and poured some of it into the glasses. "Unfortunately, your uncle still could not fight his jetlag. I can see you haven't slept yet, so I thought you would like some."

Amelia suppressed her laugh, afraid it would wake up uncle Gardiner or their other neighbour. She took the glass from her aunt's hand and offered her a cheer before sipping it.

"I know Fitz has some wine business in Australia. Do you remember Sharon, my childhood friend? She is married to a guy who now works for Fitz's aunt in Barossa Valley."

"Right." Aunt Marie nodded while sipping her wine and gave her an attentive look from the rim of the glass. "So, what is happening between you and Fitz?"

Somehow Amelia had expected the question, but it still did not stop her from feeling a flush of adrenaline tingling in her body. The time they have recently spent with Fitz and Georgie had shown some obvious signal that Fitz seemed to care for her.

"Nothing." She looked down, avoiding her aunt's look. "We're just friends. What we've gone through after dealing with Gerald and the court hearing makes us closer. As a friend."

"I can see the way he looks at you. Exactly the way your uncle looks at me," beamed Aunt Marie.

Amelia's shoulder was quaking as she tried to repress her laugh.

"I believe he has a feeling towards you. More than just friends," added Aunt Marie.

Amelia knew her aunt was waiting for her response as she was still trying to swallow her remaining laughter. The warm gaze from her aunt was consoling, which reminded her of her dad's and Lana's when they tried to soothe her when she was a little girl and upset with her little left limb. She felt a sudden lightness in her heart, especially at this time when her head filled with all her doubts and thoughts on Fitz's intention.

"You know exactly who he is, aunt. It's impossible between us," she murmured. She sat with her shoulders curling and a bent spine while shaking her head.

"I know what you mean. From our interaction recently, he seems like a decent and nice guy. I know you're intimidated by the fact that he's more than that with his position, status, and wealth. But I believe you like him as a person regardless of his attributes. I believe that's what Lana feels too towards Charlie. I haven't had an opportunity to see Charlie, but you know him well, I suppose. You won't let Lana be together with Charlie if you think Charlie is just an arrogant snobbish person. He must be down to earth too. Like Fitz."

"You're right about Charlie. And Fitz too. He's just more reserved than Charlie. Charlie is more bubbly."

"Right. So, why can't you be like Lana and Charlie? Does Lana have any concern over Charlie's wealth attributes too?"

Amelia nodded while sipping her wine, which made her aunt's eyebrow shoot up in surprise.

"It's a long story. But yes, Lana loves Charlie as a person, not because of his possessions. She will ask for a prenup agreement before they tie the knot, to show that she's with him not because of his money."

"Oh?" Aunt Marie gasped in surprise. "That's an audacious move. You could do the same too."

"You speak as if I'm going to marry Fitz soon, even before we have a relationship!" chortled Amelia.

Aunt Marie burst into a laugh. "Well, I may be thinking too far. But what I mean, there it goes, there's always a solution, right? I know people talks, but who doesn't? Just ignore them."

"I'm not Lana, aunt." Amelia felt her heart tightening. She lifted her little left limb with a cracked voice. "I also have this, remember? At least, Lana, she is beautiful, graceful, clever and physically perfect."

Aunt Marie gave her a weak smile, put down her glass and slowly encircled her arm on her niece's shoulder. "Why do you always think so little of yourself, Liz?" she whispered, and Amelia could feel her breathing on her head. "Don't you know that you're also beautiful? You may only have one perfect hand, but your courage and resilience shine through your character. People could see how smart and kind you are. I believe that's the reason Fitz falls in love with you."

Amelia went silent. The warmth of aunt Marie's embrace warmed her heart, and her words made her eyes well up in tears. Her aunt spoke the words Lana and her dad have always told her since she was little when she was upset with people's mockery of her. She realised now that not only Fitz struggled with his feelings, but she herself struggled with her inner demon. The insecurity of her little left arm.

They cuddled up in that position for a moment before slowly aunt Marie straightened up and released her. She squeezed Amelia's hand gently before she walked towards the door back to her room.

"You are a courageous woman, Liz," said Aunt Marie softly before she disappeared at the door. "I hope you think about that carefully. I hope things between you and Fitz can work out. I think what you need is not only to give him a chance, but you also have to learn to give yourself a chance. A chance for happiness. Because you also deserve it as well as any other person in the world."

Amelia sent her aunt off with her darted glaze as her words resonated in her head. She knew what her aunt said was true. She never believed that she deserved a romantic relationship with any man. That was the reason she buried herself with work, trained herself in self-defence, and tried to be independent as much as she could. Deep inside her heart, she sometimes felt tired and hoped to have a shoulder to lean on. She did not dare to have such a dream. When that possibility came up, she was too afraid to take the chance. Aunt Marie was right, it was not only giving Fitz a chance, but she also had to give herself a chance.

CHAPTER FOURTEEN
A Different Perspective

It was another beautiful morning on the day of the ball. Amelia went out of her room and, fortunately, could find her way to the back garden after passing some Pemberley staff and asking for direction. Her body ached for some exercise, and with her track pants and t-shirt, she started her jog.

She was unsure whether she was looking forward to the ball, though she was excited about meeting Sharon. Her friend had arrived last night with her husband and Mrs De Boyville too, and they were expected to join them for breakfast, as Georgie told her yesterday. She did not have a chance to message Sharon about her extended stay in Derbyshire with so many things in her mind recently. She was sure Sharon would be in great surprise to see her here.

As she jogged along the garden while sniffing the fragrance of summer flowers that she passed by, she did not pay attention to her direction and how far she had gone. She stopped when she saw a beautiful lake, caught her breath for a moment, and enjoyed its tranquillity.

As if like an eternity, her breath was getting steady. She turned her body, ready to walk back to Pemberley. Though she was not sure exactly which way she took, the magnificent building of Pemberley was within her eyesight, and she just believed in her sense of direction to take her back.

Internally, she complained that she had jogged too far as her tummy started grumbling. However, she had no other choice but to just keep walking as quickly as she could and only curse herself inwardly for not bringing at least a nut bar to fill up her empty stomach.

Her feet grounded to a halt as she heard thumps and a horse neigh in her direction. Before, she noticed that some guests at Pemberley did some horse riding, and she thought that could probably be one of them. Her breath stalled as she recognised the person who rode a big black horse galloping steadily towards her.

"I guess you've walked too far." Fitz pulled the horse rein and jumped down to be precisely in front of her.

"I jogged," she replied with a timid smile, "Jogged too far, yes." And she continued her walk again, letting him catch up with her pace.

"How about I take you back on the horse ride?"

The offer tempted her. Of course, riding a horse would be much quicker than her walk, and she was too hungry to jog back. Even if she could jog back, it would not be as fast as being on the horse ride. The problem was she had NIL experience with horses.

"No, thank you. I'm fine. I just walk. You can ride back."

"You're not scared of horses, are you?"

"Nope." She shook her head. "I just never ride one."

"Don't' worry about it. I'll hold the rein."

She stopped and looked at him hesitantly, and tried to think carefully about whether that would be a good idea. They would be sitting in such proximity, and she wondered whether her heart could handle it.

"Come on." He offered his hand. "You don't want to be late for breakfast, for sure. Your aunt and uncle will look for you."

She had to admit that he was right. She noticed that the morning sun was getting higher, and if she insisted on walking back, she might reach before lunchtime instead. Hesitantly she took his hand and let him lift her petite body to the horseback before he joined in sitting behind her.

As she expected, their body touched, and she could feel the warmth of his chest behind her. She felt nervous while at the same time embarrassed as her t-shirt was wet because of her sweat. Her head was dizzy, which disallowed her to think anything else except for how close he was. His body even leaned closer to her as he took the horse rein. She could feel the warmth of his breath on her neck, which sent a slight chill to her spine.

"Do you want to try to hold the horse rein?" he asked while the horse was galloping lightly. She did not answer but only nodded her head and hesitantly took the rein from his hand. When he let her take full of it, she squealed in panic.

"Don't let go of the rein!"

He laughed softly behind her ear. "Don't worry. He's a good boy." And he enveloped her hand under his, so their hands hold the rein together. She cursed inwardly, feeling stupid. Their touch made her even more nervous as her heart was hammering hard. She wondered whether he could hear it.

For a moment, there was only silence between them as they fell into their own deep thoughts while enjoying the scenery that they passed through.

"So, when are you going back to Melbourne?" he asked as they were approaching Pemberley.

"We'll spend time in Nottingham for about three weeks before flying back to Melbourne."

"Right." He took a breath. "Can we still see each other in Melbourne?"

"We will anyway. Lana and Charlie's wedding is coming up."

"Their wedding is still six months away." He sounded disappointed.

She was not sure what she should say. She knew it did not sound fair, but to see him now, even as a friend, was a bit hard for her. Perhaps what she needed was time, but she was unsure when it would be.

"Next month, I'll be in Sydney for some business meetings and have a little break for my birthday, with Georgie and some close cousins and friends. Charlie and Lana will be there too, I suppose. I hope you can join in too." As he spoke, his thumb caressed her hand that was enveloped under his.

"I may need to work," she replied, and her words were like hanging in the air. She was too scared to move from her position and checked on his reaction. She could sense his disappointment.

As they got closer to Pemberley, her sight caught something familiar when she looked up to the upper ground balcony facing the garden. That was where the breakfast buffet service would be for most of Pemberley's guests. She saw from the distance her aunt and uncle were already seated and waved their hands toward her. Her smile immediately faded when she noticed other familiar faces. She recognised Sharon, Colin and Mrs De Boyville. The last-mentioned person looked at her coldly, and she could feel that the woman was not thrilled at all.

As their horse reached the stable, Fitz jumped down and helped her come down. He caught her waist as she descended, and she held her breath, realising that she landed exactly in front of him and his face almost touched her cheek. She took a step back slowly to ensure that her movement was not too abrupt and obvious, and walked into the lobby.

"Thanks for the ride back. I'll get freshen up first and join you at breakfast." She glanced at him, who was behind her. Now she could see his disappointed look but quickly turned her face away and walked straight to where her room was located.

She was almost running when she saw the sight of her room door. Once she was in, she tried to recompose herself while leaning against the door. She had to admit that she liked their closeness earlier, but she was still scared. And now, with more of his family and friends here for the ball, her apprehension was intensified. She would be potentially scrutinised more. The look from Mrs De Boyville was one example.

She tried to ward off her negative thinking. There was nothing official between them, though she could feel Fitz's caring attention was still unchanged. Perhaps this ball would change his mind again. As he had mentioned before, his family's expectation was one of his biggest concerns if they were in a relationship. If Fitz doubted his feeling again after this ball, perhaps that was for the best. She had been disappointed over this before. It hurt, but it would not break her.

Within fifteen minutes, she went out again from her room with her summer V-neck tie knot front blouse and short jeans, and found her way to the breakfast area. It was a lovely sunny morning. Georgie had organised an outdoor setting breakfast on the balcony for close friends and family, including herself, aunt Marie and uncle Gardiner. She guessed it was the same balcony where she had seen them earlier.

When she arrived, most of the people were engaged in their own group circles of conversation, including her aunt and uncle, who were speaking with a couple of their similar age. Georgie was also talking with some group of people, and she could not find Sharon. A tall man in his polo shirt and shorts with his sunnies on, approached her while smiling at her warmly.

"You must be Amelia. I'm Richard, Fitz and Georgie's cousin. Their father is my father's brother." The man was perhaps as tall as Fitz. He lowered his head and gave her a peck. "Nice to finally meet you. Georgie and Fitz have been talking about you."

She smiled sheepishly, did not expect such a warm gesture. "Nice to meet you too, Richard."

For the next minutes, she had Richard on her side. He took her to where the breakfast food was displayed in buffet style, while they talked about when they arrived and what their next itinerary plan was. Richard had a sharp nose and a similar square solid jaw feature to Fitz, perhaps it was something that ran in the family. However, his light brown round eyes were full of mirth and constantly flickered with mischief.

From their small talk, she found out that Richard was mainly based in Europe, handling the family business related to some Dalton business. Richard was a funny man, full of jokes to be thrown into the conversation, and she had to admit he was friendly and charming. His communication skill was much better in contrast with his cousin, but she could sense it was not filled with fake pretence as she felt with Gerald before.

She took her plate and squeezed it between her left limb and her chest while spooning the scrambled eggs from the food display when a waiter came forward and offered help. She shook her head, declining the offer politely while smiling in gratitude. From the corner of her eyes, Richard was watching the short exchange.

"I would like to apologise for asking perhaps a delicate question to you," began Richard while they were seated at one of the tables in the corner. Amelia glanced around, wondering whether her aunt and uncle would join them. She had not even had the chance yet to say 'hi' to Sharon. However, she could sense Richard wanted her for himself. She wondered whether he was sent on a mission by the rest of the family to interrogate her.

"Go ahead," she replied without hesitation. She knew what he would ask as his eyes travelled to her left limb.

"So you were born with this little hand?"

"Magic hand," she chuckled at her own words while piercing a baby sausage and mushroom with her fork.

He snorted while clearing his throat. "Yes, your magic hand. It seems you could do a lot of things with that too."

"Of course. But to answer your question, yes. I have had this since I was born."

"Do you know why you got it?"

"It's a jackpot in the family." Her eyes sparkled while her lips drew a bemused smile.

Richard burst out into huge laughter, drawing raised eyebrows from other guests around them. His laughter lasted for at least half a minute before he composed himself still with his remaining ones on his face. He lowered his head to her and whispered, "Now I know why Fitz is into you."

She was startled, but his eyes looked up to someone approaching behind her. She thought it could be her aunt and uncle, but her heart started racing when it was Fitz who came and took a seat at their table. He put down his breakfast plate while giving his cousin a stern look.

"What are you guys laughing about?"

"Nothing, Fitz. Relax," replied Richard with a witty grin. "I'm just getting to know your girl here. Don't worry. She's still yours."

"I have to disagree with you, Mr Richard," protested Amelia, hearing the word 'your girl'. She was not someone else possession. Even if she was married one day, she would not like to be addressed that way.

"Fitzwilliam," Richard corrected her. "My last name is Fitzwilliam. I know it's confusing that my last name is Fitz's first name. It's just the old English family tradition, using the same name circling between first, middle, and last names."

Amelia tried to make her face straight, seeing his comical face while saying those words, but she focused back on what she wanted to say earlier.

"You spoke as if I am a property to be owned. Is that how you usually address a woman? As someone's possession?"

"Well, I did not mean it that way. However, when two persons are married and together, like your aunt and uncle as an example, or my parents..." He glanced to where aunt Marie and uncle Gardiner were sitting, two tables away from them, together with another old couple which Amelia guessed as Richard's parents - Fitz's uncle and aunt. "...they practically own each other, don't they? Don't tell me that you are practising or supporting all sorts of polygamy?" He giggled and winked at her.

Amelia couldn't help but chuckle. She still wanted to argue the point, but they were interrupted by another young couple who approached their table to join in. The young couple was one of Fitz's close friends since university. Fitz introduced them to her and Richard before they began some casual conversations about work and business. Amelia noticed how the girl glared at her and her little left arm occasionally, which was a common thing that she usually received from someone who had just met her for the first time. She quietly finished her breakfast and excused herself to leave.

While she was on her way to get some drinks, she was startled when Colin suddenly stood beside her.

"Hi, Amelia. I hope you can join us at the corner table. Mrs De Boyville is asking for you."

The words sounded more like an order to her than a polite request. She gave Colin a raised eyebrow, but he seemed uneasy and did not dare to return her look.

"Okay." She finished her juice and walked towards the corner where Mrs De Boyville and Sharon waited for her.

Her lips broke into a smile when she saw her friend, who welcomed her with a beaming face and a hug.

"I can't believe to see you here," whispered Sharon to her ear. However, she released her quickly as Mrs De Boyville cleared her throat.

"Mrs De Boyville, how are you?" greeted Amelia politely. However, her greeting was hanging in the air as Mrs De Boyville did not respond but moved her head to signal her to take the seat in front of her.

Amelia chose to stand. "Do you wish to speak to me?" She could sense that this woman was going to confront her. As her conscience was clear that she had nothing to hide, she did not feel that she had any obligation as well to obey her.

"I believe you're having a great time here, Miss Bettney."

Amelia held herself from giggling, hearing she was addressed with her last name. She even did not expect Mrs De Boyville would know her last name.

"I believe these are not something you always have?" Mrs De Boyville gave her a smirk.

"Fitz and Georgie have been good friends and hosts," she replied tactfully.

"I wonder what a coincidence you could be in this part of the town."

"My aunt, if you have met her, used to live in this little town when she was little. We are also visiting her daughter soon in Nottingham."

"What is holding you here then?" Mrs De Boyville tilted her head with a squinting smile on her lips.

Amelia swallowed. From the corner of her eye, she could see that Sharon had taken her cup of tea with a shaky hand while Colin looked away.

"Unfortunately, something happened to my cousin's house that she is not able to host us sooner than planned. Therefore, we extend our stay here."

"What a mischievous plan."

Amelia raised her eyebrow, could hardly believe what she heard. "I beg your pardon?"

Mrs De Boyville took her teacup and sipped it elegantly while still giving her a contempt look and a jutting chin. "I believe you heard me, Miss Bettney. You've planned this very well to have a chance to stay in the grand place like Pemberley for free."

Amelia could feel heat flush through her body. She pursed her lips while clenching her fist behind her. She drew slow, steady breaths before replying.

"As I have said before, Mrs De Boyville," she tried to keep her voice even. "Your nephew and niece have been great hosts. Don't you think the baseless accusation that you just threw at me would be an insult to them? They invited me and my uncle and aunt to stay here."

"They are young and naïve. They could be easily taken advantage of."

"So are you saying that all their friends are here to take advantage of them? I think you give very little credit to them."

Mrs De Boyville sucked a quick breath, wordless for a moment, before releasing a scorned huff. Amelia tightened her fist behind her back while maintaining her stony glare at the lady.

Suddenly they were interrupted when a couple around Mrs De Boyville's age, approached the table and greeted her. Mrs De Boyville's face, which was initially stiff, broke into a smile when she saw the intruder. Amelia could feel an unexpected release of all the tension in her muscle. Sharon rose and gripped her hand to walk away, not bothered by what Mrs De Boyville would think of her absents. Colin followed his employer, talking with their new acquaintances, which distracted Mrs De Boyville even more.

"It seems you have been on excellent terms now with Fitz," teased Sharon after they managed to walk further to the garden. Sharon leaned to her and enveloped Amelia's little left limb in her hands. It was a habit they used to have every time they walked back from school when they were teenagers.

Amelia believed Sharon must be referring to what she saw earlier this morning when she was on a horse, riding with Fitz.

"I told you before he likes to stare at you. When you were sick in Adelaide, he was very caring and attentive to you, ensuring that you would be taken care of. He even stayed vigil while you were feverish." Sharon stopped the walk and looked at their surroundings, ensuring no one was close for eavesdropping. She lowered her voice. "Annie told me. Luckily Mrs De Boyville left early on the wedding day itself. You can see now how protective she is in regards to her nephew."

Amelia took a small intake of breath. Fitz stayed vigil while she was sick at that time? She remembered vaguely what happened when she was ill. She could only remember when she was under the warmth of someone's arm, which she thought was only in her dream because it could not be her father. But could it be that it was actually Fitz? She remembered now that she could smell his masculine scent in that dream, which she knew did not belong to her father.

"I believe she wants the best for her family," Amelia responded flatly.

"You don't know yet. She has an ulterior motive. She wants an advantageous marriage for Fitz and Georgie. Someone that would be her choice and she could control, so she could enjoy the benefits for having related to Dalton family."

"Isn't it a common thing in a wealthy and respectful family like theirs? They want to make sure they keep the people within their circle."

"But, what is your plan with Fitz?" Sharon smiled mischievously. "I will not believe if you don't feel something for him. He is very handsome, isn't he?"

Amelia shook her head. "I think you already know the answer, Sharon. It's impossible between us."

"But he's so attentive and caring to you," argued Sharon.

"You do remember I have my magic hand, don't you?"

Sharon released a soft laugh. "Love is blind, Liz. You see, it's like Colin and me."

Amelia's eyebrow knitted, wondering whether Sharon was actually being sarcastic or not. She remembered that she raised her concern before whether Colin would be the right person for her. She always thought Sharon deserved someone better. However, she respected her friend's choice.

"Don't get me wrong, Liz," added Sharon as if her friend could read her mind. "I'm happy with Colin. I can close my eyes to everything that he is lacking. I don't mean to change him, but in the end, in marriage, what you need is compromise."

Amelia went silent, unsure what to comment on that. She never thought about having a relationship, let alone a marriage. Looking at her parent's marriage, it was not a pathway that she would like to follow. Her father intentionally kept being ignorant of her mother's behaviour, and her mother did likewise. They somehow just made a pact on what they could agree on together and stayed out of each other for something they both disagreed with. Was it called a compromise? On the other hand, looking at aunt Marie and uncle Gardiner's marriage, she could feel generous affections exchanged between them and mutual respect even though they were not a young couple anymore. That would be something she was after if she was to get married. However, marriage was something that she doubted could happen to her, given her circumstances and birth defect.

Their short stroll had to cease when Colin's voice was heard calling Sharon from the balcony. Sharon gave her an apologetic smile which she only responded with a hug and soft squeeze on her friend's hand.

"I'll see you tonight at the ball."

And they parted with sparkling eyes and mutual understanding that they were going to have an exciting time together like last time.

* * *

Amelia looked at her reflection in the mirror and almost could not recognise herself. Aunt Marie and Georgie had helped her with her make up today for the ball. The first full-on face make-up and hairdo that she perhaps ever had. Luscious mascara highlighted her round brown eyes and eyelashes, the powder and liners highlighting her newly shaped eyebrow and nose lines, and a soft pink lipstick on her thin lips. Her slight over the shoulder curly brunette hair was also tied up with a few strays behind her ears.

Aunt Marie also lent her a couple of jewellery for her ears and bare neck. She received them with wrinkled brows since she did not expect aunt Marie to bring such expensive jewellery pieces for a holiday trip. Her aunt brushed off her questions and dashed off from her room with the excuse she had to get ready too. Amelia caught her aunt and Georgie exchanging glances before disappearing from her room.

Amelia looked back at the mirror. She was unsure whether she should put the jewellery on. They were a classic three sapphire pendant diamond necklace with a pair of matching earrings. The colour matched well with her dress. The design seemed too young for her aunt's taste. However, she did not want to get queried later by her aunt if she was not wearing them.

She put on her prosthetic hand and hid the joint part behind her sleeve. With a slow smile, she felt relieved for not forgetting her prosthetic hand behind. She brought it for the trip because she did not wish to frighten Aunt Marie's grandchildren with her left limb. It seemed the prosthetic hand came in handy before it was needed.

She took another glance at her reflection in the mirror. It would be her first masquerade ball, but she was not sure what she should feel. She still could not believe that she was at Pemberley, and she could not think how she ended up in this place.

Her earlier conversation with Mrs De Boyville was one example she would encounter if she became a part of Fitz's life. The objections from his family. However, the earlier conversation with Sharon on how strong Fitz's feeling towards her made her chest feel flooded with warmth. He had harboured that feeling since almost a year ago, and how he had been trying to fight the feeling. He had told her that he had overcome his doubts and firmly decided to pursue their relationship. She was the one that was unsure whether she was ready for the relationship.

She had to admit that she probably liked him too. However, reality kept kicking her about how much background differences they had and how her disabled hand would not make things easier. Probably Fitz would give up on her eventually with many objections waiting for them, even now before they began anything.

The soft knock from the interconnecting room door severed her thought. Aunt Marie appeared and smiled radiantly at her. Uncle Gardiner followed her and whistled, "I think I just found a princess here."

Amelia chuckled and pushed both of her favourite people to the exit door. It seemed they had been waited, not only by Georgie and Fitz but also by the close family of Dalton. Richard was standing not far from his cousins, smiling charmingly at her. His parents, who somehow had made friendships with aunt Marie and uncle Gardiner, stood arm in arms while approaching them.

"What an honour being surrounded by amazing beautiful ladies here," stated Richard while glancing through all the people around him, but his eyes lingered on Amelia longer. Amelia returned it with a sheepish smile.

"Shall we?" cued Georgie while pulling her cousin's arm. Richard reluctantly bowed to Amelia before Georgie pulled him away. Meanwhile, aunt Marie started walking with uncle Gardiner together with Richard's parents.

Amelia could sense that her aunt and uncle, as well as Georgie, had set her up again with Fitz. As she expected, Fitz approached her and offered his arm.

"Shall we?" asked him in his deep baritone voice.

Amelia lifted her eyes to his tall figure. He was dashingly handsome in his penguin suit and warrior metallic masquerade mask that fitted perfectly, covering his surrounding eyes. The mask colour made his umber eyes even darker and his gaze on her was intense as if scorching on her skin and sent a pleasure shiver on her nape. She took his arm with a lowered head, trying to hide her blushed cheek.

As they approached the ballroom, her own heartbeat seemed loud in her ear. She came to realise that walking into the ball on Fitz's side would bring all the attention to them straight away. As the steward was about to open the double door for them, intuitively, she pulled her hand. But Fitz held it back while warmly squeezing her and gave her a firm, soft gaze as if pleading to her not to let him go.

"Thank you for walking with me tonight," he whispered in her ear.

The door was opened simultaneously, and she could immediately feel all the eyes drawn to them. Some started to whisper and smiled mischievously, while others gave a disdainful look. She felt her chest tightening but quietly took a breath to calm herself. Her eyes could not help but catch the sharp glare from Mrs De Boyville, who stood not far from the entrance.

Georgie made her opening speech, and the attention was drawn away from them. The ball was organised mainly as a tradition by Georgie's and Fitz's mother. However, the purpose was to raise funds for their chosen organisation charity this year. Georgie mentioned in her speech that the preferred charity would be kids' cancer research, which was applauded warmly by all the guests who seemed eager to provide their support. The ball then started with some fascinating magic and acrobatic performances. Amelia was carried away by the performance for the next hour, not realising that she began to get comfortable as her hand was still on Fitz's arms.

At the end of the performance, slow music cued in, signalling the guests to start mingling around while enjoying the canapes. Amelia felt her cheeks warm, realising that she had been too comfortable. She let out a relieved breath when Fitz's attention was diverted as Georgie signalled him to attend to one of the guests who seemed important. Amelia took the opportunity to slide her hand off his arm as he excused himself for a moment. She chose to roam around to find her aunt and uncle. She could not find them, but when she entered one part of the ballroom in the corner, she saw Sharon standing near the bar and gleefully approached her.

"Glad to finally see a familiar face here," she said while giving Sharon a brief cuddle.

"You look great, Liz," commented Sharon after pushing her within arm's distance so she could look at Amelia's dress thoroughly.

"Thanks. You also look beautiful," she replied with an honest comment too, finding Sharon's purple dress matched well with her skin. "Where's Colin?"

"As usual, talking with some people that he recognised. Most of the people here have been involved in business with the Dalton family for quite a while since Fitz's parents' time."

Amelia nodded in understanding. She halted the server, who carried a tray full of glasses of wine and took two glasses for herself and Sharon. They cheered their drink together.

"For our friendship."

"Forever."

As they sipped their wine, from the corner of her eyes, Amelia noticed someone in a white ball gown was approaching. With everyone in their masquerade mask, she could not immediately recognise the person. However, upon closer look, she slowly discerned that it was Clare.

"Cheering for your grand entrance, Amelia?" snickered Clare with her usual smug smile.

"I'm not an attention seeker, Clare. I'm cheering for perhaps something you never have. A friendship," she replied calmly.

Clare scoffed. "I do have friends, of course."

"I believe you have, but not always a true one."

"Do you think just because you entered the ball with Fitz, you are going to be with him?" Clare lifted her chin and looked her under her nose. "You know you won't last long. Do you think people like you could be with him?"

Amelia rolled her eyes. She already had an unpleasant conversation with Fitz's aunt this morning. Now she had another unpleasant encounter with a jealous woman like Clare. Obviously, Clare came to her only to confront her. She gave a signal to Sharon to walk away. Sharon nodded in agreement.

"Where do you think you are going?" Clare raised her voice which started to attract guests' attention around them. Amelia was startled and did not expect aggressiveness. "You know, elite social people like us hate disguised people like you," she hissed with gritted teeth as she walked closer.

Amelia felt a raised blood pressure within her while giving her sister's future sister in law a cold glare. Clare's eyes at her were full of intense dislike, but she did not want to fight with another woman over a man. As much as she wanted to punch that woman, she tried to remind herself that Clare would be Lana's future sister in law. She had to respect Charlie's family too. She decided to take a step back, pulling Sharon along and turned away.

However, she did not anticipate what Clare was capable of doing as a jealous woman fuelled by hatred. Suddenly she felt her prosthetic hand was grabbed. It was disconnected from her left limb and fell to the floor. A choir of gasps erupted in that small corner, including the shock on Sharon's face as she covered her mouth in horror while looking at the prosthetic hand on the floor. Amelia understood that Sharon's reaction was more due to Clare's outrageous behaviour.

Clare laughed in triumph with a disgusted snort. "Let people see who you really are. Stop disguising yourself," she sneered and walked away, leaving her bully victim behind.

Amelia only took a sigh. The guests around them started murmuring while watching her. She could not interpret the meaning of their look, perhaps some were pity, concerned or just disgusted by what they saw. She was used to those mixed reactions when some kids were abusing her during her school time. It would be no different this time, she knew it would be her curse for a lifetime. In the past, she would be in tears, but this time she only closed her eyes briefly, shook her head, not understanding why people could be so mean. She walked towards her prosthetic hand on the floor and bent down as if picking up a dropped toy. However, another hand picked it up before her.

"Are you alright?" Fitz held the prosthetic hand with a concerned look in his eyes at her. His eyes moved briefly to their surroundings which made the spectators slowly disperse.

"Yeah, I'm okay." She avoided his eyes and was about to take her prosthetic hand from him. But it seemed he did not plan to give it to her and firmly held it. She was taken aback. "Let me put my prosthetic hand back in my room."

"Alright, I'll go with you." His hand was on her small back, ready to move her to walk. But, instead, she put him on a halt.

"I can go back to my room by myself. You are the host of this event. You have many guests to be attended to." She tried to keep her voice down so only both of them could hear. She was fully aware that many eyes were still watching them, including Sharon, who awkwardly stood not far from them and seemed unsure what to say. Her hand reached out to Sharon to ensure her friend stayed with her. "Sharon will accompany me."

"I don't need to entertain everyone. I regret letting such a thing happen to you at my party," he insisted. She could feel his stern voice behind his words.

"You don't need to feel responsible for what happened. I'm used to it. And you know Clare. Look, I should be the one to apologise for making your guests freak out. Please stay and don't let me embarrass you more."

As she finished her words and looked at him, her body stiffened with the tightness in his expression. His face became dark, his body tensed and he clenched and unclenched his fist while drawing a steady breath. She realised she must have said something that made him upset.

Sharon's voice interrupted them. "I think I need to find Colin. I believe he's looking for me anyway. I'll catch up again with you later, alright?" She winked and fled away before Amelia could even say a word.

"Let's go." Fitz took her small back and motioned her to walk toward the exit door that would bring them to the centre wing, hence their rooms. Amelia did not want to create any scene and obediently followed.

There was an unnatural silence as they walked towards her room, passing through a couple of high ceiling hallways before reaching her room door. Amelia could feel that he was still trying to restrain his anger, which made her hesitant to look at him. Once they reached her room door, she turned around, ready to take her prosthetic hand from him, without lifting her eyes. But he held it back. For a moment, both of them were gripping the prosthetic hand tightly without anyone wanting to let it go first.

"I want you to know...." Half panting, his voice was trembling, "I am not embarrassed by you, especially not because of your hand."

She closed her eyes and took a breath quietly. She did not mean to say those words to make him upset. It was an embarrassing scene for sure, an evil scheme from a jealous Clare. She did not care if she became a laughingstock like Clare perhaps expected. Instead, she was afraid she had embarrassed the host and made all the guests freaked out.

She opened her eyes only to feel her eyes well in tears. She did not know why she had to feel this way. She did not want to look up to him and let her head down while still holding her prosthetic hand tightly. She hoped he would release it and let her go inside.

"Please promise me that we will go back to the ball after this," he whispered. This time his voice sounded calmer and light with a hint of pleading.

She could not utter any word. She did plan to leave the ball for good after this if not because he insisted on escorting her. She knew her absence would disappoint Georgie and now him too. However, they could not blame her for leaving the ball. She did not belong here anyway. Who was she to them if she was not merely an acquaintance? But now, she knew that she was being unfair for thinking that way. Even though they were only friends, still, she should not have run away after being cordially invited.

Reluctantly she nodded her head. Fitz slowly released his grip on the prosthetic hand.

"Thank you."

She burst into her room and turned on the light. Fitz was standing at the doorway, waiting for her while holding the door. Once she placed her prosthetic hand on her bed and turned around, his umber eyes gazed at her tenderly, stirring her heart.

They walked back to the ball in silence again, but she let his hand on her small back throughout the walk. Once they reached the ballroom, he offered his arm to her to hold onto. Hesitantly she took it, but as his hand enveloped hers, her heart pulse became calm, and she took a content sigh. It was the same feeling that she once tasted when they had a kiss. She felt her cheeks become warm from her thoughts. She hoped her blushing would be concealed under her mask.

The ambience at the ball was still lively, with many people still chattering around, drinking and dancing. Amelia could feel that almost all the eyes turned to them as they walked through the people. Without her prosthetic hand, her little left limb became more apparent. She was not intimidated by people's reactions, she was used to it. Again in her thoughts, she was more concerned whether she had embarrassed Fitz.

As they walked towards the dance floor, the music was changed into swinging jazz. The presenter announced that the host – The Dalton – with his close family would begin the dance. Amelia felt giddy, realising what that meant as Fitz was still holding her hand.

"May I have a dance with Miss Bettney?" Richard approached them with his congenial smile that was betrayed by his cheeky glance at his cousin. "After you, of course, cousin."

"Thanks, Richard. The decision is hers. " Fitz released her arm and turned to her while giving her hand a light kiss. "May I have the honour of the first dance, Miss Bettney?"

Amelia felt a flush creeping across her cheek, making her stutter, unable to reply. She was confused with her own thought. Rejecting the host a request for the dance, or exposing the host to an awkward dance with a disabled person? But she could only nod and follow as Fitz led her to the dance floor. She glanced at other dancers and found Richard was dancing with Georgie. Richard's parents followed, and the rest of the guests followed, including Aunt Marie and Uncle Gardiner, who both winked at her.

Amelia felt the temperature in the room seemed too warm for her as Fitz's hand circled on her waist and his other hand again held her hand gently. The moment of their first dance came back to her mind. She smiled to herself, remembering how the dance ended poorly with their little argument over his accusation of her involvement in the pub attack. She even wondered at that time how on earth he could ask her for a dance? Could that be possible he already had feelings towards her at that time?

Her mind focused back on the present. She could feel his breath on her forehead, sometimes sweeping away her fringe, and his lips occasionally brushed against her forehead skin. She was again brought back to when they were in an embrace, in their 'accidental' first kiss. Her heart swelled with warmth, which made her feel a surge of happiness within her. She had never felt this way before. It never crossed her mind that someone could show his care and love, which made her feel like floating in heaven. Did she deserve this? This was just too good to be true. She closed her eyes, enjoying the music, enjoying the warmth of his chest on her face and hoped she could just stay like this forever. Even if this moment was only temporary, she just wanted to hold on to the moment.

Unfortunately, the music slowly cued to the end of the song. She flew her eyes open and stepped back as his hand slowly released her waist. As the band played the next song, Richard suddenly jumped in.

"I suppose it's my turn now," said Richard gleefully.

"Has she said yes?" Fitz looked at him quizzically, but that did not deter his cousin from sliding in between them and motioned Amelia's body away from him. Amelia threw her head laughing as Richard gave his comical blowing raspberry mouth at Fitz.

"I suppose my dear handsome cousin has not complimented you today," remarked Richard as he twirled her body around.

"I don't understand what you mean," she responded as a matter of fact.

"Fitz and I grew up together. We are close even until now. He's like my next brother, although I have another older brother who unfortunately can not join in tonight. I know Fitz is a person with few words, but his action always speaks louder. I can see how the way he looks at you and treats you tonight, but I believe he hasn't told you that you look absolutely stunning tonight."

Amelia suppressed her smile. Richard was a funny, charming person. She always giggled every time he spoke, anticipating his next jokes or comical facial expression. She even perhaps never took his words seriously, and it seemed this time he meant his word but could sense that Amelia did not realise it.

"You don't believe me, do you?"

Amelia did not reply, wishing the question would be left in the air. Richard was not as tall as Fitz, so her eyes were just on his nose level. She glanced away, avoiding his stare, but she could feel he was still waiting for her reply.

"Look, I hope you would give Fitz a chance." His voice was heard again. It was soft but clear enough to her ear. "I know it's not going to be easy for both of you. But I already saw him suffering when you avoided him. Never, never in my entire life since I knew him that he was that broken."

Amelia turned to him with a furrowed brow, didn't understand what he meant.

"He had been drinking. More than usual."

She was stunned. Fitz started to drink because of her? Was it the time he struggled to fight his feelings towards her because he knew it was against his better judgment?

"I believe he has stopped now," continued Richard. "I can see his mood changes recently since you're here."

Amelia briefly closed her eyes and took a deliberately quiet exhale. She could not believe that someone like her could bring such turmoil to someone like Fitz? Was Richard just making this up?

"As I said, if you're together, I know it's not going to be a smooth journey. However, you have to give him a chance. I'm pretty sure he would do anything that he could to protect you. My father is the brother of his late father. He was surprised to know that Fitz is into a girl like you. However, in the end, Fitz has control over his own life."

Amelia smiled weakly. "But he cannot deny who he really is." She finally opened her mouth to speak.

"No, he does not deny himself. However, he hopes you can be part of his life. I believe he's not asking you to change too." Richard smiled warmly.

They went quiet for the rest of the dance as Amelia reflected Richard's words. When the music stopped, Richard took her to the side and became her companion for the rest of the night until the guest started leaving. During that time, Amelia quietly observed Fitz from a distance, who seemed occupied with the guests that surrounded him. Fitz was talking with them, mainly with Georgie on his side. However, she noticed that some young girls tried to get his attention. There was a moment that he seemed restless, and his eyes roamed around, and their eyes met. The tension on his face seemed to disappear the moment he saw her. His lips broke into a smile. She returned the smile, assuring him that she was not leaving the ball as promised.

"So, I heard you're leaving tomorrow afternoon?" asked Richard as he gave her a glass of wine. Amelia felt she needed one to help her have a good sleep tonight.

"Yes, to my cousin's place in Nottingham."

"I hope we can still have a catch-up tomorrow morning during breakfast."

Amelia nodded. "Yeah, me too." She took a quiet breath, looked at Fitz direction who was still occupied by his guests. "I probably need to go back to my room now."

"May I escort you?" Richard offered his arm.

"Thanks, Richard. That's not necessary. Please let Fitz and Georgie know that I need to pack up for tomorrow."

"Will do."

Once again, she took a glimpse of Fitz before she firmly strode to the door connecting the hallway to her room. She wondered whether aunt Marie and uncle Gardiner had turned in as well. But she felt she did not want to worry too much about them. Too many things in her mind now as too many things happened today.

She walked through the hallway as her heels made an echoing click-clack sound on every step. Her eyes gaze blankly at the high ceiling with its beautiful highly detailed architecture, luxurious art paintings, and sculptures. Probably she should have been thrilled. However, in the stillness of that grand hallway, she felt so small and alone.

CHAPTER FIFTEEN
An Unwelcomed Visit

Amelia switched off her car engine once her car landed smoothly on her house driveway. She furrowed her brow as she saw a luxurious limousine car parked outside the house. That type of car did not belong to this place, especially not in her suburb, which was predominantly occupied by low-income earners. She wondered who on earth came to this suburb with such a luxury car.

It was pouring rain outside. She had just finished her Sunday work shift, and the time had already shown five o'clock in the evening. She slid open her mobile phone to find a message from Fitz asking her how she was. She took a quiet breath, thinking about how to answer it.

It had been three weeks since she came back from England. That meant it was almost six weeks ago from the last time they met. The day after the ball, they still saw each other for the last time at breakfast. It was also an opportunity for her and her aunt and uncle to properly express their gratitude for their hospitality. After all their luggage had been packed into their small rental car, he motioned her away from the rest so they could speak privately.

"I hope you had a great time during your stay here," he began.

"Of course I did. Thank you again for having us here and inviting us to the ball."

"Can I occasionally call or message you?" There was a meekness, a tentative smile and a yearning look when he asked the question. She felt like she was seeing a shy teenage boy who gazed at her adorably.

"Yeah, sure." She nodded nervously. In return, he smiled in relief.

She extended her arm for a friendly hug, which he returned with more vigour that almost lifted her petite body from the ground. He pressed his lips on her head crown, which lasted for a couple of minutes. She could sense that he was reluctant to let her go until she was the one who tried to push her body away. He gave her a light peck on the cheek before he squeezed her hand and took her back to where aunt Marie and uncle Gardiner were waiting for her. From her car side mirror, she could see him, Richard and Georgie waving at them until their car disappeared from their sight.

When she was in Nottingham, Fitz sent her a couple of messages. They had a chat briefly afterwards, but aunt Marie excitedly shared their pictures in Nottingham with Georgie. Amelia assumed Georgie showed those pictures to Fitz too. Since then, there had been at least one message from him almost every day. He shared that he was staying in Pemberley for quite a while after she left and went to London for some business. Today his message was saying that he was flying off soon to Sydney. He asked her again whether she could come to Hunter Valley, together with Charlie and Lana, for his short birthday break. She had not replied yet, because she still did not know the answer.

Lana had asked her the same question. Returning from England, she had been drilled down by her sister with all her trip details, especially on her relationship with Fitz. She was sure Lana must have heard it from aunt Marie or perhaps Sharon.

"I heard you had a dance with him, and he was like your date that night," giggled Lana. Her eyebrows were wiggling, her eyes were full of tease, and her lips displayed a wide grin.

"That's not exactly true," responded Amelia tactfully. "He and his sister were the hosts. They had so many guests to attend to."

"Still, you entered the ballroom as his date!"

Amelia winced. "I think you're interpreting it too far. He was being polite because we were his guests, who came all the way from down under. And, because I am your sister, you're going to be his best friend's wife."

Lana smirked, not giving up yet. "Alright. Then, what will you say now that he is even inviting you to his little birthday party in Hunter Valley next week? He is ready to organise a private helicopter for you. He has asked me whether I could persuade you to go."

"I may have a shift work that day," answered Amelia flatly.

Lana threw a cushion at her and laughed. "I can see you're also falling in love with him!"

Amelia looked at her sister with a raised eyebrow. Then, something came up in her mind to stop her sister's teasing.

"Didn't you know that Fitz was one of those who tried to separate you and Charlie?" she prompted the question but cursed herself inwardly afterwards.

"Yeah, I know." Lana nodded lightly, which surprised her. "He called me to apologise. Oh, I didn't tell you, did I?

She was puzzled. "Did he? When?"

"I don't remember exactly when. But it was the time when Charlie wanted me back. I think he regretted it, and his sincere apology touched me. He's a nice person, very caring towards his close friends and family. But I think I know now why he apologised." Lana gave her a mischievous smile. "Because he realises he's falling in love with my sister!"

With the endless teasing, Amelia flew away, leaving her sister, who was still giggling at her.

She was falling in love with him. Lana's words suddenly resonated again in her head. She closed her eyes and thought for a moment. Perhaps indeed, she was in love with him too. He had singled her out during the ball, and even before that, his small touch, the way he looked at her and spoke to her tenderly, she had to admit she liked it. She felt a swamp of happiness of being adored. She did not expect he would even apologise to Lana for separating her from Charlie. Did he do that because she confronted him or because he had feelings towards her too?

But who could not fall in love with someone like Fitz? So many girls were eyeing him. Would he regret his decision to pursue her? Had he really given deep thought to the consequences of being with her?

Richard's words came to her mind again. "It will not be a smooth journey, but he would do anything to make it work. You must give him a chance." She wondered why from all the girls that he could have, he had to fall in love with her?

She had to admit that he had proven his words. Despite doubting their big social gap and background differences, he was not hesitant to pursue justice for Georgie and Leah by letting his family's name become the centre of media scrutinisation. As he said at the ball, he was never embarrassed by her physical condition. He had shown her that he genuinely accepted her for who she was. The answer now rested on her.

She shook her head and realised that she had not moved out of her car. She looked at the message from Fitz again, still unsure what to reply, before finally closing her mobile phone screen and putting it inside her bag. She jumped out of the car, and half hopped on the grass, avoiding the rain to enter the house. When she opened the door, she was startled that someone was sitting in the living room. Someone who was not any of her family members. Someone who she did not expect to be in her house, in her living room.

The guest was also startled when she saw her coming in, but lifted her chin and looked at her under her nose.

"You're finally here, Miss Bettney." There was a sense of false modesty from her greeting, something that Amelia would expect from Mrs De Boyville. "I wish to speak to you privately," the snobbish lady snickered with a scornful glance to where all her family were standing, signalling that she wanted them to be left alone.

Amelia noticed that both of her parents, Lana and even Leah were apparently in the same room as well, but all of them stood up on the sideline instead as if their guest was a lion that was by accident sitting in their living room. Each of her family's facial expressions mixed with anxiety, except for Leah, who was unsure what was happening.

"I have to remind you, Mrs De Boyville. This is not your house. There's no secret in this house," Mr Bettney replied with a firm tone. Amelia was pleasantly surprised to hear such a response from her dad. It was probably ages ago the last time her dad defended her when some naughty kids bullied and mocked her when she was in school.

Mrs De Boyville seemed taken aback, but she did not waver and kept looking at Amelia under her nose. "I come here to make you a very generous offer that I believe you cannot refuse. This is very important for your future." She took out a piece of paper from her clutch and put it down on the table. Amelia slowly sat on the opposite and looked at it with a furrowed brow, figuring out what it was.

It was a blank cheque.

"You could write down how much money you want, Miss Bettney. Whatever amount that you need. Think carefully about how this money will help, not only your future but your family too. You only have one chance. In exchange, stay away from my nephew."

Amelia froze and stared blankly at the cheque for a moment before glancing at the shocked expression from her family.

"I am not sure what sort of allurement that you use on my nephew. Though I understand why Charlie could fall for your sister's beauty and charm." Mrs De Boyville's eyes sneaked to where Lana stood, and her sister shifted uncomfortably with that scrutinising look. "But I believe you're smart enough to understand that your relationship with my nephew is reprehensible. You will never be good enough for him. He even knew that from the beginning."

Amelia pursed her lips. The word 'never good enough' was not unfamiliar to her. She remembered how Fitz even spat out that word the first time they met, even before he knew about her little limb. When she heard that, she was upset with herself. But this time, hearing those words from Mrs De Boyville boiled her blood with anger. How dare this woman offer her money in exchange for an opportunity to insult her?

"If you think my relationship with your nephew is impossible, why do you have to offer me money?" she challenged her with a raised eyebrow.

"As I said, I want to help you, Miss Bettney." Mrs De Boyville's lips upturn with contempt. "I am well known as a generous person. I believe you heard that a lot from your best friend too. You should think carefully, if you are with Fitz, you may be happy in the beginning. However, down the track, you will realise that you don't belong in his life as much as he doesn't belong in yours. Before you fall into false hope and disappointment, I am offering you something much better. You only need to name the price for your happiness, freedom from your family's financial burden. Afterwards, you don't need to trouble your heart with a relationship that will never work out."

Amelia swallowed and started thinking. Every word spoken by this woman sounded true and realistic. She could not deny that it had been in her mind all this while it would be impossible between Fitz and her. Richard even said it before, it would not be an easy journey, though he tried to convince her that Fitz would do anything to make it work. But wouldn't that be easier for Fitz if she never existed at all in his life?

She stared blankly at the blank cheque that was still lying on the table in front of her and took a quiet breath. If she took the money, it would solve all their financial problems. She could finally breathe in peace, knowing all her father's business debts were settled, and they would even possibly have extra for their future. Perhaps for an overseas holiday, a new house, a new beginning, away from Fitz, so he did not need to find her again. He might hate her anyway if she took the money. Could she live with the knowledge that he hated her? The thought of it suddenly made her heart ache.

"You have to remember, Amelia." Mrs De Boyville's voice was heard again in an even tone but still full of her haughtiness. "Fitz even knew from the beginning that it would be impossible between you and him. Now he may seem serious toward you, but after all the difficulties and obstacles that both of you will face, which is very much foreseeable, he may change his mind again."

"She's probably right, Liz." It was her mother's voice this time, sounded hesitant but clear.

"Mum!" Lana and Mr Bettney reprimanded her at the same time, giving her a glare.

"What?" Mrs Bettney lifted her chin in defiance. "I'm thinking about her own happiness too. She has to be realistic."

Mrs De Boyville smiled triumphantly, knowing someone in the room was finally on her side.

Amelia closed her eyes briefly while rubbing her temple. She could not blame her mother because her words reminded her of who she was. Yet her heart was still stung by it.

"Listen, Liz. I'm speaking this for your own good too. You've been hard on yourself all this time, trying to help our family's financial distress. This is a ticket to your freedom, too," continued her mother.

She had to admit that sometimes she felt tired, but it never crossed her mind that the solution was by accepting someone else's money with the sacrifice of her own feelings.

"Enough!" Her father's voice roared in the room. "You said it just for the sake of your own convenience! None of us has complained about our current situation as much as you do!"

"Well, I do agree with mum," Leah chimed in innocently. "I want to go for overseas holidays too like my friends."

"Just shut up, Leah," hissed Lana.

Amelia saw that their guest seemed to enjoy their family's argument. Mrs De Boyville took the cup of tea prepared for her and sipped it with a victory smirk. Amelia watched her with a tightening chest which made her unable to utter a word. She clenched her fist until her fingernails bit into her palm, but she knew it would not be wise to use physical violence against such a person. She felt dizzy hearing her family's argument, something that was actually common in their family. Still, at this time, she did not need this. Her head almost exploded.

She grasped the blank cheque and the pen that had been prepared on its side. Her action made her family gasp and then go silent. She frowned for a moment, thinking what nominal she wanted to write on the cheque. Mrs De Boyville waited on her expectantly with her victorious smile on her lips. She stared at the paper again for a long minute before she lifted the pen and scribbled on it.

Another choir of gasps again. She lifted her eyes to see her guest gifted her a bewildered expression.

"Thank you for your generosity Mrs De Boyville. But we don't need your charity." Her voice sounded cold and clear in the stillness of the living room. She could hear a deep exhale from Lana and her dad.

Mrs De Boyville looked at her with a trembling chin. "You will regret this!"

"I won't," she replied calmly without wavering. "On the other hand, I think I will regret it if I have to live under your generosity. In rejecting your offer, it doesn't mean I will end up with your nephew anyway. The decision does not rely on this."

"You must promise me that you will not be with him!"

"I won't make such a promise. Especially to you."

Mrs De Boyville scoffed. "Do you think you could make my nephew happy? Your presence in his life is only polluting his family's good name! You're such a selfish, headstrong, proud fool! What are you thinking? Do you think you can give him heirs? Disabled kids like yourself?"

Amelia clenched her fist again, wishing she could punch something to release her anger. Wishing not to make any physical attack instead, she stormed to the door, swung it open and glared at her guest coldly. Her hand on the door handle was shaking in her effort to restrain herself.

"I think it's time for you to leave, Mrs De Boyville," she hissed. "You have insulted me in every possible way in our humble home. We cannot accept such inappropriate behaviour in our house. You are not welcomed here anymore."

Mrs De Boyville's mouth was hanging open. For a moment, she was frozen in her seat before slowly standing up nervously. She briefly glanced at the Bettney family before returning her angry look to Amelia and walking towards the door.

"I never been treated like this in my life!" she fumed, then fled away. Amelia scoffed while watching her guest enter the luxurious car and take off. As much as her head was dizzy because of her effort to control her emotion, seeing Mrs De Boyville gone was like getting rid of a huge stone from her heart. She closed the door with her shoulder down as if all her strength had gone.

A soft touch on her shoulder startled her. She just remembered that all her family were still watching her.

"I thought you were going to take the money, Liz," said Lana while giving her a tight hug. She saw her father standing not far from them, watching them with a proud smile on his face.

"You know I'm too proud of doing that." Amelia released a self-deprecating chuckle. "Perhaps she's right. I'm a proud fool."

"Perhaps you are," her mother chimed in with rolling eyes, followed by a stony glare from her father.

Amelia squeezed her father's shoulder, preventing him from speaking out again to start a quarrel.

"I'm very proud of you, Liz," her father said while planting a kiss on her forehead. "Whatever your decision regarding your relationship with Fitz, I will support you."

"Thanks, dad."

"Like I have said before, since you were a little. You deserve happiness as much as any other people, regardless of who you are or what you are."

She nodded, but her heart still denied those words. She excused herself for a shower and rest. The shower seemed to melt away her anger and pain in her heart as she recalled every little thing that had happened earlier. Mrs De Boyville's insulting words still resonated in her head, and she felt like being stabbed in her heart, realising how valid those words could be—giving Fitz disabled kids like her? She smiled bitterly. She even had a full doubt about beginning a relationship with him, let alone thinking about marriage and having kids. Of course, it would be her dream to build a family one day with someone she loved but was it fair for him if she only gave him disabled kids?

Still, with that sad thought, she stepped out of the shower and dried her body. When she was already in her pyjamas and ready for bed, Lana came in and sat at the edge of her bed.

"I hope you don't take into heart whatever that rude woman said," said Lana. "In the end, what you must focus on is what Fitz feels about you. Like Charlie and me, Liz. You know Charlie's family has not approved us a hundred percent yet, even till now. Though we are proceeding to a wedding, I can sense more obstacles coming to us. Clare is one example." She chuckled as the name was mentioned. "But the most important thing is we don't lose our self-respect." She squeezed her hand and stroked her hair gently. "Don't belittle yourself just because of your hand. If he loves you the way you are, then you have to give him a chance. You also have to give yourself a chance."

Amelia closed her eyes while listening to her sister's words. Her tears threatened to roll down, and she quickly buried herself into the pillow. Lana's words reminded her of Aunt Marie's words to her as well. She had to admit that it was not about giving Fitz a chance, but it was also giving herself a chance, and it seemed harder for her to do the second than the first one. She knew that it was the demon within herself that she had to fight in the end. She was unsure how and if she would have the courage to take the chance.

She could feel Lana stroking her arm gently before leaving the room. She opened her eyes only to let her tears roll down her cheeks. She wiped them away, but her tears kept rolling down, and she started sobbing. She let herself drift to sleep still with the remaining dry tears on her cheeks.

CHAPTER SIXTEEN
Undecided

Amelia fixed her eyes on the road ahead of her while occasionally glancing at the passing scenery. The green pasture and farms with sheep, cows, and horses made her feel fresh and warm, combined with the beautiful sunrise on the day. She had been driving for six hours away from Melbourne on her way to Hunter Valley. She was about to reach Canberra, where she planned to take a rest. She drove alone as she intended to, with no one knowing where she was, not even Lana.

Lana's ticket was still in her bag, but she did not touch it. Lana knew she did not like to go by plane for interstate travelling, however her sister still pushed it to her anyway since the ticket was from Fitz. To her sister's knowledge, she went to work instead. She started driving straight from work after she finished her shift last night. Although she had driven for six hours, she still could not make up her mind whether she would turn up in Hunter Valley or not.

Lana had informed her of the duration of their stay, the address of the accommodation and even the itinerary plan. Lana had left yesterday morning, and Fitz's little birthday party was held last night while she was still at work. She planned to send Fitz a message, wishing him happy birthday, but she was hesitant. Perhaps she should not do it, to stop giving him hope. But on the other hand, she wished at least they could be friends, especially after what they've been through. She was torn with her own feeling.

The driving was supposed to give her ample time to make a decision, but the closer she was to her destination, the more anxious she was. She still did not know what to do apart from just keep driving. Perhaps that's what she was supposed to do with their relationship. Giving him and herself a chance, keep running it until they decided to give up if they had to. There would be a broken heart, and she was unsure how it would feel. Perhaps it would be like when they were at the park, and Fitz said the words she interpreted as him asking her to go away. Perhaps it would hurt that much. It was really painful, but time healed her. She wondered if their relationship did not work out, would it be more hurtful to part, especially after they spent more time together? But would it break her?

She remembered when Lana had a break-up with Charlie. Lana was shattered for quite a while. Despite her sister's soft appearance, Lana managed to rise up again. Even though she was still fragile, time healed her. Things turned out better than she or anyone expected. The pain was somehow worth it. It made her stronger and even more than ready to be with Charlie against all odds and objections from his family.

Then why should she be afraid? Because she was disabled? She chuckled inwardly. Despite her disability, she was physically stronger than her sister, especially with her black belt in taekwondo. Why she had to be scared of love?

She smiled to herself. She knew now that she would turn up in Hunter Valley anyway. She wondered what Fitz's reaction would be. Would he be disappointed in her because she did not come last night, not even send him a message? Or perhaps he had moved on. She had no idea who had been invited to this little party. Perhaps Clare would be there too and perhaps some of his girlfriends. Perhaps he changed his mind again. Regardless, she had no regret for coming for him now. Like she thought earlier, at least they could be friends.

She pulled up her car for breakfast when she reached a small town centre. She scrolled her mobile phone's screen to see a message from Lana asking whether she had woken up and gone to work again. She wondered what Lana would think if her sister knew she had been on the road on the way to Hunter Valley. She chose to ignore the message and gave her a surprise later.

The next half of her journey was more difficult than she thought. The rain started pouring heavily, so she drove slower than planned. She looked at the time and realised that she would reach Hunter Valley late afternoon. For a moment she wondered what Fitz and his friends were doing in this heavy rain. Perhaps he was talking with Clare or other girlfriends? Would her presence become a disturbance instead? She tried to shake her crazy thought by making the music volume louder as her car crawled on the road.

As predicted, she reached her destination when it was already dark. She felt exhausted, but she felt she had a mission to finish. There was a moment she thought perhaps she should go back instead. She must be looking horrible, dusty and filthy after such a long journey. Perhaps she could find a place to freshen up a bit before turning up. She wondered whether she should call Lana instead and inform her about her coming.

Her head was in a mess, and for a moment, she just sat in her car at the accommodation car park and fell into deep thinking. The rain was still drizzling heavily outside.

Her eyes suddenly caught a familiar figure within her sight. If she could believe her own eyes, it was Fitz entering the accommodation. She jumped out of the car, hopped as if that could make her less wet, and entered the accommodation. Her eyes again caught Fitz's familiar figure walking further inside, greeted along the way by the staff to the pathway that probably led to his room. It seemed he was walking in a rush, which made her unsure whether it would be a good time to see him. She quietly followed him anyway and cursed herself for acting like his stalker. She was determined to let her presence known once she found the right time.

Her guess was correct as he walked to one of the villas with an umbrella in his hand. She put on her hoodie, hopped on again between the puddles of water, trying to avoid the drizzle and followed him. He went inside and disappeared behind the door before she had chance to call him.

She stopped outside the villa and let herself soaked under the heavy drizzle. Her second thought came back again. Would this be wrong? Would this be right? Was he with someone at the moment? She was ready to knock on the door, but she could not do it. She closed her eyes briefly and took an annoyed breath while cursing herself for acting so silly. She reminded herself why she finally decided to be here. If he changed his mind, at least they could be friends. And she promised herself she would not blame him or take it too hard because she knew she had to be realistic. She kept reminding herself that there was nothing to be embarrassed about, whatever his reaction would be.

She finally took a deep breath as if it would give her strength. She closed her eyes again briefly before lifting her hand. But before her knuckle touched the door, suddenly the door flew open. She was startled, and the person who opened the door was equally stunned to see her.

"Amelia.." He was staring wide-eyed at her.

She chuckled nervously. "Hey there. Happy birthday." She did not even know how she could get her voice out. The next thing that happened was beyond her expectation.

Her hand was suddenly pulled. She fell into the embrace of his arms, and her body was lifted and twirled. Her face was only an inch away from him, and she could feel his warm breath on her while slowly their lips met. He held her tighter, buried his hand in the back of her hair as he tried to kiss her deeper. She was not aware anymore of her surrounding, immersed herself in the warmth and security she always liked under his embrace. Her head felt light, and she was in seventh heaven.

She was not sure for how long they were in that position. When they were out of breath, slowly, he put her back on the floor without letting her go. When her feet touched the ground, it reminded her of where she was. A flush of heat crept over her cheeks, realising what they had just done, and she wondered whether there was anyone else in the villa watching them.

She then realised how wet her clothes were when she saw his shirt was wet too.

"I'm sorry," she chuckled. "I'm soaking wet, and now you're wet too."

He pushed her away gently within an arm's distance and gazed at her radiantly. Then he took her hand and pulled her inside.

"Let's get you changed."

They entered the first room with the double door, probably the biggest room in the villa. He gave her his clean shirt and showed her the bathroom while waiting outside. She obediently followed his suggestion, entered the bathroom, and felt tempted to take a warm shower. She heard his voice from outside as if he could read her mind.

"Take a warm shower if you want to. Don't get yourself sick."

She did not answer but quickly undressed and get herself into the shower box. The warm shower was indeed like another heaven for her. Her mind was wandering around, she still could not believe what happened earlier, another kiss they shared. And now she was in his room, in his bathroom, taking a shower and wearing his shirt. She could smell his scent again, and she giggled at it. She went out of the bathroom to find herself alone in the room.

The king-size bed in that room looked inviting to her. It looked cushy and comfortable. After the shower, she felt all the bones in her body loosen out, and she could not wait to lie down. She sat at the edge of the bed, stroking the smooth cold of the bedsheet and slowly started to lie herself down without being able to resist it.

She felt warmth and content. The way he lifted her earlier and kissed her made her heart swell with contentment. She wanted to be with him, and she could not wait for it anymore. She closed her eyes, trying to remember that particular moment again over and over while putting her cheek against the pillow, without realising that sleep had started to overtake her.

She opened her eyes when she felt the warmth of the sunshine peeping through the window. Intuitively, she rose and watched her surroundings, trying to recognise where she was. Had she just been dreaming? But this was not her room. Was she in the place that she was thinking of?

She was startled as the room door opened and a familiar figure that she had been expecting appeared with a food tray in his hand. She blinked a couple of times, ensuring that she was not dreaming.

"Good morning," he greeted while placing the food tray on the bed and sitting next to her at the edge of the bed. "You slept like sleeping beauty last night. You must be exhausted."

Amelia felt her cheeks warm. How could she fall asleep last night after they just shared a kiss? How embarrassing. She had to admit the long drive was tearing her down.

"I'm sorry...."

"No, don't be," he smiled. The sweetest smile that probably she had ever seen from him. This was a new side of Fitz again that she found.

She lowered her eyes to find the food on the tray not far from her feet. It looked like breakfast for her: a poached egg with pale yellow sauce was covering it, some mushroom and sourdough underneath it, and a cup of juice. By looking at it, her tummy started to grumble.

"I bet you're hungry." Clearly, he heard the sound from her tummy.

"May I?" she asked hesitantly.

He released a soft laugh. "Of course. That's for you."

She grabbed the cup of juice first as she felt her mouth dry. "Did you cook this?"

He nodded still with his smile and soft, warm gaze at her. She focused on her food while trying to calm her pounding heart. Never did she imagine someone would cook breakfast for her. With her busy daily routine, she only had two slices of toast for her breakfast and ate them in a rush. She even sometimes did not indulge herself in a cup of juice or coffee in the morning. But this time, she felt she was treated special.

She took the plate from the tray and squeezed it between her chest and her left limb, while her right hand held the spoon, scooping the food from the plate into her mouth. When she lifted her eyes, she realised that he was still staring at her without blinking. This was the first time she felt nervous being observed that way, as before, she never cared. She carefully put the plate on her crossed-legged lap.

"Have you had your breakfast?" she asked sheepishly.

"Yes, I have," he nodded. "I bet you drove all the way here and abandoned the flight ticket that I've prepared for you." He seemed amused as his eyes twinkled with mirth.

She chuckled. "Well, I don't like to take flights. Unless it's an overseas trip, of course."

"Yeah, I should have known that. I remember that you drove all the way from Melbourne to Sydney to visit Lana when she was sick."

She raised her eyebrow in disbelief that he still remembered it. She looked much worse than yesterday after that long drive, and yet he was the first person she met when she reached the accommodation where Lana stayed and fell sick.

"I thought you would never come. Lana said you had work. But I thought you decided not to see me anymore after what my aunt did to you." His voice tone sounded grave as he lowered his eyes.

She was puzzled. "You know that? Lana told you?" She would not believe her sister would tell him about Mrs De Boyville's visit. She had made her promised not to mention it to anyone, and her sister had agreed to keep that to themselves.

He shook his head. "No, it wasn't Lana who told me. It was my aunt herself."

She looked at him bewildered.

"In her anger with you, she came to me and told me about her visit to your house and how you rejected her gracious offer and chased her out."

She sucked in her breath. Her mouth opened into agape.

"She said she had never been so insulted in her life. And she said how your behaviour was outrageous."

She closed her mouth, and her heart began racing. She looked at his impassive countenance that she could not again interpret. She was trying to understand what he thought about the whole situation. She read on the news before that Mrs De Boyville was like a second parent to them since their parents passed away. There was a glimpse of embarrassment and slight regret for still turning up here after she insulted one of his closest family members. Her eyes were sneaking into the exit door of the room.

"I am sorry for her behaviour." A pained expression was evident on his face as he lowered his gaze.

Amelia was stunned. She did not expect to hear an apology instead.

"She was the one with outrageous behaviour. I had assumed that my aunt's sharp tongue caused you to decide not to come here yesterday." His voice was trailing off. "When Lana told me that you had work and couldn't come, I thought that was the answer. You do not want to see me again. I had a thought about it overnight about what I needed to do to make it up. I was about to pack up and fly to Melbourne to see you. But instead, you appeared at my door."

She was breathless as he took her hand that was holding the spoon and squeezed it gently.

"I was so thrilled. I am still." He moved closer to her, lowering his face as his palm pressed lightly on her cheek and planted a soft kiss on her lips. She closed her eyes to savour each tingly moment on her lips while he deepened the kiss.

"When?" she whispered as they pulled apart while their foreheads rested against each other. "When did you start having feelings for me?"

"I have no idea exactly when. Perhaps from the first time I saw you. The feeling gradually became stronger the more interaction that we have." He gazed at her while his finger was skimming at her cheek. "Has anyone told you that you have beautiful eyes?"

She startled and moved back, giving him a frown. A flash of Gerald's words came into her mind straightaway. He was probably the first person who told her about it. She did not take it seriously at that time, knowing he was just flirting. But now it was Fitz saying it. She saw it in a different light.

She stammered, torn between lying or telling the truth and bringing Gerald's name to the table.

"Your eyes are sparkling beautifully every time you talk and even much more fascinating when you're angry," he continued, not sensing her internal turmoil.

She did not expect the compliment and blurted out, "But on the first day we met, you said I was not good enough for you. You said that to Charlie."

He looked at her bewildered. "You heard that?" He covered his face with his hand and groaned.

She winced. There was a glimpse of regret in her heart for bringing that up, which perhaps was too harsh. She did not mean to say that she harboured resentment toward him.

"I'm sorry you heard that. I...," he stuttered and took a heavy sigh. "I am not someone who can easily talk with other people that I've just met. That night Charlie was such a pest, kept pushing me to pick up any girl." He lifted his guilt-ridden eyes. "I did not mean to insult you."

Looking at his pinched expression, she could feel how terrible he must have felt. "That's alright. I guess I did not leave a good first impression either. I'm just surprised that you even said it before knowing about my left limb. So I suppose I'm not that attractive after all. It makes me curious why you could say I have beautiful eyes."

Suddenly, he raised his hand, cupped her face, and pulled it, so their forehead met again.

"I admire you, Amelia," he said softly. "You have a relentless spirit within you despite...." He sounded hesitant." Your physical condition. You're smart, mature and responsible, and you even became the breadwinner in the family. You are not afraid of anything and ready to fight for your loved ones. Like when you fought me because of Lana and Charlie's breakup."

She grimaced at his last sentence. "So, you like me because of my impertinence? I suppose I'm the first woman in your life who had kicked you."

He laughed softly. "You can do that anytime when you think I deserve it. I was a proud fool, thinking that I knew everything. I separated Charlie and Lana partly because I wanted to avoid seeing you more often. But, perhaps without realising it, I was mesmerised by you from the first day we met. Even after I know about your hand, I can't take my eyes off you. Your strong character and resilience make you shine, and it makes me never pay attention to your little left hand." His hand travelled to her left limb. "Even when we had that fight, I totally forgot that you have only one full hand."

He lifted up his head and looked at her with his hands moved to behind her neck, holding her face close. "I love you," he whispered.

She could feel her body trembling, her heart flooded with warmth. She heard those words from his lips again, said in a very earnest way. She closed her eyes, still thinking that she was probably dreaming. When his lips were on hers again, she felt like floating.

The spoon in her hand slowly dropped with a clinking sound that made him pull away. He seemed to realise that there was a plate of food sitting between them.

"I'm sorry that I have stopped you from eating your breakfast," he chuckled.

"It's alright. I'm..." She bit her lips, unsure what to say. She still had a lot of questions in her mind. Not that she doubted his feelings towards her, as both of them were mature adults, she was fully aware of who she was and who he was.

Her mind trailed as he squeezed her hand again.

"I suppose that you're here, you are giving me another chance?" he asked with a yearning gaze at her.

"Are you sure? You're a Dalton." She looked away, suddenly daunted by her own question and the answer she would get.

"I know what is bothering you is me as a Dalton." He gripped her chin and turned her face to him, so their eyes met again. "I cannot change who I am. But I am still human despite I'm a Dalton, Amelia. I'm just a man who's deeply in love with you. Please don't hate me that I tried to fight my feelings towards you before. But you know I'm changed now. I am more determined than ever to win your heart."

She pursed her lips, hoping it would stop her tears from rolling out.

"What made you change your mind?" Her voice was trembling, and she hated it. She took a deep breath. "What made you decide to pursue our relationship?"

He took a long exhale. "I think it was my parents."

Her brow knitted in confusion.

"Yes, my parents have passed away," he smiled. "Their deaths become a constant reminder for Georgie and me that our wealth and good name could never patch the hollowness in our hearts after losing them. That was the reason Georgie brought Gerald to the court too. She wanted to bring justice to those who Gerald had harmed."

He lowered his gaze and swallowed before lifting his eyes on her again. "Georgie and I decided to be at Pemberley a few days before the masquerade ball because it was close to the death anniversary of our parents. We made a pact to do this every year to remember them. That time I was reminded again of what I had failed to understand. I drowned myself in alcohol for quite a while, and I beat myself up. I was almost a wreck. Thank God you appeared in my life again at the right time. When we bumped into each other at Pemberley, it was like a wake-up call for me that I have to make it right this time."

She suddenly remembered what Richard said about Fitz almost becoming an alcoholic before their accidental meeting at Pemberley. She could not believe that she had such a great effect on his life.

"Yeah, Richard told me." She took a quiet sigh. "That you had been drinking."

He smiled sheepishly. "It was not my best moment."

She raised her hand and touched his cheek softly with her knuckle. She realised that from all the intimate moments they had shared all this while, he always initiated them first. She always wanted to do it, but she was never sure because she never felt that he was going to become hers. But this time, everything seemed so real. All her doubts seemed answered. She knew one thing that she should do now for them to move forward.

"Please, tell me that you are here to give me another chance," he said again with his pleading eyes.

She smiled with radiant joy and full of certainty within her heart. "No."

He stared at her wide-eyed, which made her release a soft laugh while pressing her lips onto his.

"I'm the one who needs a chance," she whispered while she threw her arm around him and pulled him closer.

And she could feel a smile on his lips between their kisses.

EPILOGUE

A Twisted Reality – A Year Later

Amelia looked at the time shown on her mobile phone, perhaps for the tenth time in the last fifteen minutes. She took a sigh, realising that it had been almost half an hour she had been sitting alone at one of the corner tables in this luxurious, elegant restaurant, sipping her almost finished wine. She started to feel restless and was tempted to stand up and leave the place. However, Fitz could come anytime soon, and she did not want them to miss each other as much as she was furious why he still hadn't turned up. She had been trying to call his mobile phone but reached his voicemail instead. She wondered whether Fitz was caught up in an urgent meeting, hence he was late. At least a text message to inform her would be nice.

She took a deep breath, trying to remind herself to be patient. The last time Fitz was late for their appointment was due to an urgent work meeting that he had to attend. He only managed to text her after she had been waiting for half an hour too. She was upset, but he apologised a thousand times, and Amelia knew that he tried to make it up by spending more time with her. She tried to be more understanding, realising the huge responsibilities that Fitz bore in running his family business. Sometimes even Lana also complained about the same thing, the lack of time Charlie spent with her after a year of marriage. Her sister wished to have a baby soon, however they spent more time being apart than being together. Amelia thought perhaps this was the risk her sister had to take to marry a wealthy businessman.

Amelia smiled to herself. She could not believe it had been a year too she started a relationship with Fitz. It had not been easy, especially with the scrutinization from most of Fitz's relatives of her physical disability and her family's financial background. However, Fitz had been on her side, assuring her of his sincerity and how he was ready to do anything to be with her. In the end, Amelia knew that they could just simply ignore what other people say and just live for themselves. However, she could not deny there was always a slip of doubt in her heart about whether they could overcome this together.

But now, after a year they were together as a couple, she had to admit that she enjoyed spending time with him, getting to know him and realising how they had many things in common. Their love for the outdoors was one of them. They had been spending time camping and hiking together. Their interest in self-defence was another thing. Sometimes, the time they spent sparring was a way for them to get their bodies close to each other comfortably. Even though Fitz did show some affection to her publicly through his small touch on her waist, hand, or the small of her back, Amelia felt the moments they held each other close privately were more meaningful to her. How far they could go in their relationship always made her ponder.

She shook her thoughts and looked at her mobile phone again. Still, there was no single message from Fitz, and now it was almost forty five minutes she had been waiting. She started to feel anxious, and somehow she felt something was not right. The ringtone of her mobile phone with Georgie's number on display immediately answered everything.

"Amelia!"

Georgie's voice sounded hoarse, mixed with sobs. Her heart suddenly pounded hard.

"Fitz had an accident. He's in the hospital now."

Her heart seemed to cease beating at that particular second. She closed her eyes briefly before she answered. Georgie told her the hospital's name, and she immediately fled the place. Her hand was quivering with worry, but she managed to calm herself while driving to her destination.

The moment she reached the hospital, it was Lana who saw her first. Charlie came a minute after her. He had come straight from the airport as he had been away on a business trip to London that week.

"He's still unconscious, but his condition is stable," informed Lana.

"What happened?" Charlie asked. However, his question was hanging in the air as they walked through the hospital corridor. Lana took them to the ward, and all of them were astonished when they saw Georgie sitting beside her brother with wet cheeks but a relieved smile on her lips. All of them breathed a sigh of relief, too, almost at the same time.

Fitz was lying on the bed, which tilted up about 60 degrees. His head was wrapped with a white bandage, and there was a couple of dry bruises on his temple and cheek. He was conscious, however Amelia could see that his eyes did not show the vigour that she would usually find in him. Whatever the accident he just had must be pretty serious, and she quietly prayed that the injury he sustained was pretty light.

Their eyes met for a moment. He gave her a furrowed brow, which she returned with a smile. Georgie's voice broke their silence.

"I'm glad you're conscious now, Fitz," sobbed Georgie. Amelia approached and hugged her while rubbing her back, trying to soothe her.

"You've made all of us worry, Fitz," she said.

"Yeah, mate. I immediately came here from the airport when I heard the news from Lana," said Charlie while shoving his hair but giving a warm smile to his best friend. "I'm glad you're alright. What happened?"

Fitz did not respond and closed his eyes with a pinched expression. Everyone was quiet, watching him with worry.

"You fell from the horse, Fitz," said Georgie softly. "Do you remember?"

"Horse?" repeated Amelia. "He was doing horse riding? I thought he was in a meeting. "

"The meeting was with Mr Smith, who also loves horse riding," answered Georgie. "However, I'm not sure what happened and why Fitz fell from the horse."

"Right." Amelia nodded. Fitz now opened his eyes and gave her a blank look. She felt something amiss. It seemed that Fitz did not know what they were talking about. She believed he must still be in shock after the accident. His countenance was filled with confusion and weariness.

"Are you alright, mate?" asked Charlie. "How do you feel?"

Fitz lifted his head and looked at his friend. "I think...I'm alright," he answered weakly. Amelia quietly felt relieved with his response, though his voice sounded weak. She noticed that his eyes shifted to Lana briefly, and he tilted his head while observing her sister with narrowed eyes.

"That's good, mate. I guess you need to have plenty of rest. Take it easy," added Charlie.

"Thanks," replied Fitz.

The room fell into silence as Fitz closed his eyes again. Amelia exchanged glances with the rest realising that perhaps what Fitz needed now was only rest. Charlie and Lana nodded understandably.

"Have a good rest, mate," said Charlie. "I just arrived today from London. I think I'll go back and have a rest now too. I'll catch up again with you tomorrow, alright?" He patted Fitz on his shoulder gently.

"Hope you get well soon, Fitz," added Lana while giving him a gentle smile.

Fitz only nodded weakly.

"I'll send you out," said Amelia while following her sister, and Charlie walked out of the room. Lana gave her a warm farewell hug before she and Charlie left. When she was about to step into the room again, she heard Georgie and Fitz conversing.

"Is that Charlie's new girlfriend?"

She did not put enough brakes on her feet as she had already appeared at the door when she heard the question. Fitz, who was initially looking at his sister, moved his eyes to her. His gaze towards her seemed foreign to her, which suddenly made her heart sink.

Their eyes locked for a moment as she walked toward him. She swallowed thickly as her heartbeat drummed loudly and reached her ear. When she noticed that his eyes were briefly travelling to her little left limb, she knew something was not right.

The last time Fitz gave her that look seemed ages ago. It was the same look that she received from him when he found out about her prosthetic hand. It was the look mixed between pity and disgust that she was used to seeing from anyone who saw her for the first time. There was a sinking feeling in her heart that now she saw the same look again from his umber eyes.

A fear suddenly crept into her heart. An unexplained feeling made her feel insecure as if she was about to fall into a deep valley. It was a similar feeling that had been haunting her since the beginning of their relationship, but it was easily brushed off the moment she was immersed in his tender umber gaze. This time, however, that feeling escalated and made her chest tight. His next words made her grip the side of her dress tightly.

"Excuse me. But ....do I know you?"

Amelia felt her body aching as if she was already at the bottom of the valley. She sucked in her breath while Georgie's soft gasp filled the air.

* * *

Amelia stared blankly at the backyard from her parents' house kitchen window. A slice of toast was on the plate in front of her, however she hadn't touched it as her mind was elsewhere despite her grumbling tummy.

It had been three days since Fitz's accident. He had been discharged from the hospital and gone home. It was Georgie who accompanied her brother most of the time, meanwhile she had excused herself with work. She knew it was cowardly to run away from this painful reality. However, she was not ready to see him again after the day of the accident.

When Fitz asked her who she was, she felt the room spinning around her. She tried to catch her breath while at the same time restraining her own emotion. She could not get herself to answer the question, though now she felt she should have. Georgie responded to the question, and his reaction was even more unbearable for her to see.

"Amelia is your girlfriend, Fitz," explained Georgie.

His brow knitted as his eyes moved between herself and his sister in disbelief. The corner of his lip slowly upturned into a smirk. "My girlfriend? You must be joking," he chuckled.

Amelia clutched the side of her dress tighter and forced herself to release a small smile. Her eyes welled in tears, which made her rush out to the door while signalling Georgie to follow her. She took a heavy breath once they were outside the room.

"Amelia..." Georgie gripped her hand softly. "He just had an accident and had some serious injury on his head. I suppose that's the reason he has some memory problems. Please don't get upset about this."

She shook her head while trying to force a weak smile. "I'm okay, " she lied. Her voice was shaking. Georgie's hand on her back, trying to soothe her, made her almost could not hold her dam of tears anymore. "I understand. But perhaps it's best I just leave. I don't think it's a good idea for me to stay around. I think it will make him more confused."

"How could you say that?" scolded Georgie. "You *are* his girlfriend. This is the time that he needs you the most."

"But he does not remember me," Amelia chuckled bitterly. "He has no memory of what happened in the past year."

Georgie took a heavy sigh. "You have to give him some time."

"Precisely. That is why I should leave."

Georgie snapped away and left her behind. For a moment, she did not understand what she needed to do. Part of her had to agree with Georgie's statement that this was the time when Fitz needed her the most. But how could she help him when he did not even recognise her? She took a deep breath, trying to get the tightness in her chest out and hoping it could clear her mind. She did not want to act emotionally, she had to think clearly, too. And she knew what the right thing she needed to do at this moment. She shouldn't just simply leave.

After drying up her tears, she gathered her courage to enter the room again. She was welcomed with a smile from Georgie while Fitz still looked at her suspiciously. For a moment, she stood awkwardly in front of both siblings. Georgie saved her from further embarrassment when Fitz almost opened his mouth, questioning her presence.

"Thank you for staying around, Amelia. We really appreciate it," said Georgie while throwing her arm on Amelia's shoulder. "I won't be able to do this alone without you."

"How about I get you some dinner from outside?" She was surprised to throw the idea. She looked at the man who had captured her heart for the past year with the best affectionate smile she could offer him. "What would you like to have, Fitz? Chicken quinoa? I know that's your favourite."

Fitz seemed taken aback that she knew his favourite food. His lips slowly broke into a smile. "Thanks. I would love to."

"That's a great idea," said Georgie. "Please get me anything from the same shop. Chicken quinoa is also fine."

With that, she managed to get herself away again from the room. She did not leave immediately when she was out of the room, but hid behind the wall, gathering her strength again. She could hear Fitz's voice speaking with his sister.

"So, her name is Amelia? And you said she's my girlfriend? Do you mean girlfriend like in a romantic relationship?"

Her chest was tight again as she heard the question.

"Yes, Fitz. Look, I know it is probably confusing for you because you don't remember her yet. But please, you just had an accident. We need to speak to the doctor about what happened with your memory and when you could get it back."

She could not stand to hear the conversation further and decided to dash out of the hospital. During the time she bought the dinner, her mind was numb. She was not sure what she had to do next. However, somehow she knew she should stick around, not only for Fitz himself but also for herself and Georgie. She took a couple of deep breaths, reminding herself that she should try to help as much as possible, even as a friend. Though it was excruciating to see the man she loved did not remember who she was and sometimes gave her a contemptuous look, not believing that they actually had a relationship.

When she came back, a team of doctors was also inside the room discussing Fitz's memory problem. With his severe head injury, there was no definite answer on when his memory could return. The doctors' advice was only plenty of rest and not to rush him with work matters.

After the doctors left, Fitz seemed exhausted and chose to sleep with no interest in touching the dinner. Amelia thought it was a good time for her to leave, as much as she wanted to hold his hand and kiss him, she restrained herself from doing so.

In the following three days, she decided not to appear too often. Instead, she paid a visit in the evening after work, bringing them food for dinner. She felt relieved that Georgie was there most of the time, so they were never left alone. Fitz gave her an appreciative smile when she came with his favourite food. Seeing the glow in his eyes when he opened the food package made her smile in contentment. At least she made him happy with this small gesture. However, he still could not recognise her, as his eyes still gave her a wary look.

Today was the first weekend since Fitz was discharged. Georgie had given her an ultimatum not to take any extra shift job and insisted that she should spend more time with Fitz, helping him slowly recollect his memory. Georgie had organised a small gathering for them, Charlie and Lana, at their house. She had to agree that it was probably a good idea to jolt his memory back.

However, her heart felt heavy. She was unsure whether she would have the strength to endure Fitz's standoffishness towards her for the whole day.

Once Lana knew about Fitz's memory problem, she immediately called her.

"Are you alright, Liz?" asked Lana. Amelia could sense the cautious tone of her voice.

"I'm not sure," she replied flatly. "I'm not sure whether this could be a sign that we shouldn't be together."

"Please don't say that, Liz. He loves you.

Amelia couldn't help but chuckle bitterly as she felt the prick in her eyes. "He doesn't remember that anymore." Her voice started to crack, mixed with a sob. " I can see from his eyes that having a relationship with me seems to be something that does not make any sense to him."

"You cannot give up on him, Liz. You know he's not himself at this stage. You have to give him time."

It was true that she had to give him time, she could not deny that. But how long could she endure this? Finding the way he looked at her warily broke her heart into pieces.

"Please don't give up, Liz," consoled Lana. "He did not give up on you, on your relationship. He always tried to work it out."

She closed her eyes, admitting that statement was true. Nevertheless, she knew she had to keep trying.

She took a heavy breath before finally having a bite of her toast. After finishing her breakfast, she left the house and drove to her destination, which she could not avoid anymore. Fitz's house was a mansion in an elite suburb in Melbourne, next to the suburb where Sharon and herself used to live. As a regular visitor of the house, she was welcomed warmly by the housekeeper, who informed her that Fitz and Georgie were in the upper floor study room. She walked up the stairs slowly, buying her more time to gather her courage and strength. However, when she felt she was ready, her confidence was instantly shattered when she heard Fitz's voice from inside the room.

"How could I have a relationship with Amelia? Where did I meet her? In Vegas when I was drunk? " There was a booming laugh for a brief moment before he continued. "Was I too drunk when I asked her to be my girlfriend?"

"Stop it, Fitz!" Georgie's voice could be heard reprimanding her brother. "Amelia has never been in Vegas. She went to Pemberley before, though. That was the time you actually showed your interest towards her."

"How could I?"

"You love her!"

Another huge laughter.

"I can't believe I fell in love with someone physically disabled like her. Unless she's rich."

"Stop it, Fitz! You love her because she's unlike any other woman who is always after you because of your money."

"So, do you mean I like her because she only has one hand?"

Amelia shut her eyes as her lungs constricted. She was not sure whether she should stay there any longer. For a moment she stood there, staring blankly at the wall. She knew she should not linger too long. She did not wish to be caught red-handed eavesdropping.

The doorbell from the ground floor shook her awake. She went downstairs again, feeling sure that the visitors must be Lana and Charlie. While she was gliding down the stairs, the last person that she wished to see appeared from the door with a smug look all over her face.

"Hi, Amelia." Clare greeted her. "I'm surprised you're still here."

"I'm surprised that you're here too, Clare. I'm not sure whether you're actually invited," she retorted without hesitation, though she was gifted with a glare from Lana, who came behind Clare, together with Charlie.

Charlie felt uneasy and made an inaudible mouth shaped 'sorry' from behind Clare's back. She only returned it with a stiff smile.

"I flew quickly here once I heard about Fitz's accident," gloated Clare. "I heard he had forgotten you."

Amelia knew this was coming. What else could she expect from someone like Clare, one of the people who were totally against her relationship with Fitz? Clare would be the first woman out there who would leap for joy if she and Fitz were not together anymore.

"I hope he hasn't forgotten you either, Clare," she muttered while rolling her eyes. The steps behind her indicate that the house owners were coming down and heard their conversation. She turned her body around to see Georgie who was trying to draw a cordial smile to her guests but was betrayed by her squinting eyes seeing Clare's presence. Meanwhile, Fitz'looked impassive, a mask that she knew that he always put on when he was on his guard.

Seeing the object of her affection, Clare did not waste her time and immediately showed her over and fake amiability towards Fitz and Georgie. As much as Amelia prayed hard, wishing that Fitz's memory did not include someone like Clare, unfortunately, Fitz remembered his best friend's sister, whom he already knew for a long time. She moved aside, letting Clare approach the hosts while she approached her sister and her brother-in-law.

"Trust me, I absolutely have no idea that she would arrive today," whispered Charlie while they watched the show that Clare put on.

"Don't worry about it," muttered Amelia. "She is not your sister if she's not inviting herself to be here."

She did not expect that Charlie would laugh at her words. However, his laughter startled the rest of them, especially Fitz, who looked amusingly at his friend. Fitz moved forward to his friend while motioning him to the game room. Georgie also motioned the ladies to follow, though she deliberately walked slower to the same pace as Amelia. Lana seemed to understand what she meant and took her sister-in-law to walk together with her.

"Think positively," whispered Georgie while enveloping Amelia's right hand in hers. "Fitz never likes Clare anyway. Perhaps seeing her would make his memory about you come back sooner than we expect."

Amelia did not respond, as she was not that optimistic.

The game room was a spacious, soundproof room in the house that Fitz converted into a place to play his favourite video games. It was where Amelia and Fitz used to spend a lot of time together, as she also enjoyed playing video games. They played competitively against each other but in a relaxing and fun way, which eventually ended with laughter, cuddles, and sometimes a couple of kisses.

Fitz asked Charlie to take the other remote to play his favourite fighting game - Street Fighter. Charlie took the challenge reluctantly, knowing he was never a good player. As he had expected, he was already on the losing side in a couple of strikes. Amelia couldn't help but whisper to her brother-in-law's ear some game tricks while trying to hold her smirk. From her peripheral view, she knew Fitz was looking at them curiously.

"You should play instead, Amelia," said Charlie while pushing the remote game to her.

"Sure."

Amelia happily took it as she had to admit that her hand was itchy to join in the game, especially looking at how meek Charlie was. She took the seat beside Fitz and started to hold the remote with her right hand, and occasionally her little left limb helped to press the button on the remote. She was engrossed in the game and did not realise that their bodies had inevitably touched, making Fitz flinch.

When her character in the game managed to win over Fitz's character, she squealed in excitement. However, her smile faded as Fitz abruptly left his seat. She felt dejected with a prick of tears in her eyes which she secretly wiped with the back of her hand.

"Let us move to the music room, Fitz," said Clare while she approached Fitz and enveloped Fitz's arm in her hands. Amelia only bit her lips watching that scene noticing Fitz did not mind Clare's flirtatious behaviour. Lana threw her arm on her shoulder, consoling her, while Georgie rolled her eyes.

"I remember you mentioned it before, Fitz," said Clare after all of them entered the music room. "Your definition of an accomplished woman. She has to be smart, beautiful, proficient in many international languages, arts and music. I'm pretty sure that would be the type of woman you're after to be your life partner."

Amelia quietly took a sigh, realising where the conversation was going. Fitz did not utter any word but only gave a small nod.

"Georgie, why don't you play the piano to entertain us?" asked Clare. "I believe playing music like a piano would not be something that could be done with one hand." She gave a mocking smile towards Amelia.

Amelia was visualising herself slapping this woman instead. Her sister and Charlie looked at her uncomfortably, seeing how Clare behaved.

"You have two hands, Clare," challenged Amelia with an even tone." Why don't you play the piano?"

Clare threw her head back while laughing sarcastically. "I do play a musical instrument, Amelia. I play the violin. Unfortunately, there is none here."

"Well, why don't you play the piano instead, Fitz?" Georgie quickly interjected. "Amelia can accompany you. I know both of you have been practising together."

Fitz seemed taken aback. Amelia would not be surprised. It was a new activity that they had just started recently before the accident.

Amelia knew that Fitz was proficient in piano, nearly as good as his sister. Meanwhile, she had *nil* experience in music. However, slightly over a month before the accident, Fitz persuaded her to understand some music notes and play the melody with her right hand while he played the chord parts. So far, there was only one song they played together, *The Beauty and The Beast*.

Remembering the song's title, Amelia wondered whether Georgie's strategy to get her and Fitz to play the piano together would be a good idea. This could be an object of a laughingstock for Clare. However, at the same time, she wanted to put effort into bringing back Fitz's memory about them.

"That's correct." She gathered her courage to speak while moving to the piano and getting herself seated. "Shall we give it a go, Fitz? It's the beauty and the beast in C major. " She looked at Fitz, who still seemed hesitant. For a moment, her heart pounded hard anxiously, whether he would abruptly walk away like earlier. However, she quietly took an exhale when he sat beside her at the piano seat. Amelia could feel that, except for Clare, the rest gave her a warm, excited smile waiting for their mini-performance.

She whispered the cue, so they began the notes together. Her heart washed with warmth as their fingers danced smoothly on the piano keys.

The moment brought her to the time they were practising the song with his right arm wrapped around her waist. It was one of the sweetest moments they had shared, and she always hoped they could do it forever. For that short three minutes, her hurt and disappointment over his loss of memory of her seemed forgotten. She hoped this moment could freeze.

The song ended smoothly with a perfect ending with high chord notes from Fitz's fingers. Enthusiastic applause was echoing in the room with warm smiles from their audiences, except from one person.

Amelia gathered her courage to look at him, wondering what he thought about their moment earlier. However, she only could sigh as he was giving her an impassive look before Clare grabbed his arm, so he involuntarily stood up from his seat.

"Let's have a stroll outside, Fitz."

"Where are you going, Clare?" protested Charlie. "We're going to the beach soon."

Clare ignored him, kept pulling Fitz's arm to the alfresco folding door, and stepped outside. What annoyed Amelia was that Fitz did not seem to mind Clare's intimate gesture and obediently followed her. She only bit her lips and stormed towards the fridge in the kitchen area connected to the alfresco door.

"He obviously needs some space. Away from me," muttered Amelia.

"I'll join them. Let's go, Lana!" Charlie's voice was heard, followed by the hustle and bustle of their hurried footsteps.

Amelia opened the fridge door and grabbed a bottle of beer. She had been in the house for the past year frequently, so she had been helping herself a lot with the things in the house. When she looked at the bottle in her hand, she wondered whether she should stop being too comfortable in this house. She was not Fitz's girlfriend anymore.

"That was a beautiful piano duet, by the way," said Georgie. "I'm glad both of you did it. I believe it may somehow jolt something in his memory."

"I hope so," she mumbled. She avoided Georgie's concerned look that she did not want to see.

A doorbell startled both of them. Georgie furrowed her brow, indicating she did not expect any more visitors today. However, when they saw the visitors coming toward them a few minutes later, Amelia was unsure what she felt. It was a mix between relief and annoyance.

"Aunt Catherine!" Georgie gasped. "Did you just arrive today?"

"I booked a flight as soon as I heard about Fitz's accident," replied Mrs De Boyville. When her eyes laid on Amelia, she lifted her chin. "I heard about his memory issue. Perhaps it's a good time to make him think straight."

Amelia scoffed. "Nice to see you again, Mrs De Boyville," she greeted with tight lips.

Catherine De Boyville had been the most prominent person in Fitz's family who was against her relationship with Fitz. After expressing her disgruntled unhappiness over their relationship, she spent most of her time in England over the past year. Knowing things started to break up, Amelia would not be surprised if this woman would take the most of it. She just did not expect her arrival this soon.

The other visitor, on the other hand, made Amelia smile. Pretending not to hear Mrs De Boyville's cold comment, Richard approached his cousin and Amelia with his arm wide open and then squeezed them.

"My two favourite ladies!"

"Don't let your aunt hear that," murmured Amelia which made Richard throw his head back and laugh wholeheartedly.

At the same time, Fitz entered the house from the alfresco door, together with Clare, plus Charlie and Lana, behind them. He was astonished by the additional guests in the house, however he nodded respectfully to his aunt before turning to his cousin. Amelia noticed that he furrowed his brow when Richard suddenly threw his arm around her shoulder, pulled her and kissed her cheek.

Amelia only winced. She was used to Richard's affectionate gestures towards her, which she assumed was because they were mates. She remembered Fitz used to look at them with a glassy stare every time Richard acted too intimate towards her. However, this time she felt Fitz's knitted brow meant something else.

For the next couple of minutes, the atmosphere in the room became stiff and formal. While Fitz was politely responding to his aunt's question, Georgie glared at his cousin.

"I'm glad you're here, but why do you bring her along?" whispered Georgie.

Richard swallowed nervously. "Sorry, dear. She overheard our conversation. She insisted on coming along with me."

Amelia, who still stood beside them, only repressed her smile. She had to admit the presence of Mrs De Boyville and Clare made things worse for her and Fitz. She exchanged glances with Lana, who gave her a concerned look, which she returned with a weak smile. She pondered whether she should drop everything and leave. Looking at Fitz's cold behaviour towards her, she did not feel she had a purpose in being here anymore.

The plan to go to the beach was scrapped as aunt Catherine insisted on having a private conversation with Fitz in the study. Richard mischievously put up a reason why he also needed to join in the conversation, to which aunt Catherine reluctantly agreed. Georgie also put up a reason to join in while asking Amelia's help to accompany the rest of the guests. She was more than happy to be with her sister and Charlie. While she was sure Clare could help herself in the house.

She took this opportunity to stroll in the backyard and thought to get Lana to come along. She went to the lounge to find her sister. However, she only saw Charlie and Clare there.

"Where's Lana?" she asked.

Clare did not even bother to lift her eyes from her mobile screen.

"She's in the restroom," replied Charlie.

Amelia went to the closest powder room, located just under the stairs. The room door was abruptly opened when she reached it, and Lana came out from it flustered.

Amelia furrowed her brow. "Are you alright?"

Lana smiled at her sheepishly while she nodded. "Yes."

Amelia noticed that her sister rubbed her hands to her skirt nervously. It was a sign that her sister was keeping something from her.

"Would you like to go for a walk with me? Just in the backyard."

Lana beamed and nodded her head.

They went to the backyard through the same alfresco folding door that Fitz and Clare went earlier. For the first five minutes, there was only silence between them. Amelia noticed that her sister was staring blankly at the pathway they were walking on.

"What are you thinking?" she asked carefully.

Lana was startled by the question and smiled sheepishly. Amelia gripped her sister's arm gently and arched her eyebrow as a sign that she was waiting. These were the things she would always do when she tried to dig a secret that her sister was trying to keep from her.

Lana chuckled. "I'm pregnant."

Amelia's eyes widened with her lips broke into a wide smile. "Congratulations! Charlie must be thrilled."

Lana shook her head. "I don't want to break the news too early, Liz, to avoid disappointment. You know we've been trying, and I had a miscarriage before."

Amelia nodded understandably. "Sure. It's between us for now. But you have to take care of yourself." She moved forward to give her sister a warm hug before they were interrupted by the voice from inside. Georgie waved at them, calling them to come back as the lunch started. Amelia quietly took a sigh. This was not the moment she would look forward to.

Lana squeezed her shoulder to console her. "Just be yourself, Liz. You know that's the reason Fitz loves you."

Amelia could not respond to that. She only smiled faintly.

The lunch arrangement became formal dining. It was something that everyone would expect with the presence of Catherine DeBoyville. Georgie was finger-tapping on the table with a pout, annoyed that all her plan for today had gone wasted. They were supposed to relax on the beach by now, especially with today's lovely warm summer weather. Even Richard joked about it, which was ignored by Mrs De Boyville.

For a moment, Amelia hesitated about where she should sit. Clare happily seated on Fitz's right-hand side, and she seized the chance without hesitation. Georgie pulled Amelia's hand to get her seated opposite Fitz, and Richard happily got himself seated beside her. Mrs De Boyville got herself placed on Fitz's left side. Amelia was unsure whether this seating arrangement was a good idea. Facing Fitz, looking at her coldly and impassively, only made her heart shatter.

"As discussed, Fitz, I think you should return to Pemberley as soon as possible. It will help you to recollect your memories," said Mrs De Boyville while they were starting their appetizer.

Amelia pursed her lips. She should have expected this. This was a way to keep her away from Fitz. It had been a suggestion from Mrs De Boyville from the beginning of their relationship.

"I will speak to your secretary to organise a private jet for you so that you can leave by tomorrow night."

Georgie's soft gasp was heard. "That soon? Surely, we don't need to leave in haste. Fitz still needs to do some check-up."

"That can be done in England. The doctors there are equally good as here," responded Mrs De Boyville.

"Perhaps we should make an appointment with the doctor before Fitz could go, aunt," commented Richard. "Perhaps having a long-haul flight is not good for Fitz's current health."

"I feel fine." Fitz's deep baritone voice was suddenly heard.

Amelia stared at him. She felt her gut was being punched. He looked at his plate, ignoring her stare.

"Oh, that's great, Fitz. Can I join you as well on your private jet?" Clare sneaked a malicious glance at Amelia. "We can spend Christmas together in England. The summer here is way too hot."

"Yeah, sure," replied Fitz monotonously.

"I think it's best to consult the doctor first." Amelia was unsure where she had the courage to get her voice out. "I notice that sometimes you still have a headache. I suppose many business matters still could be done remotely from here."

"I agree with Amelia," followed Richard quickly while munching his food. "I understand your good intention, aunt. But there's no rush. Fitz has just been discharged from the hospital yesterday. He can leave next week instead, and who knows?" He shrugged his shoulder. "His memory is back to normal by then."

"Thank you for your concern, Rich," added Fitz curtly. "But as I said, I feel fine. I think being at Pemberley would help me better to recollect my memory. I feel I can be myself when I'm there."

Amelia swallowed thickly while restraining the turmoil in her heart. She did not care about the contemptuous look from Mrs De Boyville or the triumphant smile from Clare. Fitz's stony speaking manner was the one that instead made her clutch to the spoon tightly.

"Why is it so hard to make one phone call to your doctor before you make a decision?" She braced herself to lift her head and give him a stern look.

Fitz seemed taken aback, but his lip was still curled upturn.

"Fitz could make his own decision without any interference from an outsider," growled Mrs De Boyville

"Aunt Catherine, Amelia is not an outsider," Georgie interjected exasperatedly.

"This is a family matter. As far as I know, Amelia is not part of the family."

"Yet." Richard quickly added in. "But she will be."

Amelia took a sigh. Her head was spinning. She appreciated that Georgie and Richard were trying to defend her, but she was unsure whether this would be necessary. Her eyes met with Fitz's cold umber eyes directed to her.

"You are not fully yourself at this stage," said Amelia while restraining the anguish in her voice. "Technically, you are not in a healthy state of mind to make a decision. Even a business decision."

Fitz chuckled in disdain. "And who are you that I have to listen to you?"

"Fitz!" groaned Georgie exasperatedly while holding her head in her hands.

"Technically, no one to you," Amelia responded in an even tone. "But I bring up a point here that I think you should think carefully, Fitz." She tried to get her emotion in check and be patient. "Perhaps Georgie and Richard could explain it to you better. But since you were in the hospital three days ago, your proxy should take over. I believe it's something that you have organised with your legal advisor before."

"Oh dear!" exclaimed Mrs De Boyville. "Are you saying you are the proxy?"

Amelia wished she could laugh at that. Richard and Georgie were practically snorting beside her. However, she maintained her stern face and never took her eyes off Fitz's.

"You don't give enough credit to your nephew and niece, Mrs De Boyville," she said calmly while shaking her head. "I'm not the proxy."

"I am the next in line for Fitz's legal representative," Richard declared. He struggled to keep his face straight as his lips broke in laughter. "So, I agree with Amelia. She has brought a valid point."

"In business matter, perhaps you could, Richie. But not with my personal life decision," retorted Fitz.

"Making a rush decision is not something you usually do, either," added Amelia quickly.

"At least you check with the doctor first, bro," pleaded Georgie.

The room went to silence. Amelia knew her words made him think. His gaze was softer, which inevitably made her heart stir. However, it was still an unreadable expression for her. She had no idea what actually ran through his mind at this moment. Did he start to remember her? She would really hope so, but she knew she couldn't raise her hope too early.

The lunch continued as Richard invited Charlie for a conversation surrounding some asset investment. Somehow it reminded Mrs De Boyville that other non-Dalton people were at the same table. After lunch, Charlie and Lana excused themselves to leave. Amelia could see that Charlie was trying to bring his sister along. Finally, after a couple of wishy-washy discussions between the siblings, Clare reluctantly agreed to leave. It was an episode that Amelia would not forget as Charlie half dragged his sister away. "I think you should leave too, Amelia," Clare snickered before heading to the door. "I think now it's the private moment for family only."

"Amelia is practically a family," responded Georgie quickly. "Don't you remember that Amelia stayed at the centre wing of Pemberley at our annual masquerade ball?"

Clare scoffed, dusted her shoes and left. Amelia sighed exasperatedly before giving her sister a warm farewell hug and whispering to her to take care of herself. After the three of them left, Amelia closed the door and fell into Georgie's arm, who motioned her towards the study room. Fitz and Richard had been retreating to that room, while Mrs De Boyville had chosen to have a rest in her room after a long flight.

"I'm glad you stay," said Georgie. "With the annoying people gone, I think now all of us can have a more relaxing conversation. I think that's what Fitz needs."

"I'm not sure about that," responded Amelia. "You can see that your brother seems to be avoiding me."

"Don't worry." Georgie squeezed her shoulder. "With Richard and I around, both of you will be fine. Just be yourself."

Amelia took a deep breath and only followed when Georgie pulled her to the study room. Richard and Fitz were sitting on the couch with a glass of cocktail in their hand.

"We just talked about going to Pemberley, Amelia," said Richard. "Fitz is still keen to go. And the more I think about it, actually, it's not a bad idea."

Amelia gave Richard a wary look. Didn't this mean that even Richard think giving Fitz some time to break away from her was necessary?

"All of us could spend Christmas day together," added Richard with a wide grin on his face.

Amelia was startled. Christmas? With all the recent happenings, she had lost track of time. The major festive season was just around the corner.

"That is a splendid idea!" exclaimed Georgie excitedly. "You have not experienced winter in England before, Amelia. This is the right time."

Amelia was not sure whether she should share the excitement. Her mouth was partly opened, and she saw Fitz seemed not to share the same excitement. He must have thought to include her – an outsider- for Christmas, that was usually meant for close family, would be a crazy idea.

"I still have to work." Amelia couldn't help but blurt out those words. As much as she was excited to spend Christmas overseas, at the back of her mind, she realised she still had to carry her responsibility.

"I'm not saying we're leaving tomorrow," chuckled Richard. "Christmas is still four weeks away. How about you depart a few days before Christmas and spend about two or three weeks there? Anyway, I suppose usually there's Christmas shutdown in your office."

"Yeah," she nodded. "About three weeks."

"Settled then!" squealed Georgie. "Oh, I'm so excited. Make sure you get your ski gear ready, Amelia."

"I'm not good at skiing," she muttered. As far as she remembered, her father only brought them to Mount Buller for simple toboggan play, but no one in the family was a serious skier. She knew it was one of Fitz's favourite hobbies, and she remembered that Fitz had planned for them to go skiing in New Zealand next winter. With the accident and memory loss Fitz was having now, she doubted the plan could be realised.

"Don't worry about it. I can teach you," said Richard as he threw his arm around her while giving his cousin a mischievous look. Amelia noticed that Fitz was again looking at them quizzically. A few minutes later, Richard made an excuse to rest while pulling Georgie to join him as well. Amelia realised that both of them tried to give her some time alone with Fitz.

For a moment her heart surged in panic. Since the accident, they had never been left alone together. Amelia preferred that way, too, to avoid the awkwardness between them. Sometimes she had to laugh thinking about this. It seemed they started everything from zero again despite having been in a relationship for the past year.

"It seems Richard likes you." Fitz's deep baritone voice broke the silence between them. Amelia turned to him, and their eyes met. His gaze on her was stern, but it was not as cold as before. She quietly felt relieved seeing that, which made her break a smile on her lips.

"He's a good mate," she replied softly.

Fitz took a deep sigh. "I hope you understand, Amelia. No offence. But I still cannot believe that I have fallen for you. It's not something that I imagine I would do."

Amelia couldn't help but winced even though she had heard him say those words before. She felt as if the conversation they had over a year ago, when he made his feelings towards her known for the first time, was being replayed again before her eyes. It hurt, but she reminded herself that this man had just suffered a heavy injury and lost his memory this time. Though sadly, why from all the memory, only his memory of her was erased from his head.

"Richard keeps reminding me that if I don't give ourselves a chance, I will regret this for the rest of my life. He told me what happened last time when I let you go."

His gaze was briefly on the floor before he lifted his eyes again. Amelia bit her lips, unsure how she should respond to this.

"I'm not sure whether anything can be done now. Sometimes perhaps the history could not be repeated easily. I hope you don't grudge against me, Georgie or Richard if ..." his voice faltered. Amelia clutched tightly to her jeans while listening. "If my memory about us never come back. And we have to part."

Amelia gathered her strength to give a faint smile. "I totally understand. I do not wish to force anyone's feelings here. My wish is that you stay safe and healthy."

Her heart skipped a beat as she saw a ghost of a smile on his impassive face. She had been missing that smile from him since the accident. She hoped she could see it one more time before they went their separate ways.

"Thank you," he said softly. He put down his glass and strode to the door as if that were all the things they needed to discuss. As his body passed her, her shoulder was inevitably brushed slightly, and she breathed in the masculine scent she always liked. She smiled bitterly to herself. How her body screamed, wanting to hold him back and fall into his warm embrace once again. However, yearning for it seemed impossible, and perhaps she would never have that chance again.

The silence became so loud as she was left alone in the room. For a moment she stared blankly at the door before moving to the room's big window. The view from this room had been her favourite. In the past, they had been spending a lot of time in this room too. She would be on the couch reading her book, while he would be doing his work. Sometimes they would snuggle up on the couch, covered with a throw while reading together. She smiled, recalling those memories, though sadly, that memory perhaps would never be repeated.

Last Christmas

Amelia zipped up her windbreaker jacket wishing it would make her body warmer. However, the cold wind that touched her face still made her inevitably shiver. She was standing outside the Manchester airport, waiting for her pickup that was supposed to arrive by now. But after standing outside for about five minutes, she almost gave up and turned back to wait inside the airport building instead. A black limo suddenly approached her, which she wished was meant for her. She had never been so happy in her life when she saw Richard hop out from the passenger seat.

"Sorry for being late, my dear," said Richard while giving her a tight hug before leading her to the car. The chauffeur helped put her luggage in the vehicle.

Once seated in the car, Richard offered her a glass of wine that she gladly received. She knew she needed it in this kind of weather.

Finally, she was back in England. The last time she was here was with her aunt and uncle. It was during summer over a year ago. That time Fitz showed his genuine intention, declared his feelings towards her and did not even hesitate to walk beside her during the Dalton family's annual charity ball. Since the beginning of the relationship, Fitz had mentioned that he wanted to bring her back to Pemberley to spend a holiday together. The plan was almost eventualised on their first Christmas as a couple. However, realising that their relationship was still in an early stage, Amelia decided not to go. She knew Fitz was disappointed, it was supposed to be their first Christmas together, but they had it separately in two different places. But this time, ironically, she came to Pemberley when Fitz perhaps did not wish to see her as their relationship was on edge.

She had been contemplating for the past four weeks whether she should be here. Fitz had left for Pemberley the day after their lunch gathering. He called the doctor to seek advice before leaving on his private jet plane with his aunt, Georgie and Clare. Only Richard decided to leave a day after them. Since then, Georgie had been messaging her and giving her an update from Pemberley with daily video calls, ensuring that she had booked her flight to England as planned. Georgie always tried to get Fitz to pop up to say Hi to her, but Amelia knew he did not wish to see her.

For the past weeks, she had not only been contemplating but also felt dispirited. Georgie and Richard had been very persistent, and the more she thought about this, she was here merely because she did not wish to disappoint them. Meeting with the Dalton family's extended relatives at this time was perhaps not a good idea either. How could she face the scrutinization from not only Mrs De Boyville, but maybe from most of them when Fitz did not even want to lay his eyes on her for a minute? Deep inside, she hated to admit that she was giving up. She hated to give up in any relationship, but things were just different when it came to Fitz and his attributes as a Dalton.

A soft touch on her little left limb awoke her from her reverie. She turned and smiled at Richard, who seemed to understand what she had in mind. There was no opportunity to sight any scenery throughout the journey because it was just pitch dark outside. However, she would presume that thick snow was everywhere, covering all the grassland surrounding them.

Her flight time was not ideal. It was almost midnight local time. She couldn't blame Richard's tardiness as much as she felt bad for the chauffeur who had to drive them in the wee hours of the morning. When they finally reached Pemberley, she admired the colourful Christmas light decoration surrounding the estate. The vast garden was illuminated with Christmas lights shaped in various Christmas characters. She felt like she was brought into a magical place and understood why Fitz had been so eager to take her here for Christmas.

They entered the centre wing, and Richard took her to her room. They passed through the quiet corridor, which indicated that most of the guests must have slept. She knew the only thing she could do next was trying to sleep, despite having her jetlag.

"I hope you had a nice flight," said Richard while putting down the only luggage she brought. "You have too little things to carry for someone who's going to spend three weeks here."

She did not respond to it, walked further inside the room and slowly took off her jacket. It was true that somehow she had a gut feeling she would not stay in this place for long.

"Have a good rest, and we'll see you at breakfast tomorrow," added Richard as he wrapped his arm around her and gave her a light kiss on her forehead. "You must be tired."

"Sure. Good night."

Once Richard left and her room door shut tightly, Amelia sighed heavily. The quietude in this large high, ceiling room made her feel empty. She remembered that she had a similar feeling the first time she stayed in this estate. Even though she was now in a different room, she still could not help the loneliness that crept into her heart. She wished Fitz could be with her and pulled her into his embrace. That was what she had wished for the next time she was at Pemberley. However, the reality was far from the dream.

She decided to have a warm shower before she laid down and tried to get some sleep. When she was awake, it was six am. It was still rather dark outside. Since she felt more vigorous, she changed into her waterproof track pants and jacket. Lana had been helping her to shop for winter attires since her sister had the experience from her last ski honeymoon trip.

She took out her boots from her suitcase, put them on and reached the door, ready to go out. She laughed as she was half tiptoeing when she needed to find her way out. She had no idea where her room was located, but when she managed to find a steward who showed her the way to the backyard, she realised that she had been placed in a room far away from Fitz and Georgie.

The fresh cold winter air splashed on her face and helped to clear her mind. The sky started to show some colour, and with her beanie and hand glove on, she started strolling. Most of the pathway had been cleared, but with her boots on, it did not stop her from walking on the grassland covered thickly by snow. Her memory of playing toboggan in the snow when her father took her and her sisters to Mount Buller was like yesterday. She smiled to herself because of it. However, she was reminded again of where she was now. And it made her steps seem heavy despite being on her Christmas holiday.

She was unsure how she would act when seeing Fitz later. There was only awkwardness as if there was a deep valley between them now. This place had brought many sweet memories from the last time she was here. It was the time that they rekindled their feelings towards each other. However, it was going to be different this time, and somehow she was scared that she would be leaving this place with a painful memory instead.

After she had walked about five kilometres away, a faint voice suddenly startled her. She looked to her surrounding to find no single soul around. It was still early morning, and she would not be surprised if no activity was happening yet. She focused on her hearing again and was sure someone was calling for help. Her heart was beating hard as she focused her mind on the source of the voice and walked towards it. When the voice became more evident, her walk became a fast run. When she reached the edge, her gut immediately told her that someone must have had an accident.

A flush of adrenaline tingled through her body when she saw who the person was. She should have guessed it, as he was also an early riser like her.

Fitz was lying helplessly on the slope with his face pinched in pain. He looked up when she arrived, and she could see that he did not expect it was her who turned up to help him. His hand clutched tightly at the cliff's edge, halting him from sliding down further. Amelia grabbed his hand to make sure that he would not fall.

"Are you alright?" Her question was probably meaningless as she noticed the tear at the bottom of his pants and the blood trickling down his legs. It looked nasty, which made her unavoidably flinch before her eyes met his.

"Perhaps it's best if you go and get some help," he groaned.

"Let me pull you up first."

"You can't!" He yelled. "You won't be able to!"

Amelia felt annoyed that he was underestimating her strength. She reminded herself that he had lost his memory of her, hence he did not know what she had been trained for.

"If I leave you now to get more help, you will be at the bottom of the hill by the time I come back," she growled. Ignoring his protests, she leaned forward further to grab half of his body and pulled him up

"Grab my other hand!" she yelled. She offered her little left limb to him. He looked hesitant, and she realised that he probably felt disgusted to touch her little left limb.

"Grab it, please! It will not bite you!" she yelled again angrily. He finally took it with a wince. It made a lot of difference to how much power she needed to pull him up. With an unladylike groan, she used all the strength she had and pulled his body up. The moment his body weighted on the safe side, inevitably, he fell on top of her.

How their faces were just an inch away brought her to the past. A similar thing happened in this place when she collided with him while having a morning jog. Throughout their relationship, she always liked the moment when she could be under his embrace. It made her feel warm and secure. However, the wariness in his eyes threw her back to the reality that he did not remember that sweet moment. She gently pushed his body to the side, realising that his pain prevented him from moving the way he wanted to.

Their bodies lied flat on the snow facing the clear morning sky while they were still catching their breaths. After she felt that her strength had come back, she got herself up.

"I'll come back as soon as I can," she said, still half panting. Before he could respond, she stormed back to Pemberley. The morning sun started to peep out, and when she was about three metres away from the estate, she yelled out, calling the first person she met. After explaining what happened, she had about five men come with a stretcher back to where Fitz was.

The morning became chaos. The estate manager promptly organised someone to call a paramedic and get a first aid box while Fitz was taken to one of the lounge rooms in the centre wing.

Amelia did not know much about first aid, though she had gone for training before. She ordered someone to get a glass of water for Fitz and get him seated comfortably near the fireplace. She examined the wound closely before finally lifting her head and meeting his anxious gaze at her.

"It looks bad, does it?" he chuckled.

She only smirked. "I think you won't be able to walk without a cane for a couple of weeks.

Something in the way he looked at her made her heart stir. It was the tender gaze she used to see from him when they were in a relationship. It made her wonder whether his memory was starting to come back.

Their trance, unfortunately was severed with the presence of other Dalton relatives. Mrs De Boyville gasped in shock to see Fitz's condition before she made a wailing about the bad omen that Amelia had brought the moment she stepped into the house. Amelia winced slightly before cursing inwardly. She had her emotion in check, realising the presence of the rest of Dalton's relatives. Richard's parents, who had met her before, smiled at her congenially. Both of them rolled their eyes behind Mrs De Boyville before diverting the conversation into something pleasant.

"Luckily, he is found alive," commented Richard's mother - Mrs Matlock. "By the very same girlfriend."

Mrs De Boyville only scoffed, but it made her quiet.

Georgie and Richard appeared afterwards. For a moment both of them looked shocked while Amelia explained what happened. While Georgie sat at her brother's side and hugged him in relief, Richard immediately crushed her under his arm and lifted her petite body in the air for a few seconds.

"You're a real hero!" he exclaimed before placing her down, cupping her face and pressing his lips on hers briefly, which was enough to make her body stiff. Her cheeks were warm, and she felt relieved that the others did not seem to notice. However, her eyes caught Fitz who saw everything suspiciously.

The paramedic came soon afterwards, examined Fitz's wound, and brought him to the nearby hospital for some stitches. Amelia accompanied him in the hospital until the afternoon when Fitz was finally discharged with the doctor's note that he needed to come back three days later for another check-up. It seemed Fitz would be unable to do much for the Christmas party tonight. He seemed resigned to sit on the couch with his leg lifted for the whole day. It was a visualisation that was enough to make Richard unceasingly laugh and mock his cousin.

The party still went ahead anyway. Amelia felt her jetlag start to get on her, however she could not avoid the party. She refreshed herself with a warm shower before getting dressed in the V-neck long-sleeved dress that she bought with Lana's help. This time, she put on her prosthetic hand and briefly took a deep breath while checking on her appearance before finally leaving her room.

She felt anxious at the prospect of meeting The Dalton's extended relatives. So far, she only had met Mrs De Boyville and Richard's parents. Perhaps, she had actually met most of them at last year's masquerade charity ball, however she was not introduced to them officially at that time. She wondered what kind of stories Mrs De Boyville had fed to the rest of

Dalton's relatives regarding her. Whatever it was, she could not change or prevent it. She just had to raise her courage for any attempt to intimidate her.

Richard came to pick her up. He offered his arm, then his left hand warmly squeezed her hand. When they entered the hall where the party was held, she noticed some people sneering at them. She took it lightly as she had expected it anyway. She followed Richard to where Fitz was seated. Fitz's eyes seemed to light up when he saw her, making her feel a jolt through her body. However, she was mortified when a woman walked past from behind her and gave Fitz a light kiss on his cheek.

Amelia felt her body stiffened, wondering who that woman was. She was beautiful and elegant with her light-coloured hair and a flattering slim lithe figure wrapped in her white sack dress. The woman reminded her of her sister, except this woman was slightly shorter than Lana with different hair colour.

"That is Anne," whispered Richard. "Mrs De Boyville's favourite girl. She works at one of Dalton's subsidiaries. Pretty chick, and of course, has been eyeing Fitz for a while."

Amelia pursed her lips, feeling the heaviness in her heart. The thought of contemplating why she came here haunted her again. Clearly, Fitz remembered Anne from the way he talked to her comfortably. *But he still could not remember me*, she thought bitterly.

Richard tried to distract her by introducing her to the rest of Dalton's extended relatives. Some of them gracefully greeted her, but some of them looked at her under their nose. Amelia knew these were something that she would face anyway if she had a relationship with Fitz. But was she still in a relationship with Fitz now?

After being introduced to all the guests, she excused herself to the restroom before stealing a glance at where Fitz was. Fitz was seated on the couch, and the beautiful Anne had herself sitting on a single couch beside him while joining the conversation with anyone who approached him. It seemed that Anne was Fitz's girlfriend, not her. The sight made her sick, and she could not wait but leave the room.

The restroom was a good brief escape to clear her mind before she gathered her courage again. While she walked back to the party, she saw

Fitz entering his study room with the help of a steward who supported him with his shoulder.

Amelia launched and offered to take over. The steward seemed hesitant, noticing that she was much shorter than Fitz but too polite to argue. Quietly Amelia felt relieved that Fitz did not argue it either.

Once Fitz was seated on the couch, and his leg was placed correctly, Amelia walked over to the console table to get him a glass of water. He took the glass from her hand while giving her a stern look. It pierced her heart, but she had to accept it. Her fingers fiddled with the side of her dress, rubbing the excessive sweat in her hand while she watched him finishing his drink.

"I wonder what your intention is." His voice broke the silence between them.

Amelia braced herself to look at him and waited. She did not understand what he meant and the direction of their conversation.

"You're here as my girlfriend, but it seems to me you are acting like Richard's girlfriend."

Her mouth fell open. *Acting like Richard's girlfriend??*

"Are you referring to when he introduced me to your relatives?" she quizzed.

"Yes, but that was not the only one. You even welcomed his affection to you. He kissed you on the lips this morning."

"He is your cousin. We are mates only," she answered after a quick breath.

He held his gaze upon her firmly while his hand moved to take a piece of folded paper from his blazer. Amelia furrowed her brow, wondering about the paper's content when he unfolded it and gave it to her.

"Regardless of whether you are after Richard or me, you are just a liar."

His intense cold gaze penetrated her heart and made her body stiff. She was unsure how she could still get the strength to take the piece of paper from him and read it.

"You have been lying to all of us for something simple, even like your name. Then perhaps you can tell me now what your real intention is. Is it money? Since now I lost my memory about you, you changed your target to Richard while gaining sympathy from Georgie? That sounds like a perfect plan, does it?"

His tense voice was like an echo hovering over her. Amelia read the paper in her hand with a shaky breath. It was a report from the Registry of Births, Deaths and Marriages regarding her official legal name. She saw the date of the report was over a month ago before Fitz had the accident and memory loss.

She did not understand. Why did he check on her legal name? Throughout their relationship, she never interfered with his legal business matters. They even discussed that she did not want him to interfere with her family's financial debt. So why did he do this instead of asking her if he had any doubt about her legal name?

"Why..?" Her voice was caught in her throat. She cleared her throat while gathering her strength to speak. "Why were you checking my legal name?"

He gave her a hard squint. "I believe because I knew that you were hiding something. It's a typical scam. You are known by another name, so you will not be easily tracked when you decide to disappear after you get what you want."

She wasn't sure whether she should laugh at that theory. That was insane! Was he thinking that she was going to steal money from him?

She made a false sound of chuckling. "So, now you think I'm going to steal something from here?"

"I know you have a much better plan than that," he responded, still with a contemptuous smirk on his face.

She could feel the prick in her eyes as her tears threatened to roll down. She bit her lips, and clenched her fist, crumpling the paper in her palm. She paced around the room, trying to restrain her anguish as her heart sank with his accusation.

As comprehension dawned on her, she laughed bitterly. "You are just trying to get rid of me, aren't you?" Her voice cracked with emotion. "I know you have every reason to fight your feelings toward me."

He seemed taken aback as his eyes blinked a couple of times with a furrowed brow. When he recovered, he was back to his impassive look. For a moment they just stared at each other. Amelia took a quiet breath, realising that her eyes already welled in tears, and he – the man she loved – only looked at her - stoic, with narrowed eyes. She had been stupid to come to this place all the way from down under, thinking that she might still be able to salvage their relationship when perhaps that relationship never existed. He never trusted her.

"Why do you lie about your name?" he pushed the question again.

She gritted her teeth in anguish. "I do not lie about my name. I am an Amelia! How dare you to investigate me," she hissed in anger.

"Just tell me how much you need," he snapped curtly. "I suppose having Charlie as your brother-in-law would help to alleviate your family's financial difficulties slightly. With my respect to him as my best friend, I will not pursue this matter further. Tell me how much you need, and stay away from Georgie and Richard."

Amelia could imagine her face blanching as her chest tightened and restricted her breath. Her head was heavy and dizzy. This was the old Fitz that she knew, who was consumed by his vanity, looked down on her and her family because of their financial disadvantage, who had accused her sister of marrying Charlie for his wealth. Her Fitz, who declared his love for her, had gone and would possibly never come back.

She gathered her courage to look at him for the last time. "Merry Christmas, Fitz," she said softly. He looked astonished. "I wish you get well soon." She forced herself a weak smile and stormed out of the room.

Though her heart and brain were still shattered, she was determined to leave without letting Richard and Georgie know. If they knew, they would try to convince her to stay. She slipped to her room, quickly packed up her luggage in a matter of minutes. One of the stewards helped her hail a taxi for her without question, thinking she was probably one of the non-private guests.

It was snowy outside on Christmas Eve. While her taxi was driving slowly to the airport, she only stared blankly outside the window. *It is over,* she thought. Their relationship was bound to end anyway. She did not care anymore if anyone thought she gave up on their relationship too easily.

She was lucky that she still could get a flight back to Melbourne that night despite being Christmas Eve. Christmas songs were echoing in the airport, accompanying her stroll to the boarding gate.

Last Christmas

I gave you my heart

And the very next day, you gave it away.

She smiled bitterly to herself. Of all the Christmas songs that she knew, she never liked that song. But many people loved it, and every year it had been a must to be played Christmas song despite it had nothing to do with Jesus' birth. She looked heavenward and scoffed, thinking that God was perhaps also laughing at her.

Before getting on board, she knew she could not simply disappear. She had to let at least Richard and Georgie know about her whereabouts, so she sent them a text. She felt guilty that she had disappointed them, however this was for the best.

Usually, she never looked forward to a long flight. However, this time she felt grateful for it. A twenty-four hours flight would help her to have some peace to herself, mauled and cried over what had happened, then gather her spirit back to put the past behind. She promised herself the moment she touched down in Melbourne, she would be herself again.

As an Amelia.

Going Back to Where It Began

Amelia fixed her eyes on the road ahead of her while listening to the upbeat Bruno Mars songs and enjoying the fresh air from the grassland on the surrounding scenery. She was on a road trip to Adelaide to see her old best friend, Sharon, who had just delivered a baby girl a month ago. Since Sharon's wedding over a year ago, she had not had a chance to visit her. So Sharon's offer to come to Adelaide and help with the newborn was quite tempting for her. Moreover, it came at a good time since she needed to escape from her family after the disastrous Christmas trip to Pemberley.

It had been four weeks since she came back from Pemberley. Lana happened to be visiting when she reached home. They knew she was supposed to be back three weeks later, but it had not even been a week, and she had come back. She avoided her sister and her father's look before hiding in her room. She thought she was ready to face them, but it was not as easy as she had thought.

Three days afterwards, Lana managed to get her to speak about what happened. Her sister was such an angel who never thought negatively of other people. She did not try to defend Fitz's action, however she believed Fitz might have another reason for investigating her legal name. No one knew the reason until Fitz could regain his memory, and no one knew when that would happen. Regardless, Amelia knew he did not want to see her anymore.

Richard and Georgie had been trying to contact her from the moment she touched down in Melbourne. She answered their video call once and hated herself for being unable to control her tears. When Richard and Georgie tried to talk her out, she abruptly ended their phone call. The subsequent phone calls were simply ignored, and any text messages never been replied to. Her only reply was her apology that she had given up.

A road trip was her favourite time to be in her solitude. However, the image of Fitz still easily haunted her. They had a couple of road trips together during their relationship, and those sweet times would be just another memory between them

When she entered Sharon's house spacious front yard, she had a little second thought. Perhaps being here was not entirely a good idea. She passed by the winery where Sharon had her wedding, and where Colin had been working. Inevitably she was reminded again of the time when she and Fitz had their accidental first kiss. She took a heavy breath and shook her head, wishing he would disappear from her mind. But she knew everything took time.

When she arrived, she noticed the dark circle on Sharon's puffy eyes. Her old friend looked exhausted, probably caused by sleepless nights with the newborn. However, the friendly and warm smile was still drawn on her friend's lips when she opened the door for her.

"Oh, Liz. It's been a while," greeted Sharon while they hugged each other tightly.

Amelia felt she had come at the right time when her friend needed her the most. Sharon's mother could not help her due to her health issue. Colin's mother lived in England; meanwhile, Colin had been busy working. Occasionally, a nanny and a cleaner came to the house, but Sharon still needed to be available 24/7 for her needy baby girl. Amelia perhaps did not know much about looking after a baby, but at least she could help to watch over the baby so Sharon could get some rest.

"Let's get you a drink," said Sharon while ushering her inside. They walked through the high-raked ceiling hallway with huge modern paintings and a wall-to-wall glass window facing the inner garden of the house, before reaching the living room with the open-plan kitchen area. In the past, Sharon had been excited to show her beautiful grand home. Now that she was here, her friend did not have any energy to even talk about it.

"Don't worry about me, Sharon." Amelia pulled her friend to the sofa to sit down. A second later, she could hear a soft whine from the bassinet in the room. She smiled while approaching the sound. Her heart immediately melted when she saw the tiny cute beautiful baby girl in it wrapped in a soft pink muslin wrap.

"She's so adorable," whispered Amelia, realising the baby's eyes were closed. "What's her name again? Adele, isn't it?"

"Yes, that's correct. Her name is Adele."

Amelia squeezed her friend's shoulder tightly. "Congratulations, Sharon. She's gorgeous."

Sharon still had her tired smile on her face and took a sigh. Her eyes were almost in tears. "She's so difficult. She always cries most of the time. I don't know how to console her. I only managed to put her down like a minute before you came. Now she falls asleep perhaps because she is too tired crying."

"Why don't you have a rest while she's sleeping?" Amelia motioned her friend away from the bassinet. "Don't worry about me."

Sharon wanted to argue, but Amelia managed to persuade her to go to the bedroom. When the house became quiet, baby Adele started to whine. Sharon stormed out of her room, but Amelia pushed her to return, assuring her that she would care for Adele.

"Don't worry. I won't lift her up if that's your concern. I will just wheel the bassinet around."

Sharon nodded and agreed with the idea. "Please wake me up in two hours. That's her next breastfeeding time," she said, sluggishly walking back to her room.

Amelia kept her promise that she would not lift Adele from the bassinet. She had never held a baby before, and she would understand if people doubted her ability to hold a baby when she only had one hand. She wheeled around the bassinet while quietly humming. It seemed to work as Adele's whinge slowly dissipated. She kept wheeling the bassinet around a few more until Adele was fully in her deep sleep. She reached for her mobile to turn on the alarm and played some soft music on it while breaking a satisfying smile on her successful trick. She sat on the sofa and closed her eyes to finally drift to sleep too.

When the alarm went off, she almost leapt from the sofa. Luckily Adele was still sleeping peacefully. Sharon's room door flew open, and her friend appeared still looking sluggish.

"She's still sleeping. Perhaps she's not hungry yet," commented Amelia. "Would you like me to make a sandwich for you?"

Sharon nodded without uttering any word as she had no energy to respond.

Amelia felt amused as she was helping herself in the house as if she lived there. She could imagine the terrified look from Colin if he saw her acting like this. She opened the fridge and took out items she could use to make a sandwich. She even helped herself with a bottle of cider while preparing lunch.

When she looked at the label of her bottle, she took a quiet sigh realising that Dalton's winery produced the drink. She should have expected this. It would never be easy to get rid of Fitz from her mind.

The shrieking sound of a door opening from the entrance, followed by footsteps coming to the kitchen area, made Sharon furrow her brow. The sound awakened Adele and made her cry. Amelia was immediately on her guard, wondering whether it was an intruder. It was not dark yet, and it seemed Sharon was not expecting Colin to get home this early. Sharon quickly took her baby into her arms while Amelia walked towards the hallway. They were startled to see their unexpected visitors but took a relieved sigh afterwards.

"Sorry, dear, I did not mean to frighten you," said Colin. He smiled sheepishly and strode towards his wife and gave her and his baby a kiss.

Amelia froze when she saw another person who came behind Colin. She held her breath as their eyes met. He was the person who had been haunting her, and she could not believe that now he had appeared before her eyes in the flesh. His expression was impassive, though she felt the way he looked at her was not as cold as before.

She wondered what he was doing here. Sharon mentioned to her before that Fitz only paid an annual visit to this winery for a short meeting. During their relationship, she planned to join him in coming here for the meeting while she could pay a visit to her friend. Obviously, as their relationship ended, the plan was never realised. So, could it be this time he was due for the meeting? She could not understand why she had been so unlucky.

"Hi, Mr Dalton," greeted Sharon politely. "I didn't know you were coming."

"Yeah, Mr Dalton just arrived this morning in his private helicopter," explained Colin before Fitz could reply. "There are a few business matters that we need to discuss." He arched his eyebrow towards Amelia. "I am sorry that you have to meet Miss Bettney here as well, Mr Dalton."

Amelia winced but pretended she did not hear it and focused back on making the sandwich. From the corner of her eyes, she saw Sharon was elbowing her husband.

A loud cry from Adele distracted all of them. Sheepishly, Sharon excused herself for Adele's breastfeeding time. With her friend leaving the room, Amelia felt bereft, as if she had just lost her protection shield. Now she had to face not only her friend's annoying husband but also the person that she desperately wanted to avoid. She tried to calm herself by grabbing her bottle and sipping it while giving both Fitz and Colin a firm look.

"Can I help you both with any drink?" she offered.

"No, thank you." Both men replied almost at the same time.

"Don't you think you should stop drinking alcohol?" Fitz's voice boomed while he strode towards her. An island kitchen bench separated them, but he shifted the bottle away from her before Amelia responded. Amelia's brows knitted seeing that.

"I don't think that's good for the baby," he continued.

Her mouth fell open before slowly breaking into a smirk. The handsome broad shouldered man in front of her, absolutely had confused her with someone else.

"Oh, Sharon doesn't drink alcohol," Colin's voice piped in. "She has stopped since she got pregnant. I believe my Sharon knows how alcohol could harm the baby."

Amelia's eyes moved to Colin before returning to Fitz, who stood intimidatingly in front of her. His stern eyes never left her, which made her wonder whether he heard what Colin said.

"The drink is mine. Not Sharon's. " She extended her hand to reach her bottle back but gasped when his hand grabbed it instead.

"What I mean is your baby," he said with a low voice.

She was probably too shocked and forgot to breathe in. Her jaw dropped, her eyes were rapidly blinking, and her mind was racing, wondering what it meant.

"I'm not....," she couldn't help but stutter. "My baby? I think you have mistaken me for Sharon, Mr Dalton. I am not Sharon."

"Georgie found a pregnancy test with a positive result in the house, not long after your last visit."

"In Pemberley?"

"No. In my Melbourne's house."

Her mind flew immediately to her sister Lana. Her lips broke into a wide grin as her body shook with her inaudible laugh, which subsequently roared. She laughed for a couple of minutes like a madwoman until her laughter subsided. Finally, she straightened her body while looking at both men's confused faces.

"Sorry, but that was....." she tried to make her face straight. "That was funny."

Colin gave her a bewildered look, but Fitz seemed displeased. "How so?"

"Can we talk outside?" she gestured her head towards the alfresco door that led to the backyard. "Just us, Mr Dalton."

Fitz did not answer but followed her after giving Colin a stern look not to disobey the instruction.

It was a fresh summer afternoon. The house's backyard was huge, with a swimming pool, a spacious lawn and a pavilion at the corner. Amelia knew the pavilion would be the perfect place for them to talk, away from any potential Colin eavesdropping effort.

For a moment there was only silence between them. Amelia turned around to see the man she loved, standing before her with two hands in his pockets and eyes down to the floor. He looked like a boy that was about to receive a verdict for the mistake that he made. It made her wonder what was in his mind now. He thought she was pregnant and was it why he was here? She thought he didn't want her anymore?

"That is not my pregnancy test result." Her voice broke the silence. He looked up at her, surprised. "I cannot tell whose it is right now. Rest assured, it's not mine. And anyway, we never did it." She took a heavy sigh. "We never slept together."

She lied. In truth, they had their first sex not long before the accident on the night after his birthday party. It was the first, and it took her almost a year to finally be ready for it. It began with gentle tentative touches, ensuring they were comfortable and enjoying it before it escalated into passionate lovemaking. Recalling the memory made her chest tight again with a broken heart.

Did it matter if she lied? His memory of her had gone anyway. With his accusation of her as a liar, a white lie would be nothing.

"Do you mean the night that we had after my birthday party did not mean anything to you?"

She was stunned. He gazed at her intently. It was the tender gaze that he showered upon her throughout their relationship. A blush slowly crept to her cheek as she realised that his memory of her might have returned. She looked at him with pursed lips and a tight clutch to the side of her jeans.

"My memory about us is still bits and pieces. But I think I remember that night," he said sheepishly.

She scoffed. "Perhaps what you remembered was not with me".

She would not be surprised if he slept with other women. They had not been seeing each other for two months since the accident. Perhaps he had even slept with that gorgeous Anne girl. She couldn't deny her heart was not only broken after that Christmas in Pemberley but also filled with jealousy recalling how he was very comfortable sitting beside Anne.

"No, I'm pretty sure it was you."

"How could you be so sure? Because you had it with a woman with only one hand? Don't you feel sick when that memory suddenly struck you?"

He closed his eyes briefly before answering with a heavy sigh. "Yes, I knew it was you. With your magic hand and your beautiful eyes." He lifted his guilt-ridden eyes while shoving his hair. "No, I didn't feel sick about it. On the other hand, I feel it was a great night that we had."

She swallowed hard. She knew it was cruel of her to say those words. Inevitably her eyes welled in tears, and her chin trembled. She clenched her fist and turned away from him.

She had enough tears on her way back home from Pemberley. She had promised herself not to shed any more tears once she was in Melbourne. She had to understand that he had an accident, and the things he said were beyond his control because of his memory problem. But on the other hand, she couldn't help but feel hurt by his recent cold behaviour towards her.

After what seemed like an eternity of silence, she heard a movement behind her, and her fingers were softly touched

"I'm so sorry for what happened," he whispered. She could feel his warm breath on her neck and his warm chest behind her. How she longed for that in the last couple of months. However, that blissful moment was unfortunately only short-lived as Collin called their names and came to them hastily.

"Mr Dalton, Mrs De Boyville has asked me to ensure you're away from Miss Bettney. With your recent accident, you are currently still confused and being with her will make it worse."

Amelia turned her face away as she rolled her eyes. Even though Mrs De Boyville was not here, Colin's presence was sufficiently infuriating. She only cursed inwardly.

"I appreciate your concern, Colin. I'm alright. Please leave us alone," replied Fitz firmly. However, Colin was not giving up.

"Mr Dalton, I'm here to assure Mrs De Boyville that you are comfortable. Please let us go inside. I will drive you back to the winery, so you can rest well there."

Fitz inhaled a long breath. "I'm comfortable here, Colin. If you don't mind, of course. I understand this is your house."

"Of course, I don't mind, Mr Dalton. But, unfortunately, this is not a good time. If it's not my dear Sharon's generous invite to Miss Bettney, certainly I will not let her be here."

Amelia's mouth was slackening before she scoffed. Colin was unbelievably rude. She couldn't believe that Sharon could end up with this man. She threw her glance to Fitz's tightening face. A couple of times he flinched while holding his head in pain.

"Mr Dalton, let me help you," said Colin while pulling Fitz's arm gently. "You need to stay away from Miss. Bettney. She only makes your headache get worse. Let me take you back to the winery."

"I'm fine, Colin!" Fitz snapped while pulling out his hand from Colin's grip. Still, it did not discourage Colin from keeping his prattle.

"Mr Dalton, I know this is confusing for you right now. Mrs De Boyville has the greatest concern for you. Please adhere to her instruction."

Fitz again shut his eyes tightly as his face pinched in pain. Amelia knew things could get worse if Colin kept talking. Before she could speak, Sharon suddenly appeared while carrying the crying Adele in her arms.

"Colin, please give me a hand. Adele just had reflux," called Sharon.

"My dear, I have an important duty here from Mrs De Boyville to take care of Mr Dalton. Could you please get Amelia away from here?"

Amelia almost couldn't believe her hearing. She was more than ready to punch that man if it was not because Sharon gave her an apologetic look.

"Colin, please. Adele is crying non-stop. I need your help," pleaded Sharon.

Amelia shook her head in disbelief and quickly approached her friend, leaving behind the pavilion and the two men. Sharon only gave her a guilt-ridden look while both of them went back inside the house.

While she was cleaning up the vomit mess on the living area floor, Sharon changed Adele's clothes and nappy. Colin and Fitz came in when she had finished the cleaning. Fitz looked tired and dishevelled while he shoved his hair agitatedly. Meanwhile, Colin was continuing his prattle. Amelia did not know whether she should take pity on him or not, but knowing Fitz's character, she knew his patience was thinning out. Nevertheless, she did not wish Fitz to say anything unpleasant to the host, especially with Sharon's presence.

"I'll drive you back to the winery," she said. Fitz's eyes lit up with the offer. However, Colin's annoying voice interrupted them.

"No, you can't do that, Amelia. You are not supposed to be anywhere near Mr Dalton. I'll drive him back, and could you please give Sharon a hand if she needs anything?"

Amelia wished she could retort that sentence back. Was he giving her an order? Again, if it was not because of Sharon, she would probably punch her friend's husband.

"Colin, please stay back. I need your help. Adele has been unsettled," sniffled Sharon.

"My dear, you should understand. I am still working here," replied Colin agitatedly.

"Colin, I suggest you stay with your wife and daughter. I'm going back to the winery with Amelia." Fitz's firm and stern voice was finally heard.

Colin shook his head like an old man trying to scold a little child. "Mr Dalton, you should listen to Mrs De Boyville's instruction. I won't let Miss Bettney come near you."

"If you prefer to listen to Mrs De Boyville's instruction rather than my instruction or your wife's pleading, then I assure you we will have a very difficult meeting tomorrow. You will not like it, Colin," growled Fitz while giving the man who was shorter than him a sharp glare.

Colin gasped but still did not deter him from opening his mouth and talking. "But, Mr Dalton, this is for your own good."

"Once again, I appreciate your concern. But I can make my own decision."

"Mrs De Boyville said you are not in the capacity to make a rational decision because of your memory problem."

Amelia felt dizzy, couldn't believe that this conversation kept going on. She felt terrible when her eyes met with Sharon's and how her friend was on the edge of tears, feeling upset too.

Fitz's jaw was tense. Amelia knew he had been restraining his anger too long out of respect for Sharon as her best friend. She knew if she did not do anything, he might say something unpleasant in front of Sharon regarding her husband. She quickly took her bag and got herself ready to go.

"Let's go, Mr Dalton. Let me drop you off. I still need to come back here as soon as possible to help my friend whose husband is reluctant to give her a hand with his own baby," she said cynically. Fitz understood what she was trying to do and followed her to the door. However, unexpectedly Colin jumped beside her and grabbed her little left arm.

"I will not let you come any closer to Mr Dalton, Amelia. You're out of your line!"

Amelia was stunned. Before she reacted, Colin's hand was snatched, so her little hand was dropped.

"Don't you dare touch her, Colin," hissed Fitz. His voice sounded deadly, and his eyes glared sharply. Colin's face immediately turned ashes as his eyes bulged, and his body was in tremors.

"Mr Dalton, please let me go, " he whimpered. "My hand hurts."

Fitz was not listening. His hand was still gripping Colin's hand tightly, which made Colin cringe in pain.

"I warn you once again, Colin," growled Fitz. "If you still do not wish to listen to my instruction or your wife's plead for help, I assure you we will have a difficult meeting tomorrow about your future career. You're the one that was out of line. Don't you dare touch my fiancé again!" He roughly released his grip.

Amelia's eyebrow shot up. Sharon's mouth fell open, and she inaudibly said the word 'fiance' to her with a hint of a smile on her face. She shook her head, indicating she had no idea at all about being engaged to anyone.

Colin's slowly nodded his head to finally understand his boss' order. He lowered his head, too embarrassed to see his guests in the eyes.

With Colin finally stopped talking, the room turned to be awkwardly silent. Amelia threw a meaningful glance at her friend, who only nodded understandably. She dashed to the door and heard Fitz's voice saying goodbye to Sharon politely before following her.

The winery was only about five minutes drive from Colin's house. There was only silence between them during the journey, and Amelia also felt there was nothing much to be talked about. She knew Fitz was still confused about them. She could see it from his wary eyes.

Amelia pulled up the car in the winery entrance driveway but did not turn off her car engine. For a moment she couldn't help but notice his appearance, which always made her heart stir. Perhaps any woman's heart would. He was dressed semi-casual in his blazer, with the top part of his shirt unbuttoned, without a tie and showing his bare neck. His attire made his broad shoulders even more prominent, and his five o clock shadow only made his jaw feature more masculine. His tousled hair made him look more boyish. She resisted moving forward to kiss him, something that she used to do during their relationship.

"Will you come inside?" His voice broke the silence as he looked at her hesitantly.

Amelia shook her head. "No, I'll go back to Sharon's."

He looked disappointed. "I think we need to talk. Many things that we need to talk about."

"I don't think your memory about us has fully come back. I don't want to make you more confused. You are still not yourself."

He winced slightly. "Why do you say that? I remember about us."

"You said it earlier. It is still in bits and pieces. I do not want to overwhelm you. You were overreacting earlier when Colin tried to stop me. I think you don't remember I am trained in self-defence. You even told Colin that we are engaged." She scoffed. "We are not engaged."

His mouth bobbed like a fish, but no words were uttered. Instead, slowly he closed his lips tightly.

"How about tomorrow?"

"I come here to help Sharon. As you can see, her husband is not very helpful."

"I miss you. I miss us."

She was taken aback, and their eyes met. His gaze upon her was tender, full of affection that she used to receive from him. It was something that she had missed from him since the accident. She quickly looked away with a tingling feeling within her.

"How did you remember?"

He took a deep breath. "I think when you were in Pemberley." He smiled sadly. "I always wanted to bring you to Pemberley since we were together, but the moment you were there, I made you leave the place."

She was only quietly listening.

"When you saved me from the edge of the hill, it brought some flashes from the past. When we argued before you left Pemberley, somehow, the fire in your eyes brought back some memories again. Since you left, I have had more headaches, but it jolted more memories about us. I know I have to find you. I returned to Melbourne a week ago, and I knew you wouldn't answer my call since you did not even answer Richard or

Georgie's call. I came here for a short business meeting with Colin. When he took me to his home, I was merely being polite to wish Sharon a congratulation for her newborn. I was thrilled that I met you instead."

She stared blankly at the shrub that was surrounding the driveway. Deep inside, she was relieved that his memory of her had recovered. However, she was unsure what it meant for their relationship. Perhaps things happened for a reason, and she was resolute that they were not meant to be.

She was startled as his hand landed gently on her arm.

"Could you please stay? There's a lot that we need to talk about."

She shook her head again. "I can't. I told you, I'm here to help Sharon. I am going back to her place. Besides...," she looked at him with a mischievous grin. "After what happened today, I'm pretty sure you will have another visitor tomorrow."

He furrowed his brow.

"We have seen to whom Colin has been most loyal to."

He scoffed while she laughed softly. Another momentary silence between them for a couple of minutes. Amelia gathered her courage to look at him again.

"Good night, Fitz," her voice was almost above a whisper. "I think you need to go."

He shut his eyes briefly before returning her look with his sad eyes.

"Good night," he replied.

Reluctantly he opened the door and jumped out of the car. He was standing in the car park, watching her reverse the car and leave.

From the rear mirror, Amelia saw his tall figure retreating. She could feel the prick in her eyes as her tears slowly rolled down her cheek. She knew she should have rejoiced that his memory of her had returned, however her doubt about their relationship had haunted her. She believed she had tried to fight for it, but with his memory loss and the last conversation they had in Pemberley, all her faith in their relationship seemed to have gone.

The Reconciliation

Amelia woke up early the next day when she heard the sound of a soft whine and cry belonged to Adele. She assumed Sharon would be attending to her baby and perhaps was breastfeeding her in the nursery room. She decided to get up and freshen up to help her friend. Instead, she found Sharon in the living room with no sign of Colin being around.

"Colin has gone to work," said Sharon as if she could read her mind when her eyes were wandering around.

"Oh? This early? Does he always go to work this early?" Amelia looked at the clock on the wall near the kitchen island bench. It was just 7 am.

Sharon nodded. "I think because Mr Dalton is here."

Amelia grinned mischievously. "Or because Mrs De Boyville is coming?"

Amelia was sure that Colin must have immediately reported what happened yesterday to Mrs De Boyville. She would not be surprised if that lady flew all the way from England to ensure she could not touch Fitz. That old lady had done it before and rejoiced in her success of separating Fitz and her.

"Mr Dalton called him for an important meeting this morning." Sharon took a sigh. "Perhaps about yesterday. I'm so sorry about yesterday, Liz."

Amelia was drinking her juice. She shook her head while her mouth was still full. "Don't be silly, Sharon," she said after she swallowed her drink.

"Mr Dalton looked very angry when Colin grabbed your hand. I had never seen him that angry before. And, is that true? You're engaged to him?"

Amelia quickly shook her head again. "No, we are not." She imagined the word engagement would sound dramatic when Colin delivered the news to Mrs De Boyville. "You know about his memory problem, right? I think he gets me confused with someone else."

"You mean there's someone else?"

Amelia shrugged. "Perhaps by now, yeah. He had the accident for over two months ago now. During that time, he was away in Pemberley for over a month. I know there is a pretty girl who has been eyeing him." The image of Anne and Fitz talking comfortably in the lounge of Pemberley came back to her mind, which made her heart burn.

Sharon held her smile. "That's not how I interpret it, Liz. From the way he looks at you." Her voice trailed. "Sometimes I wish Colin would see me that way."

Amelia could sense the sadness in her friend's voice. Was it a regret? She remembered her mission here. She would try her best to lift her friend's spirit again. Having a baby could be quite overwhelming for a first-time mother, she heard. There could be a feeling of remorse and distance, especially with the partner. Though she was not experienced with babies, at least she could relieve Sharon throughout the day so her friend could have her own 'me' time

And that was exactly what she did for the whole day. While Sharon had her breakfast and lunch, enjoyed morning tea and afternoon tea, and sometimes watched TV and drifted to sleep, Amelia diligently attended to baby Adele. She played with her, hummed for her and wheeled the bassinet for her to sleep. She had to admit that Adele was not easy to settle. She also helped to prepare lunch for both of them with whatever she could find in the fridge and ensured that the house was tidy and clean. It was a tiring job, and she now understood how much a baby could take so much of her mother's time.

When the time showed 4 pm, Amelia was startled to hear the sound of the door opening. Colin came immediately to the living area where they had been lingering around. Adele just had her feed and looked content. However, she whined when she saw her dad. Amelia would not be surprised if the baby treated her own dad like a stranger. She believed Colin perhaps never even helped to change a nappy or even bothered to try it.

What surprised her was Colin smiled beamingly at them. She did not expect to be one of the recipients of that warm smile. The smile made him look like a sympathetic guy.

"Mrs De Boyville is inviting us for dinner tonight. In the winery restaurant," informed Colin.

Amelia laughed inwardly. She knew this would happen. Colin must have fed Mrs De Boyville with very interesting news yesterday. And the old lady would not let even a second slip away to come here, ensuring she would not be able to get close to Fitz.

"Oh, she's here?" Sharon was carrying Adele in her hand and walked towards her husband to let him give a small kiss to his baby, which made Adele whinge away.

"Yes! And she's inviting all of us to dinner. Including you, Amelia. She knows you're here and is looking forward to seeing you."

Amelia raised her eyebrow. "Is she?" The reason Mrs De Boyville would be excited to see her was either to scrutinise her or laugh at her for her failed relationship with Fitz and her refusal of the generous offer extended to her last time. However, her courage would rise to any attempt to intimidate her.

Colin instructed his wife to get ready, and Amelia felt that was a signal for her to get ready. Thirty minutes later, all of them were already in Colin's car and ready to depart. Adele looked adorable in her pink little tutu bodysuit, which made Amelia smile. She sat in the passenger seat together with the baby and played the rattle to entertain her. Adele initially cried when she was placed backward in the baby seat with her mother out of sight, however when she saw Amelia, she seemed entertained.

Amelia was relieved to listen to Lana's advice to bring along at least one summer dress. In general, she did not like to wear a dress, though she tried adding more dresses to her wardrobe since she was in a relationship with Fitz. Fitz had been inviting her along for some social events. She usually tried to find an excuse not to go, but she knew she could not keep doing that. She was not shy to see new people, but she was always afraid of being an embarrassment to Fitz. Some of Fitz's business acquaintances would give her mocking looks, but some would genuinely talk to her respectfully. Though she wore her prosthetic hand most of the time, it did not stop people from also talking behind her back about her background and how she was not from the same high-class circle as Fitz. The only reason she had the strength to face them was actually Fitz. It made her realise that she only needed Fitz's reassuring love and would not be afraid to face even dens of lions. However, when Fitz's memory of her was gone, she felt lost. She knew she did not belong to that society.

When they arrived, the waitress took them to their table. There were other customers filling half of the restaurant. The waitress took them to the best seat in the restaurant, near the semi-circle glass window, facing the winery scenery. Adele's bassinet stroller was placed near the table before they were seated.

A minute later, Amelia held her breath as she watched Fitz walking towards them. He was dazzlingly handsome with his dark grey casual suit and the white shirt beneath it. *As usual*, she thought. It was not that she was attracted to him solely because of his good looks. However, she had to admit that any woman would be attracted to him. She even noticed a couple of young ladies turning their heads to him when he stepped in. It was not the first time she always had a slip of doubt about why he wanted to be in a relationship with her. She felt his feeling towards her was genuine until the report about her legal name was found.

Amelia felt hurt every time she remembered that report. In the back of his mind, he must have still thought that she would somehow be eyeing his wealth, which was why he was investigating her life. He had the same thought about Lana before and tried to separate Lana and Charlie. She hated that his wealth attributes stood between them like a little thorn. It would be much easier if he were just an ordinary bloke.

She took a deep inhale, realising that he came closer to her, bent himself down and gave her a light peck on the cheek. She only returned it with a small smile while watching him do the same thing to Sharon.

The same waitress that helped them seated earlier came and took their order. Amelia furrowed her brow noticing that they had started ordering despite the absence of Mrs De Boyville.

"My aunt would be coming late. She sent her apology," informed Fitz.

No one questioned why. Amelia did not bother to ask why. She wondered, though, why Colin did not say anything. In fact, he was quieter than usual. *Was the threat from Fitz yesterday holding him back?*

Fitz took his seat exactly opposite her. With only four of them at the table, her choice was to see him directly face-to-face or sit close beside him. None of the options could make her pounding heart settle. She hated it and tried to take a couple of quiet deep breaths while hiding behind the menu book.

"The seafood here is the best," said Fitz. Amelia could feel, rather than see, that his eyes were at her. He used to know that she seldom eats seafood because she felt the price was dearer than other proteins. She was in fact, only started eating seafood because Fitz ordered it for her.

"That's true, Mr Dalton. I would recommend that you should give it a try too, my dear." Colin looked at his wife endearingly. Amelia noticed that Sharon blushed. *What made him so different today?* However, that was a good sign, especially remembering Sharon's little complaint this morning.

"We are very fortunate to have one of the Michelin star chef winners in the house tonight," declared Colin. "He will be here only for a couple of weeks. So we should not miss the opportunity to taste his best creation."

"Oh, who is he?" asked Amelia curiously. Sometimes she watched some cooking show, so perhaps she would recognise the name of the chef.

"You'll find out. He's coming out later to say 'Hi'," replied Fitz. As he spoke, a man with his white chef uniform walked towards them with a glowing smile on his face. He approached their table and nodded politely to all of them, though he addressed Fitz and Colin first.

Amelia could not believe her eyes. He was one of her favourites! She grinned like a little kid as he addressed her and asked what she would like. Amelia could feel the excitement within her as they spoke. After taking each of their order, he excused himself to the kitchen and prepared their order. Amelia thought it was like a dream to meet such a celebrity chef. She was giggling to herself when she realised that Fitz's eyes were on her watching her amusingly. Her cheeks became warm.

She did not understand why she felt this way. She could not deny that he had a different effect on her. There was a moment she thought that at least they could stay to be friends, especially now Lana and Charlie were married. There would be many occasions that they would likely bump into each other. However, her heart stirred most of the time when their eyes met. It was silly. It was like the first time when they started their relationship. It was not that those sparks had gone, however she felt silly, feeling like a young teenager.

Their appetizer came, accompanying their small chat about how the restaurant was run. Fitz politely asked Sharon about Adele and how things had changed since Amelia arrived. When their dinner came, Amelia started to feel odd as Mrs De Boyville was still absent.

"Your aunt is not here yet. Don't you think you want to check on her?"

Fitz swallowed his food carefully before he answered, "Yeah, perhaps I should. She told me earlier that she was a bit tired. Perhaps she had overslept. Colin, would you mind checking on her after you finish your dinner?"

Colin nodded his head immediately. "Of course."

Colin did not finish his dinner in a rushed manner and directed the conversation into some business matters. Amelia could feel he fidgeted several times before finally getting up from his seat. She felt the urge to go to the restroom too, so she also got up and excused herself.

When she was done in the restroom and ready to walk back to her table, her mobile phone rang. It was from Sharon. Her mind immediately thought that something was not right.

"Liz, I'm sorry that I have to leave first. Adele is very unsettled."

Amelia could sense the anxiety in her friend's voice, though she wondered what caused Adele to be unsettled. Adele looked alright before she went to the restroom earlier. However, she could not undermine a mother's instinct.

"Alright," replied Amelia. While waking past the reception area, she could see Colin's car leaving the driveway. It only came to her mind that she was left behind. How would she go back? However, she did not want to bother her friend and did not protest when the phone was hung up.

She thought she could walk back. It was not a short walk of ten kilometres, but she was sure she had the strength for the journey. However, when she saw the dark cloudy sky, she realised it would not be that straightforward. It seemed it was going to rain soon. Her only option was to ask Fitz for a lift. She returned to their table and saw Fitz standing up from his seat, welcoming her.

"I believe Sharon has told you that she has to rush back home because of Adele," he said. Amelia held her gaze at him, and whether it was her imagination only or not, she saw a ghost of a smile from the corner of his lips.

"Are you planning this?" she asked with a raised eyebrow.

Fitz only gave her a furrowed brow, seemingly not understanding what she meant. She knew he was only pretending. She recognised the very same expression before when he tried to trick or tease her. She couldn't believe now she had seen it again.

"Mrs De Boyville is not here, is she? Why do you use her name to get me coming here?"

"Because if I used my name to invite you here, I have a doubt you would accept the invitation."

She had to admit that he was correct. The reason she accepted the invitation was not that she wanted to see Mrs De Boyville obviously. She accepted it because out of respect for Sharon and Colin.

"I'm going to walk back." She swirled and dashed to the door. Unfortunately, the weather was not on her side. When she got to the porch, the rain poured down heavily.

"If you walk back in this weather, you would only get yourself sick." Fitz's voice was heard just behind her. "It happened the last time you did that. And you slept in my villa, on my bed instead." He gave her a mischievous smile.

She looked at him, astonished. He remembered! How much more of his memory about her had come back? She understood that he wanted her to stay this time because last night he failed to persuade her.

"I'm going to wait till the rain stops," she said firmly.

"If you want to wait, why don't you wait inside? We can have our dessert first. I think you'll love it because your favourite chef made it."

The offer tempted her. He knew she was a sweet tooth. And looking at the rain pouring, it would be a while until it stopped. By then, the street would be muddy and far from ideal for a walk. She was thinking about whether she could get a pair of boots to replace her summer shoes. Perhaps having a dessert before thinking of all those hassles was not a bad idea.

Hesitantly she entered the restaurant again, and this time she could feel his hand softly touching the small of her back. She closed her eyes briefly, realising how she missed that touch so much and how it made her heart tremble. However, she tried to remind herself that she would not be easily giving out her heart again. It had been crushed.

The dessert was served a few minutes after they sat in silence. It was her favourite dessert, the dark chocolate tiramisu. He knew it was her favourite and he had planned this for her. Her heart felt warm, and when their eyes met, she knew he was her Fitz again. She smiled bitterly.

"It seems your memory has come back fully," she said quietly while scooping the dessert with a small teaspoon into her mouth.

"Yes," he nodded. "I would say for a hundred percent. I remember the first time we met." He looked at their surroundings briefly. "When you confronted me over Charlie and Lana's breakup here. When we had a kiss afterwards."

"You kissed me," she corrected. "I did not kiss you."

He released a soft laugh. "That's right. I kissed you. And you fell sick, and I had a chance to cuddle you."

"It seems you took advantage of me a lot at that time."

She could see that he tried to make his face straight however his eyes were full of mirth. "That was the day I realised how strong my feeling toward you was," he said while giving her a soft deep gaze, which made her heart stir. She lowered her eyes to avoid it.

"I'm surprised your aunt is not here yet. I'm pretty sure Colin must have informed her that I'm coincidentally here as well with you. She must have thought I am trapping you like the time I was accidentally in Pemberley at the same time as the masquerade ball."

"Richard and Georgie managed to hold her back. And I had a good talk with Colin."

She raised her eyebrow with a smirk. "Are you threatening him?"

"Kinda," he chuckled.

"It seems to work. He did not try to stop you from organising this trick, right?"

"I told him that he needs to start using his parental leave. He hasn't used it since Adele was born. I think this is a good time."

"I'm here to help Sharon. I know she has been exhausted since she has Adele."

"That is why I said to him it's a good time. Sharon doesn't need you. She needs her husband." He took his glass and drank it, but his eyes never left her. "And you know Colin. He did not realise that. What he needs is a little nudge."

She smiled and had to admit that Fitz was correct. She would not be able to be here for the long term to help Sharon. In the end, it was Colin as her husband, who needed to work as a team with her to raise their baby.

Suddenly Fitz's hand was already on her hand that was holding the spoon. She was startled and enjoyed the first minute of his warm hand. However, she slowly pulled it while avoiding his eyes. She could hear his sigh.

"Amelia, I'm sorry for what happened. You know the accident was beyond my control. I never planned to lose my memory afterwards. I hate myself for having forgotten you. Please, you have to give me another chance." His voice was raspy with desperation.

"I don't blame you for the accident and your memory loss," she replied while slowly gathering her courage to lift her eyes. "It's just...." She could feel the prick of tears in her eyes and restrained herself not to blink. "I think it's better if we just stay as friends."

"I want to be with you. I don't want us just to be friends. Since the moment I had lost my memory, you were always around for me, though I hate to admit that my behaviour towards you was inexcusable. But ..."

His voice faltered, and he shifted his seat towards her closer. She was wondering with high apprehension what he was about to do next. Her hand was again enveloped closed with both his hands. He knew she wanted to pull her hand again, but he held her back.

"Please listen to me, Amelia." He lifted her hand and held it close to his lips. "You make me fall in love with you all over again. Despite my memory loss, I started to have feelings toward you. I admitted I was confused looking at how close you were with Richard, which somehow made me feel jealous without realising it."

"But you tried to keep denying the feeling." She couldn't help but smile bitterly. "Like you did last time too."

"You must understand that I was not fully myself." He quickly interjected and closed his eyes briefly in anguish. "I was still in disbelief that

I could be in a relationship with someone like you, but the more I tried to fight the feeling, the more it jolted the memory about us. Initially, I thought it was just infatuation, but then slowly, I realised we already had something together, and it was real. I realised how much error I've made, and I immediately flew here with a determination that I want you back. I almost lost you last time, and I do not want to lose you again."

Amelia pursed her lips and did not dare to look at him. She could feel the heat from his intense gaze on her, and the way he still held her hand in his while softly rubbing his thumb on it, made her heart tremble. It was his habit that she adored. She closed her eyes briefly, trying to strengthen her heart. During the long flight from England back to Melbourne, she was determined that they could not be together again like before.

She was not sure for how long they were in that position. It must have been a while because the restaurant was almost empty the next time she looked around, with only some staff cleaning up. The sky was getting dark, though there was still a remaining red colour sunset. The rain seemed to have stopped too. Amelia knew that if she wanted to walk back to Sharon's house, she had to begin the journey now before the road became too dark.

"I need to go now," she said while quickly standing up and twirling away. However, before she could step forward, his sturdy arms wrapped around her shoulders and waist. She gasped as she could feel the warmth of his breath as he buried his face at the back of her neck.

"Please don't go," he whispered. "Please stay."

She briefly closed her eyes, gathering her strength to release herself from the warm embrace she used to like. She missed him so much too. She pulled down his arm and turned her body around to shove him away. However, instead, he caught her body closer to him and sealed her lips with his.

The time seemed to have stopped as she was paralyzed. It was not for the first time. His kisses always made her breathless, light in her whole limbs, and she felt like floating. And it had been a while since they had it, which ignited further her desire. She let herself be carried away for a couple of seconds as he lifted her body until her feet were mid-air and deepened the kiss.

The kiss melted away all her doubts, fear, pain and hurt that she had felt for the past couple of months since his accident. As his firm lips moulded hers, his masculine scent took over her senses. There was a huge sensation of warmth and security as if he was telling her everything would be alright.

The dam of hurts in her heart seemed about to explode, and it was her tears that broke the kiss apart. She buried her face in his chest while uncontrollably sobbing in his arms

He carefully put her down but swiftly scooped her body up to the couch near the mantlepiece. He had himself seated with her on his lap while his fingers kept stroking her hair and her arm. His lips kept sending her butterfly kisses all over her face. And they were in that position unmoved for what seemed like an eternity until her cry slowly subsided. The kitchen and the restaurant floor were empty, with the only lights on was near their table and the mantlepiece.

There was a peaceful bliss within her heart, a solitude that she had missed since Fitz's memory of her had gone. Now knowing that it had come back, she felt a sense of relief and a sensation of being flooded with warmth and happiness. However, she could not deny that deep down in her heart, there was still a doubt that this blissfulness could easily slip away again. She never cared about Fitz's family's scrutinization of her as long as she had him on her side. However, once he was gone, she felt so lonely, felt like a little reindeer in the middle of dens of lions.

Could she do this again, fearing that he might forget about her again?

"When Georgie found that positive pregnancy test result, I was so thrilled." His deep baritone voice finally broke the silence.

She was startled but did not move, still burying her face in his chest. "The baby could be disabled like me," she muttered.

She could feel that he lowered his head to look at her and planted a kiss on her forehead. "It's still our baby."

She smiled bitterly. "It was not my pregnancy test result."

"I know. I think now I can figure out whose it is. Charlie just informed me of the good news."

Amelia smiled. Lana finally broke the news. That meant the pregnancy had been good so far.

"I know you must be wondering why I have been checking on your legal name," he stated.

She held her breath. Sometimes she was surprised that it seemed he could read her mind.

"I notice that your family always call you Lizzy. You mentioned that only people close to you would call your childhood name. It makes me slightly envious why you do not let me call you Lizzy instead. So, I went to check on your legal name. Then I find out that the name Amelia is not anywhere in your legal name."

She scoffed and pulled her body up so she could see his face. "Why don't you just ask me? Why did you have to check it behind my back?"

He was looking at her in his usual calm manner. "Because I have other reasons too."

She furrowed her brow and tried to read his meaning.

"I need to prepare some legal documents. For us."

She was even more confused. "What legal documents?" Something struck her mind that made her furious. She pushed herself away and was ready to jump down from his lap. But he was quick enough to catch her waist and pull her back.

"Let me go!" she hissed. "I know exactly why you did this. You are worried I'm eyeing your wealth, aren't you?"

"No, Amelia, please listen." He held her tight closer, and his warm breath was on her neck again. He did not continue his words until she stopped struggling. She hated to admit that despite being trained in self-defence, his strength was still above her.

"I'm preparing for our future. If anything happens to me, I want to make sure that you will be well taken care of."

"You don't need to worry about me. I can take care of myself," she retorted with a pout on her face.

"It's not only for you. But it is also for our kids too."

She turned her head and looked at him, confused.

"Aarrgh....," she groaned exasperatedly and struggled to escape from him, but he held her even tighter. "I think your brain still has some issues, Mr Dalton. We don't have kids! I'm not pregnant!"

"I know!" He laughed while burying his face in her neck. "I mean after we get married."

Amelia's heart seemed to cease beating for a second. *Married?* She turned her head again with disbelief. He slowly turned her around, so this time they were facing each other while she was still sitting on his lap, close to him as he wanted.

"I love you, Amelia. I want us to be together forever. I want to marry you," he said softly while his finger stroked her hair fringe before travelling to her cheek. "On the night of the accident, I was supposed to propose to you. It was supposed to be the happiest night of my life. Unfortunately, what happened was the exact opposite." His voice faltered." I almost lost you instead." He held her face firmly, making sure that his eyes never left her. "But now I don't want to lose that chance again."

He dropped his hands to reach for something within his blazer's pocket, and within a second, a dark blue velvet little box appeared in his palm.

"Will you do me the honour of taking me as your husband, Elise Amelia Bettney?" he whispered while opening the box.

For a moment Amelia couldn't catch her breath. Was this real? She felt blessed for their relationship and never thought too far of getting into the next step of marriage. It was not because she did not want it, but perhaps she was too scared to think about it. Somehow, in the back of her mind, their relationship would end one day, and they would just end up as friends. She accepted it. She loved him too much to demand anything from him. She knew it would be unfair to him. Sometimes she wondered whether she was being unfair in this relationship instead.

The classic aquamarine diamond solitaire ring inside that little box mesmerised her as it flashed before her eyes. She was not a jewellery lover and had absolutely no idea about the technicality of a ring. However, she could not deny that the little item was exquisite and must have been customised to her liking. Blue had been her favourite colour, and he knew it.

There was only silence between them for a couple of seconds as she could not utter any reply. She was overwhelmed and trying to clear her headspace. When she looked up, he was waiting for her with his yearning gaze on her.

"Are..," she couldn't help but stammer. "Are you sure?"

He beamed as his eyes were glimmering with tears. "Is that a 'yes'?" His voice cracked with emotion.

She closed her eyes, lowered her head and rested on his chest again. She could hear his heartbeat, which was enough to make her realise that this was real. She just wanted to hold onto this moment as much as she could.

His hands slowly lifted her chin so their eyes met again, and he sealed her lips with his. She smiled in between those kisses and whispered, "Yes."

An Amelia

The bright sun shone through the window on the white gown hanging next to it, which made the beads glimmer and attracted the eyes of the owner. Amelia stared at her wedding gown for what seemed like an eternity while she let the make-up artist style her curly hair. She still could not believe that this day had come.

It had been another year since she said 'yes' to Fitz's proposal. It was the happiest moment in her life, and sometimes she wondered whether she deserved it. Since then, more happy occasions have been lined up. Lana's first newborn, Leah's graduation, Georgie's engagement and Richard's new girlfriend. It had been a great year, and she couldn't stop being grateful for it. Meanwhile, she and Fitz had spent a lot of time together, not only preparing for the wedding but also for their future. She enjoyed every bit of it. And today was her wedding day. It was not the peak of happiness but only the beginning of their life journey.

The soft voice from the make-up artist startled her from her reverie. Her eyes automatically moved to the mirror, and she almost could not believe seeing her reflection. The makeup artist who stood behind her, smiled with the satisfaction of her creation.

The reflection in the mirror was someone that she did not recognise. Was it her? Her curly hair was pulled up with a few strains down. Her face was on full make-up: long luscious mascara, soft but full eyeshadow, eyeliner, and a couple of lines on her nose, plus a thick layer of powder on her face. She looked like someone else, except that little left limb stayed the same.

The makeup artist squeezed her shoulder. "It's time to put on your wedding dress. Let me help you."

She stood up and followed the directions to get herself into the dress. It was a long ball gown white wedding dress, with a deep V neckline and bareback, that fit her lithe body perfectly. Both her arms were bare, and her little left limb was on full display.

She wondered what would be the guests' reaction if she turned up without her prosthetic hands. Fitz never mentioned that she had to wear it.

It was her mother who reprimanded her when she was joking about not wearing it. But today was her day, and she decided to be what she was.

The soft knock on the door came at the right time when she finished dressing up. All her family turned up at the door with a squeal of excitement once they saw her. She burst into laughter while her eyes caught her father's red eyes with some traces of tears.

"You look gorgeous, Liz," said her father while planting a kiss on her forehead. "I can't believe that I have to let you go."

"I'm still your daughter, dad. You know that." She smiled cheekily, wishing to lighten him up. Luckily her mother's comment distracted their melancholy moment.

"I love your choice of wedding gown, Liz," commented her mother. "Good taste. Everything that has quality must be expensive. And it always looks good on you, regardless you have a perfect body or not."

Amelia stole a glance at Lana, who winced hearing her mother's words. She repressed her smile. This was her day, and her mother's comment would not easily ruin her good mood today.

"Oh, don't forget your hairpiece, Liz," exclaimed Leah, which jolted the make-up artist lady to bring the mentioned item and carefully plant it on Amelia's hair.

Amelia softly said thank you to her sister.

Soon after, another soft knock was heard. Michael, the wedding organiser, informed them that it was time to get ready. Everyone seemed to know what to do and immediately fled the room, except Leah, who would be her bridesmaid today. Her sister helped her with the train of her gown while she walked towards the church foyer entrance.

While waiting for the next cue, Clare suddenly appeared in the foyer and approached her. Amelia knitted her brow, wondering what would be the next mischievous thing that this woman would do to her. To her surprise, Michael suddenly stood tall between them, which made Clare cringe.

"I just want to wish you a congratulation, Amelia," said Clare while swallowing thickly and feeling intimidated by the tall man in front of her.

"Thank you for specifically delivering the wish now, Clare." Amelia could not hold the edge of her voice. Her eyes were observing Clare's body language, whether she would do something unexpected. However, Michael blocked her view and purposedly walked towards Clare, making her walk backwards and almost stumbled back. Amelia repressed her laugh seeing that scene.

"Please return to your seat, Madam," ordered Michael firmly.

Clare seemed not to give up. She was still trying to have a sneak peek of the bride. "I took a peep at your marriage certificate. It doesn't have the name Amelia on it. I thought Fitz is going to marry another woman," she sneered.

Amelia smiled to herself. "Sorry to disappoint you, Clare."

"So, where does the name Amelia come from?"

Michael touched her left arm softly and gestured her to move forward to the closed door that would lead her to the church aisle. Her father stood beside her, squeezed her hand warmly and gave her his arm. She looked to the side where Clare was still standing, unmoved from her position, with two arms folded on her chest and a lifted chin.

Amelia knew the question was to provoke her. But today was her day, and she would not let her emotion spoil it. Her eyes were radiant with joy, and her lips upturned into a smirk before she replied, "Because I'm an Amelia."

Acknowledgement

To my parents, sisters and brother: despite our distances, I am eternally grateful for your presence in my life, ceaseless prayer, and support. Without all of you, I would not be what I am today.

For my beloved husband: even though you are not a bookworm, thank you for your love and understanding, allowing me to pursue what I always dreamed of.

For my kids: you complete my life.

For all my friends around the world: thank you for our friendship and your faith in me.

And last but not least, Nina Christina, a newfound equally enthusiastic friend in Pride and Prejudice, my first book reader and fantastic diligent proofreader.

About The Author

Based on The Big-Five Model (B5M) of five broad personality dimensions described by Dr John A. Johnson, the assessment test was conducted in Raylene's workplace. She was identified with a high level of imagination. That means she perceived the real world as often too plain and ordinary, but it does not mean she is oblivious of things that happen around the world: war, terrorism, natural disaster and the pandemic.

Since then, Raylene has started expressing her fantasy through writing to create a richer, meaningful world apart from her daily job as a part-time office all-rounder, a baker, a mother of two energetic kids, and a wife to her - unfortunately not a bookworm - but a factual oriented husband. Obsessed with Jane Austen's Pride and Prejudice, Raylene loves to write contemporary drama stories surrounding pride and vanity.

Visit www.ldraylene.com to get the latest updates on her new books.

www.ingramcontent.com/pod-product-compliance
Lightning Source LLC
Chambersburg PA
CBHW022158170626
46807CB00005B/2257